STAR OF STONE

CENTURY
QUARTET
BOOK II

The Century Quartet
Ring of Fire
Star of Stone

STAR OF STONE

CENTURY
QUARTET
BOOK II

Pierdomenico Baccalario
Translated by Leah D. Janeczko

Random House   New York

Translation copyright © 2010 by Leah D. Janeczko

Visit us on the Web!
www.randomhouse.com/kids
www.CenturyQuartet.com

Educators and librarians, for a variety of teaching tools, visit us at
www.randomhouse.com/teachers

Library of Congress Cataloging-in-Publication Data
Baccalario, Pierdomenico.
[Stella di Pietra. English.]
Star of Stone / by Pierdomenico Baccalario ; translated by Leah D. Janeczko. — 1st American ed.
p. cm. — (Century quartet; bk. 2)
Summary: In their continuing adventures, Elettra, Sheng, and Mistral meet Harvey and Ermete in New York City and follow clues to find the mysterious Star of Stone.
ISBN 978-0-375-85896-3 (trade) — ISBN 978-0-375-95896-0 (lib. bdg.) —
ISBN 978-0-375-89227-1 (e-book)
[1. Good and evil—Fiction. 2. Friendship—Fiction. 3. New York (N.Y.)—Fiction. 4. Mystery and detective stories.] I. Janeczko, Leah. II. Title.
PZ7.B131358St 2010 [Fic]—dc22 2009030416

Printed in the United States of America
10 9 8 7 6 5 4 3 2 1
First American Edition

This book is for my grandmother,
who sees the stars from very close up.

CONTENTS

Why should we lament that fire ravaged the universe,
that the Earth's blaze burned from city to city?
When the sparks from the chariot gone astray
drifted wayward, the sky itself was scorched,
and set ablaze with unknown flames were the nearby stars,
which still today bear signs of the havoc wrought.
—Manilius, *The Song of the Stars*, vv. 744–749

You ask me what reward we may gain from this task.
The greatest one of all: an understanding of Nature.
—Seneca, *Naturales Quaestiones*, VI

CONTACT

A STRETCH OF BLACK ROCKS SWEPT BY A WIND HEAVY WITH SLEET. *The lead-gray sky. The sea is a vast expanse crashing against the reef. Crests of stone seem to chase each other as they're swallowed up by the water. Mesmerized, the woman watches the fury of the elements battling among themselves. Water, wind, fire and earth, the fickle sentiments of this remote isle: Iceland.*

She brings the sled to a halt. The six wolves curl up in the snow, the brass bells on their leather harnesses jingling one last time before falling silent.

The woman has just left the shelter surrounded by ice and the three others, her friends. She told them that Century would begin in Rome. Irene suggested they have the children meet in her little hotel. They tried to imagine how to do it.

New Year's Eve.

A good idea.

They made their plans and then said goodbye.

At the top of the cliff, the wind makes the woman's clothes billow. The hardened lava from an ancient eruption trembles beneath her boots. It's the blood of the planet, its wounds sealed by salt.

Then she gives the order to leave. The wolves spring forward and pull the sled swiftly across the snow. They dart toward tall columns of steam that stand out against the gray sky like phantom cathedrals. The wolves run, letting out resounding cries. Suddenly, amid the clouds of steam, an expanse of blue, boiling hot water appears. It's a thermal spa surrounded by prancing sleet.

The woman guides the sled up to a wooden hut. She unhitches the wolves and gives them a few commands with a harsh tone.

Then she goes inside. She takes off her damp clothes and puts on a swimsuit. Her long hair tumbles down her back. She goes down a few steps and sinks into the hot, hot water, half-closing her eyes as the steam caresses her. She swims over to the uncovered side of the pool.

She waits there, surrounded by snow.

A long while later, a man silently swims over to her, barely making the water ripple. He calls her by name.

"It's me," she replies.

The man introduces himself. His name is Jacob Mahler. His hair is the color of spiderwebs, and he's crouching down in the hot water a few steps away from her.

"This isn't what we'd agreed," she says. "I was supposed to meet Mr. Heremit—"

Jacob Mahler's hand shoots out of the water. "Never say that name."

"What nonsense," the woman retorts.

"It isn't nonsense."

As her only reply, she sinks down into the water. When she rises back up to the surface, the man is still there, perfectly still, beside her.

"I don't have time for jokes," the woman states bluntly, staring at him through strands of her wet hair. "I'll be setting sail soon."

"Your ship can wait a few more hours."

"I need to go on a long journey."

"Spitsbergen Island, Norway; Kamchatka, Siberia; the Bering Strait. A long voyage through the cold."

"I love the cold. It preserves the past."

"Spoken like a true archaeologist . . ."

"I'm not an archaeologist," the woman says.

"A few years ago, a tribe of Siberian Evenki found a mammoth that had been perfectly preserved in the ice. They boiled it and ate it piece by piece before anyone could even study it."

"Food is the first basic human need."

"What's the second one?" he asks.

"Power."

"Which is the reason we're meeting."

"I don't need to talk to you, Jacob Mahler."

"He won't leave his skyscraper. But he wants to know. If you don't want to talk to me, that means you'll have to come see us."

The woman doesn't reply. She wipes her hair away from her forehead.

"In Shanghai," Jacob Mahler continues. "Once you've finished your expedition. We can greet you with something nice and hot. Plus excellent music."

"Do you play?"

"A little. The violin."

She stares at the man's hands as they skim the surface of the water like strange, drifting animals. She thinks it over a moment and then answers. "Tell your boss I'll come."

Mahler nods. "We'll be expecting you." He smiles. With this, he sinks down into the cobalt-blue water and disappears.

Five years have passed since then.

3

1
THE ROPE

THE SUBWAY'S 3 TRAIN OPENS ITS DOORS, AND HARVEY MILLER steps off. His long, messy hair hanging down over his eyes, Harvey waits for the crowd of passengers to disperse. Then he grouchily shoves his hands down into his pockets and walks over to the stairs leading outside. On the street, the air is filled with a strong burning smell. The asphalt glistens with rain. The sky over the rooftops of Harlem looks fragile.

The boy pulls a slip of paper out of his pocket and checks the address. There are potholes in the street. A tangle of roads makes its way down to the river.

New York, January, northern Manhattan.

Harvey walks along. At the address he was looking for he finds a brick building with a basement. Closed windows sealed off by thick curtains. On the wall, graffiti. A family sitting at the top of the stairs waiting for who knows what. On the corner, some abandoned trash. Farther down, other stairways, other closed windows.

All around it are old, anonymous, grim-looking buildings. Farther down the block, a bar, a greengrocer's, a Middle Eastern diner. On the lampposts on the corner, posters for Black History

Month are splattered with white paint. Harvey breathes in an air that's filled with anger. The perfect neighborhood for a boxing gym.

It isn't hard to find. The gym's name is written in big letters on a dark awning. On the first floor, there are a labor lawyer's office, a few numbers and some indecipherable initials. There's no mistaking it. Number 89. The same number he's got written down. Still, Harvey hesitates. He walks partway past the building, leans against a rusty railing and stares at the door to the gym for a few moments. All the lights are on in the basement. Harvey checks his watch. It's five o'clock. The sky is almost completely dark.

What should he do? He can't decide. . . . He doesn't have an appointment, and he doesn't need to see anyone in particular. But he's had that address in his pocket for a week now, ever since he saw the black-and-white poster plastered to a column in the Columbus Circle station. At the top of it was the drawing of a guy wearing shorts and a sweatshirt. Written on his boxing gloves were the words:

OLYMPIA GYM — BOXING AND
GRECO-ROMAN WRESTLING

He'd liked the poster and had copied down the name and address. The idea of coming all the way here had been stuck like a pin in his head ever since. He'd imagined himself throwing punches, and the thought of it had made him smile. It was a good idea for him to learn to defend himself and be sure he could take on a stranger. Especially after what happened in Rome at New Year's.

Harvey rolls up on the balls of his feet and straightens his back, like he does whenever he has a problem.

Not far away from him, an old crow flies down and perches on a railing. It has a pointy beak and one eye is in terrible shape.

Harvey ignores it. He heads back and tries going down the flight of stairs leading to the basement. At the last step, from the other side of the door, he can hear the squeal of gym shoes on linoleum. Voices of people talking.

He's found the gym.

He knocks, spots a doorbell, rings it.

He waits. He glances back at the street above him.

The crow is still perched, motionless, on the railing. It scratches at its cloudy eye with one foot. Then, when the gym door starts to open, it flies off, disappearing among the rooftops.

Standing in the doorway is a young black woman. "I don't know you," she says to Harvey with a hint of a smile. She's very pretty. Short hair, damp with perspiration on her forehead, and big hazel eyes. Her slightly crooked nose gives her a rough-and-tumble look. She's wearing a gray sweat suit, a sweatband of the same color around her head and a pair of bright, lilac-colored kneesocks. She doesn't have shoes on. And she's really heated up.

Harvey takes an almost imperceptible step back, thinking he's made a mistake. What's a woman doing in a boxing gym?

"My name's Harvey Miller and—"

Something crashes to the ground behind her. She whirls around and shouts, "Michael! You be careful with that punching bag or I'll make you buy a new one!" Then she turns back to Harvey and says, "Sorry. You were saying?"

Harvey runs his hand through his thick tangle of hair. "Never mind . . . ," he grumbles, feeling an irresistible desire to get out of there. "I guess I just misunderstood and . . ."

7

"What is it you think you misunderstood, Harvey Miller?" she replies, looking him up and down. Her tone of voice is sharp. Typical of someone who likes to provoke people. "Did you misunderstand because you don't really want to be here or because you realized you don't have the guts?"

"Hey!" Harvey protests. "I didn't say that. . . ."

As her only reply, she takes a little step to the side, letting him see a dirty gray linoleum floor, a wall lined with two rows of empty hooks, a few jackets and a wooden bench with gym bags resting on it. "You didn't say anything, but your face did. Want to come in?"

Harvey's head sinks down between his shoulders and he hunches over suspiciously.

"You look shorter standing that way, Harvey Miller."

"You sound just like my mother."

"Your mother's right."

Harvey stands up straight, offended.

"That's better," the woman remarks. "Well?"

Harvey throws his hands up. "Well, what? What do you want me to say? I just came by to take a look."

"And what do you see?"

"I see you standing in the doorway!"

"So you came here to a boxing gym to see a woman standing here in a doorway?"

"No!" Harvey snaps impatiently. "I came here because I wanted to see a boxing gym!"

She nods for him to come in, a perfectly satisfied look on her face. "Rule number one," she says, "whoever loses his cool and his concentration loses the match. Rule number two: If you want to come to a boxing gym, you come wearing sweats and a T-shirt, not dressed up for school. In any case, I might have something to lend you."

"But I—"

"You don't need to pay for the first lesson. If you like it, you can keep coming. Otherwise, no hard feelings. Follow me."

A little confused, Harvey steps into the gym.

"And shut the door!" the woman yells without turning around. "You want us all to catch colds?"

Inside, the gym is pretty big. It's lit up by rows of white neon lights. No machines. No mechanical equipment. Just dozens of blue mats lying on the floor, wooden chin-up bars on the walls and a bunch of punching bags in all different sizes hanging from the ceiling. A teenager with his face hidden beneath the hood of a gray sweatshirt is jumping rope, crossing it beneath his feet.

In the center is the ring: a white platform encircled by thick ropes. Two people wearing blue and red foam rubber headgear are duking it out in a practice match. He can hear their gloves hissing through the air and the smacking thuds of their blows hitting their padded helmets.

The moment he sees them, Harvey stops, fascinated. The two have on tight-fitting shirts, silky-looking shorts and socks trimmed in dark blue. They're moving around on their tiptoes like ballerinas, but what they're doing isn't a dance. It's a battle.

"Terence and Evelyn are going to have their first real matches in a month. Both featherweights, but different tournaments, naturally," explains the woman, a few steps in front of Harvey.

"Evelyn?" he asks, noticing only then that one of the boxers is a young woman.

"Yeah, Evelyn . . . who happens to pack the strongest punch

9

in this place." Then, noticing Harvey's surprise, she adds, "Did you think boxing was only for guys?"

When Harvey pulls his eyes away from the ring, he sees that the woman is holding her hand out to him. "Nice to have you here, Harvey Miller. I'm Olympia. I run this gym."

Olympia is leaning against the wall outside the men's locker room. Harvey can see her silhouette through the door's frosted glass panel. The walls of the room are covered with graffiti written by other boxers. The only shower seems to have lost its mixer tap long ago, and the overall smell is a combination of mildew, sweat and clogged drains.

Sitting on the wooden bench, Harvey anxiously puts on a pair of worn-out gym shoes. He slides his thumbs around inside the heels to stretch them out a little as he shoves his feet in. He checks out his reflection in the mirror. He looks ridiculous, partly because nothing he's wearing is exactly his size. None of it is exactly clean, either. But he doesn't care.

He comes out of the locker room and walks over to Olympia, who doesn't bother with small talk. "We can start now if you want."

"How'd you know I was going to stay?" Harvey asks, following her over to the mats.

"Some things I can tell at first glance."

"Yeah? How?"

"You came alone. No dad dropping you off, telling me he was a boxer when he was your age, before he joined the army. No mom sniffing the locker room, letting me know the gym's too dirty."

"Yeah," Harvey remarks, thinking of his parents.

"We're here to box, not to do housecleaning," the trainer

continues. Then she leads him over to the opposite corner of the gym, where a giant black punching bag is hanging from the ceiling. She hugs it and shows it to Harvey. "This is going to be your enemy. But before you learn how to hit him"—she shoves it at the boy, bashing him square in the face—"you need to learn to take his punches." The bag gently swings back into her hands. "And before you learn to take his punches, you need to learn to dodge them."

Harvey rubs his cheek, where he can still feel the sting left by the bag's rough canvas. "Sounds like a good idea," he grumbles.

"To learn how to dodge them, you need to understand your body's natural balance. Legs, arms, shoulders, torso, neck. And there's only one way to do that." Olympia bends down and picks up a rope from the floor. She hands it to Harvey. "Start jumping," she orders him.

The boy grabs it, disappointed. "No gloves?"

"No gloves. Just a hundred jumps done well. Then push-ups, chin-ups and another hundred jumps. When you're done, we'll see if you're still standing. You do know how to jump rope, don't you?"

Harvey positions the rope behind his ankles, whirls it over his head and jumps over it with an awkward hop. "I can learn."

Olympia looks at him with a critical eye. "You got friends, Harvey?"

He doesn't stop jumping. "Some. Why?"

"Just curious."

2
THE SONG

"MIGHT I KNOW WHERE IT IS YOU'RE GOING, LOOKING SO UNPRE-sentable?" Linda Melodia asks Elettra right outside the front door of the Domus Quintilia hotel. She leans on her broom and peers at her niece with a critical eye.

"What's wrong?" the girl asks with a groan. A cascade of raven-black hair falls over her dark, dark eyes. She wears a close-fitting white ski jacket, gray slacks and a pair of black and purple sneakers.

"Your shoes," Linda remarks, pointing at them with the tip of her broom.

One after the other, Elettra raises her feet, which are clad in brightly colored Asics. "They're gorgeous!" she protests.

"They're filthy. What's that on the heels? Mud?"

"Auntie! How could anyone avoid the mud on the streets? The snow just melted."

"A well-dressed young lady always wears clean shoes."

"Well, I'm not a well-dressed young lady, then!"

"If your mother—"

"Could see me right now, I know! Whatever! Auntie, I've really got to go." Elettra rises up on her tiptoes, gives her aunt a kiss and darts out the front door.

Elettra walks across Piazza in Piscinula and from there reaches Viale Trastevere, where she gets onto tram number 3. The trip doesn't last long. Once she gets off at her stop, she looks up at the rooftops, searching for the eleven little pyramids of the facade of Santa Maria dell'Orto Church. She goes over to the entrance and checks the time. It's four o'clock sharp.

Sheng is waiting for her between two white pillars. Black hair in a pageboy cut, mysteriously blue eyes, a shiny silk sports coat worn with jeans and gym shoes. "Man, I'm sorry. This is my dad's jacket," he says, greeting her.

"It isn't exactly . . . um, fitting for the occasion," the girl remarks, giving him a quick hug.

"I don't think anybody will complain," Sheng says, leading the way into the church. "In fact, I don't think anybody's even here."

The church is dark and freezing cold, but strangely intimate. The two friends press up against each other and head toward the altar. Between the rows of pews, resting on a metal stand, is a black wood coffin.

There are no flowers. And no people, with the exception of a woman in the front row, a tiny woman wearing a hat with a peacock feather and a gray sheepskin jacket, which make her look like a giant turtledove. It's Ilda, the owner of the newsstand in Largo Argentina.

Elettra and Sheng sit down beside her. They smile at each other and clasp hands. "I'm sorry . . . ," the woman says in a feeble voice. "I'm so, so sorry."

13

The priest looks at them from the little doorway of the sacristy, coughs and then goes to change. The smell of incense begins to waft through the silent air. The loudspeaker crackles and then begins to fill the church with warbling, melancholy music.

"Maybe we should've brought a flower . . . or something . . . ," Elettra whispers, suddenly overcome with sadness. The sound of shuffling footsteps makes her turn around. The gypsy woman from Via della Gatta has arrived, too. She's wearing a gold earring that glimmers through her hair. She rests two stolen flowers on the coffin and hides herself away in the back of the church, in the shadows.

Then a man walks in. It's the waiter from the Caffè Greco. He didn't want to miss Professor Alfred Van Der Berger's funeral.

Outside the window, the rooftops of Paris are a flow of dark shingles lining the dormers and round windows of the garrets like chocolate on a frosted cake. A few starlings are perched in the shade of a bow window, snuggling up to each other to warm themselves. Others are whirling through the sky beneath clouds as fluffy as cotton.

At the back of the classroom, Mistral is staring out at the Seine and the domes of the churches.

Then the singing teacher's voice summons her back to the real world. "Miss Blanchard? Are you with us? Or have you set off on another one of your long journeys?" she asks with a snobbish tone reminiscent of schoolmarms from the last century.

Mistral's classmates snicker. She snaps out of it at once and smiles, too dreamy to be annoyed. She looks around at the class-room, takes a step forward, does up the top button on her V-neck sweater and asks, so innocently that she almost seems imperti-nent, "Is it my turn?"

The singing teacher is sitting at the piano. She's wearing very heavy rouge, her gray hair is held up in a bun by a big, gaudy hair-pin and her full, ruffled black dress seems to have trapped her between the stool and the pedals.

"Of course it's your turn, Mistral! It has been for a few minutes now!" She slams her heel down on the parquet floor to make the other pupils stop laughing. "What is your piece this week?"

Mistral walks over to the piano and hands her some sheet music. "I've prepared 'Woman in Love,' ma'am, by Barbra Streisand."

"American, hmm? Is that all you discovered during your New Year's vacation in Rome?"

The other girls instantly fall silent, curious to hear her reply.

"No, ma'am . . . Well, actually, there is one thing I discovered."

The teacher twirls the top of her stool around a few times until it's at just the right height, shoves the sheet music down on its stand and asks, without the slightest bit of interest, "And what would that be?"

"I don't think I enjoy classical music anymore. Or the violin, either. Mahler, in particular."

"Is that why you want to sing American songs?"

"That's one reason, yes," replies Mistral. The teacher doesn't comment. Not that she could say anything relevant. No one could know what happened in Rome.

The piano lets out the first chords. The girl takes a deep breath, waits for her cue and then starts singing. Her voice is clear and perfect. None of her classmates are snickering anymore. Outside of the window, on the rooftops sloping down toward the Seine, some birds fly in closer to listen to her.

"Thirty-one . . . thirty-one fifty . . . thirty-two dollars!" says Ermete De Panfilis as he gives the taxi driver the last two coins in his collection of American change.

The cabbie, who looks like he just got out of prison, doesn't seem very pleased to have been given all those coins. Without lifting a finger, he waits until the Italian has unloaded the last of his massive suitcases and then peels out through the slush.

"Hey!" Ermete protests, trying to dodge the splash of dirty water. "How rude!" He looks down at his corduroy slacks, shrugs and moves his luggage to the safety of the sidewalk. Written on the airport tags are the words NEW YORK, JFK. Here he is at his new home: Thirty-fifth Avenue, Jackson Heights, Queens.

It's a residential neighborhood. An apartment on the second floor of a little redbrick house with a reassuring look. It's not far from the former home of a true American legend: Alfred Butts, the inventor of Scrabble, Ermete's favorite board game.

Bags and backpacks slung over his shoulder, the engineer finds the right key among the ones given to him by the real estate agency, takes half of his luggage inside, comes back out, grabs the other half and has just enough time to explore the foyer before his cell phone starts ringing.

"Hi, Mom!" he answers, stepping over a suitcase. "No. Yes. Of course . . . I just got here. Just now. Very nice. It's raining. Pouring.

16

There's a tornado. No, come on! I was kidding! Yes. No, really . . .
a stupid joke. I know you worry. . . ."

Ermete sinks down into a comfy sofa, grabs the remote and
turns on the television to a channel discussing the upcoming
Super Bowl.

"What's that? It's just the TV, Mom. In the U.S. there are televisions everywhere. No. No, you can't come visit me. There's no
room. Sorry . . . besides, the trip here is terrible. It's really, really
long. No, even more than that. Even longer."

Ermete turns up the volume on the TV and checks out the
bedroom, the bathroom, the kitchen, the fridge. Which is empty.

"Sure I've got friends, Mom. Sure. I'll call them. I won't be all
alone. Don't worry. Great. Okay. Bye. Yeah. Bye." The engineer
hangs up and tosses his cell phone onto the cushions on the
sofa. Then he takes out the phone book and looks up the name
Miller.

There are ten pages of Millers.

"Maybe it's not a good idea to call Harvey right now. . . ."

Ermete goes over to the window and looks outside. There's
nobody on the street. "Besides, it isn't safe to use the phone for
important messages," he continues, talking to himself, as if he
were playing a part in a spy movie. "There are better ways to
communicate in New York."

He reaches into his bag and takes out the most prized possession in his movie collection: *Ghost Dog* by Jim Jarmusch. The
story of a mafia hit man who receives orders from his bosses by way
of carrier pigeon.

Ermete places the movie on an empty bookshelf in his new
American apartment. Then he looks around. The television is

still showing the game. He pulls a padded parcel out of his travel bag. He unwraps it with the utmost care until he finds himself holding a round mirror set in a bronze frame.

He rests it on the sofa and picks up the phone book again.

"Pet shops . . . ," he murmurs, thumbing through the pages.

3
THE CROW

THE NEON LIGHTS IN THE GYM SEEM TO QUIVER AGAINST THE darkness looming outside. Harvey is sitting on a wooden bench, almost unable to move. His muscles are aching. He rests his head back wearily against the wall and closes his eyes.

"First week?" a voice asks him, making him start. It's a guy wearing a hooded sweatshirt. Michael. He sits down next to Harvey and holds out his hand.

"Yeah." He smiles. "And I'm beat."

"This is nothing, believe me. Just wait until your next lessons."

"I can't believe it could get any more exhausting than this."

Michael laughs. "That's because you've never tried running around carrying a punching bag on your shoulders."

"You kidding?"

"Nope."

The two stare at the ring. Olympia's wearing a pair of boxing gloves and is about to fight one of her students, elbows raised and gloves held right in front of her nose. At the gong, they start circling around each other. The man throws a halfhearted punch, and then another one, but he seems intimidated by the idea of hitting his female trainer.

She urges him on, telling him to swing harder. And faster.

"That's it!" she says. Then she quickly pummels him with three, four blows that make him stagger backward, stunned and aching.

"Way to go!" cheers Harvey.

Michael smiles. "He didn't even see it coming."

Olympia dances around the ring, only the tips of her feet touching the ground. She dodges the blows, blocks them with her gloves, moves her torso with the litheness of a snake. All the while, she keeps talking, egging on her student. A big, round clock hanging on the wall shows the seconds ticking by one by one.

"When you're in there," Michael explains, pointing at the ring, "it's the longest minute of your whole life."

Harvey nods. Then one of Olympia's punches hits the man square in the jaw. They hear the soft thud of his mouth guard hitting the ground.

"Ow!" Harvey groans, massaging his own jaw. "What a wallop!"

"She barely touched him," Michael remarks. "But she let him know how she could hit him if he keeps defending himself like that."

Confused, Harvey looks at the man in the ring, who's wobbling around like a bowling pin.

"Trust me. He's fine," Michael insists. "You only really get hurt when they hit this," he says, pointing to his nose, which is sticking out from the hood of his sweatshirt. "If your opponent breaks your nasal septum during a match, you lose. In fact, some trainers will break yours before letting you fight in a tournament."

Harvey shakes his head as a shiver of imagined pain runs down his spine. "I want my nose to stay in one piece. I don't want to fight. I just want to learn to defend myself."

"That's what I thought, too, when I signed up. And then . . ." Michael nods toward Olympia. The match is over and the woman's climbing out of the ring.

"And then what?"

Michael rests his hands on his knees and pushes himself up to his feet. "And then Olympia told me, 'Living doesn't mean staying in one piece. It means fighting.' "

"How we doing, Harvey Miller?" the trainer asks, walking over to him. "I see you met Michael." She holds out her wrists, asking him to unlace her gloves.

"I'm exhausted." Harvey smiles.

"But . . . ?"

"But happy."

The gloves drop to the floor and Michael picks them up. Olympia massages her fingers.

"You sure taught him a lesson!" Harvey exclaims, pointing at the guy in the ring.

"We didn't really hit each other. Still, he's got to learn to keep his defenses up. His concentration isn't the greatest and he's always lowering his guard. You lower your guard even once and . . . bam! You were asking for it."

"Got it," Harvey remarks, heading toward the locker rooms with her.

"Well, am I going to see you again, Miller?"

He nods. "I think so."

"Then starting next time, it'll be forty bucks. Three times a week, otherwise it's like you aren't coming at all. Plus, you need to do exercises at home. A little bit every night. The first two days you work out, and the third you put on the gloves. Then we'll see how do you. Okay?"

"Okay."

The days pass. And the weeks.

Every time she walks out of the Domus Quintilia, Elettra notices the gypsy woman, who's moved from begging in Via della Gatta to begging in Piazza in Piscinula.

"What are you doing here?" she asked her the first time, taking her a hot coffee.

The gypsy smiled. "I'm keeping watch," she replied.

Every week Elettra collects all the tips from the hotel's guests and finds a way to get them to the woman without her knowing where the money came from.

This is how they look out for each other.

For Sheng, who has extended his stay, the months spent on cultural exchange in Rome are a sort of war. Catapulted into a family with three girls who are younger than him and completely hysterical, the Chinese boy often shuts the door to his room, where he practices his written Italian and studies. Stars, mythology, history . . . there's nothing that doesn't fascinate him. At night, he pulls his wooden top out from under the bed and turns it over and over in his fingers.

Staring at it, mesmerized, he thinks back to what the professor said. "What difference does it make which road you follow as you seek the truth?" he murmurs like a prayer, closing his eyes. "Such a great secret is not to be reached by a single path."

His nights are tormented by unstoppable dreams filled with terrifying animals. One time there were hunters tracking down a huge, ferocious bear. Another time he was in a desert riding a wild bull. He dreams of enormous wolves that howl melodies of the cold at the moon and whales that dive down to the endless depths of the ocean, seeking out the past in ancient underwater ruins.

In February, his father returns to Rome and tells Sheng about the big news at his company. Their cultural exchange program for children is a success, and Mr. See-Young Wan Ho is euphoric, to say the least. Back at home, he's turned Sheng's room into an office, where bookings keep pouring in. There are countless parents in Shanghai determined to send their offspring to study with families in cities throughout the West.

"But we need to check the host families out one by one!" Mr. See-Young Wan Ho explains fervidly. "We need to know exactly what kind of people they are. If we get it wrong, no one will ever trust our agency again!"

"But I . . . ," Sheng groans, already guessing that his father is planning on using him as a guinea pig. "I'm not going to travel the globe, skipping from one crazy family to another!"

Mr. Wan Ho does everything he can to convince his son. "I'm giving you the opportunity to see the world!"

"But I'm learning Italian," says Sheng. "I've made new friends. I like Rome and I'd like to stay here longer!"

"We already know everything about Rome!" his father cuts in, determined. "This family's fine. Now we need to move on to the others. We're missing Paris, Buenos Aires, New York, Madrid. . . ."

Sheng sighs. "I can't promise you anything, Dad," he says, trying again. Despite everything, he's showered with open-ended airplane tickets for Johannesburg, New York, Paris and dozens of other places, with notebooks containing the addresses of families to try out and booklets of vouchers for luxury hotels, in case he needs them.

In Paris, the water in the Seine is the color of well-steeped tea.

Every Thursday, Mistral attends the private institute for singing, posture and dance lessons, but more and more often she finds herself lost in thought, gazing out the window, following the flight of the pigeons and starlings. She's discovered that the starlings imitate the sounds of the human world. Some of them mimic honking horns or the noise of the heavy traffic on the outskirts of town.

Maybe they once imitated the songs of poets, Mistral muses.

She vents her melancholy thoughts in drawings, which are becoming increasingly detailed and colorful and help her pass hours of lessons and evenings spent all alone. Her mother works late creating perfumes, and many times she comes home right before Mistral goes to sleep.

Meanwhile, in New York, Ermete has gathered a squadron of carrier pigeons, training them in the icy parks in Queens. He spends his days on the Queensboro Bridge, teaching them to cross the river and delve down among the skyscrapers of Manhattan.

Now he can finally trust them with his secret messages.

The first note he's had delivered among the rooftops of Grove Court, to Harvey Miller's aerial address, reads:

Hi, Harvey. Want to meet up for pizza?

March. New York is still gripped with cold. Harvey is still going to the gym. He goes there every chance he gets, without even mentioning it to his parents. He often stays there late.

One night, Olympia pulls him aside. "I was watching you practice on the punching bag."

"Am I lousy?"

"No. You've really improved, but you've got some strange anger going on inside you. I know it's none of my business, but have you got it in for somebody?"

"No," Harvey replies. "I wouldn't say that."

"But it isn't normal for a kid your age. . . ."

"I'm paying you, aren't I?"

"You're spending more time here than at home."

"I like it here. It makes me feel good."

"Three times a week. An hour a day. Not a minute more!"

Harvey stiffens as a stabbing pain runs through his shoulders. "I don't see why."

"You got any brothers or sisters, Harvey?"

"Not anymore."

Olympia raises both hands in a gesture halfway between an apology and a sign of surrender. "I'm sorry. I didn't know."

"It isn't your fault."

"Let's pretend I never said anything."

Harvey shoots her a withering glance.

"I get it now," Olympia continues. "If you want, go ahead and keep punching away at the bag until it's in shreds."

The door to the locker room opens and closes again. The water in the shower streams out like an icy waterfall. Harvey doesn't even try to get it to run warmer. He clenches his teeth and doesn't think about it. He knows how to empty his mind.

Later on, in the subway, Harvey is zooming southbound. It's six o'clock. When the train reaches Central Park, the cars fill up with people. Harvey stubbornly remains in his seat, even though he knows he should leave it for some elderly person.

Nobody pays any attention to him. Engrossed in their books, their newspapers and the colorful displays on their iPods, thousands of indifferent strangers let themselves be whisked away down the tracks. Muffled music can be heard coming from dozens of earphones. Aching, Harvey leans against the backrest and patiently waits for his stop: Christopher Street, in the heart of the Village.

Olympia's voice is clear in his memory. *I'm sorry. . . . Keep punching away at the bag . . .*

Harvey clenches his teeth, thinking how much he'd love to be able to hear his brother's voice with that same clarity. Instead, nothing. Only silence. And noises. Millions of useless noises.

At the Twenty-third Street station, a girl gets on. She's very tall and is wearing inebriating perfume. Looking at her, Harvey thinks of Mistral and her mother, who designs perfumes. He should call her. He should call Elettra, too. And answer Ermete's messages. Go out for pizza with him for once.

But he doesn't feel like doing any of that. It's been a long time

26

now since he's thought of the days spent in Rome, his three friends (who all shared his birthday, Leap Day), the Ring of Fire, the tops, Jacob Mahler's lurking shadow and Alfred Van Der Berger's delirious messages. A few times he's even managed to convince himself it was all just a bad dream, a surreal, imaginary adventure. But each time the train lurches on its tracks, Harvey can feel a vague dizziness inside. It's the memory of the professor's building collapsing all around him.

The girl beside him reaches into her purse, pulls out a little gold compact and checks her impeccable makeup. Even that brings back memories of New Year's to Harvey's mind. The old bronze mirror that Elettra found in the Basilica di San Clemente. They call it the Ring of Fire and they're convinced it isn't just any old mirror, but something much more important. Something different. When Elettra looked at her reflection in it during those last few minutes of the year that had just gone by, something happened. Something that none of them understood but that seemed to have been understood by Rome. And by the world around them. Rome had switched off; the electricity had disappeared, as if the whole city had gone centuries back in time. Past and present. And the darkness surrounding both of them. Sure, it was crazy. Harvey told himself that every day. It was probably just as crazy as bringing the mirror to New York and entrusting it to the least accurate of scholars imaginable, the only one willing to believe it had been found by following clues from a crazy professor, a gypsy woman, four toy tops and a trunk full of human teeth.

He arrives at Christopher Street.

Harvey gets off the train car and walks down the platform. Once he's outside, he huddles up in his coat. The windows of the cafés are lit up, and behind them, dozens of businessmen are enjoying a break. Greenwich Village is a little labyrinth of short brick houses and ailanthus trees. It's the neighborhood where they shoot all the love scenes for movies. Maybe because it doesn't look like any other neighborhood in New York. Its streets are narrow and curvy; the houses rise up only a few floors and have wooden shutters and little gardens. Around here, people even walk a little more slowly than in the rest of the city.

Harvey heads toward Grove Court, lost in thought. He's got a nasty feeling he can't shake. . . . He stops, listens and looks behind him. Cashmere jackets. Eyeglasses with designer frames. Glittering jewelry. Black clothing. The tick-tack of high-heeled shoes. He tries to figure out what's causing the nasty feeling inside of him.

A shadow turns down Bleecker Street, together with dozens of other shadows.

They're following me, thinks Harvey.

It's crazy, naturally, but he keeps thinking it. Sensing it.

He stops to look at the reflection in the window of a bakery that specializes in quiche, searching for suspicious figures on the other side of the street. But he doesn't see any. Either that or he sees too many of them.

He walks past the gate to his house twice before deciding to go inside. Six old red houses, their windows and doors trimmed in white, look out over a pretty garden.

Harvey makes his way down the private path without turning around, his head bowed as he walks beneath the tree branches on which the first buds have already appeared.

His house is number 11. Once he's reached the front door, he takes one last look behind him. The garden is a series of shadows standing out against the distant lights of the bars and restaurants. Overhead, the sky threatens to rain at any moment.

"You've got to cut it out," Harvey grumbles, unlocking the front door. It was Ermete who gave him this contagious obsession with spies and the paranoid feeling of being followed.

The front door opens with a groan. A photocell detects his presence and lights up the stairway. He climbs up to the second floor. "Nobody's following me," he repeats to himself.

He walks into his house and calls out, "I'm home!"

His mother is bustling about the kitchen. The air is filled with the smell of soup. Harvey hangs his jacket up in the foyer and takes off his shoes. Inside it's hot, stifling. Mrs. Miller always keeps the heat turned all the way up. But it isn't only a question of temperature. It's stifling because of an empty room, one that none of them can walk into without feeling awkward. His brother's room.

Outside, on the sidewalk, a man's imposing shadow is sectioned off by the gate's metal bars. His massive hands disappear into the deep pockets of his dark gray mail carrier's uniform. When they reappear, they're clutching a small, round tin canister. The man opens it with unexpected grace and takes out a piece of green candy. He chews on it slowly. It's mint flavored. He stares at the garden and the door through which the boy disappeared. Then he pulls out a notebook and scrupulously jots something down. Time, address, date.

Finally, he slips it back into his pocket and calmly finishes sucking on his mint. He looks at his watch. It's almost dinnertime. He lets out a long, wavering whistle. A crow flies down and perches on the top of the gate, a few steps away from him.

"Will you stay and stand guard, Edgar?" the man dressed in gray asks it. One of the crow's eyes is cloudy. It finds a comfortable position and huddles down among the iron bars of the gate. Taking this as a reply, the man turns around, buries his hands in his pockets and walks off into the darkness.

4
THE CATALOG

"HELLO, HARVEY," HIS MOTHER SAYS THE MINUTE SHE SEES HIM.

"Hi. Dad isn't here?"

"He's in his study. Would you go call him? Dinner's almost ready."

"Cabbage soup?"

"Broccoli."

The boy limps out of the kitchen.

"Harvey, are you okay?"

He stops by the doorway. "Why?"

"You're walking funny."

"It's nothing. I didn't sleep well."

George Miller's study is at the end of the hallway, to the right. Standing guard at its sides are two Roman amphorae, a gift from a Turkish university. Leading to the room is a little antechamber. This is where Professor Miller has his students wait when they come to submit their research work to him.

He teaches dynamic climatology at NYU. Which means everything and nothing to Harvey. His father's area of expertise is cataclysms. Volcanic eruptions, storms, anomalous waves, research that can predict earthquakes. He makes highly complicated cal-culations on the drifting of the continents. In his mind are all the planet's figures. Temperatures, heights, depths. He's a walking encyclopedia with a passion for statistics, a penchant for sports coats and bow ties, and a prodigious memory.

He wants only perfectly flawless data. In their attempts to provide this to him, his students show up dragging along back-packs full of figures. The professor welcomes them into his study, nods, double-checks . . . and then, without fail, he finds some kind of fault, an inexact detail, and his students need to start all over again.

"I'm telling you, it's twelve *per mille*! One point two percent!" George Miller's voice booms through the hallway with a tone that is peeved, to say the least.

Harvey sighs, tired of his father's never-ending agitation. He pauses between the two amphorae and waits for the conversation to end.

"It's simply impossible!" his father's voice insists. "Why don't we stop kidding around?"

There are some framed photographs on the étagère in the hallway. Even though Harvey knows them by heart, he looks at them for the millionth time. In the one taken at the Rocky Mountains are the two of them, standing side by side. His brother is on the right, blond, twice as tall as he is and six years older. Dwaine.

Dwaine was good at everything. He could fix anything at all, an electrical appliance with a piece of string, a car by tightening a few bolts. . . . He spent last winter putting back together, piece by piece, a grandfather clock from the 1700s he'd found at an

32

antiques shop in Queens. Harvey remembers perfectly well its gold face, its pointy hands that looked like arrowheads, the springs to be inserted one by one with needle-nose pliers, the cogwheels and gears to be positioned just so. The clock is still at the end of the hall, in perfect working condition, but it's never been wound again.

In the study, Mr. Miller is still ranting. Harvey decides to interrupt him. "Dad?" he says, opening the door slightly and peeking into the room. Inside are four walls lined with books. His father is in the middle of the room, sitting at a glass desk that's as shiny as a mirror. When he sees his son, the professor gestures for him to come in and keep quiet.

"Of course, Matt," he's saying on the phone, "but there's no such thing as *possible* findings. Either they're right or they're wrong. And this one, if I may say, is simply ludicrous. It's impossible for there to have been an increase of that magnitude over the course of only three months. The temperatures weren't recorded accurately, that's all. . . . How should I know where the error is? Faulty instrumentation, kids not paying attention . . . you figure it out!" He waves some sheets of paper in front of him, flustered. "The fact remains that the documentation you sent me is worthless. And the university doesn't finance an oceanographic expedition in the Pacific just to be given worthless documentation. If you don't want to stick around there sunbathing anymore, all you have to do is say so! What . . . ?" George Miller straightens his bow tie, staring up at some imaginary spot to his left. Meanwhile, he waves Harvey over to one of the two chairs in the study.

Harvey sits down stiffly on the edge of the leather armchair.

His father's desk looks like the frozen foods section in a supermarket. There's not one item too many. Nothing is out of place. There's not even a pen resting crooked on the desktop. There's just a big green book and the sheets of paper, which he picks up and waves in the air as if they were an eviction notice.

After his millionth outburst, the professor suddenly calms down. "Listen, we'll talk about this next week when you have the new data, all right? I'll be expecting it. But make sure it's right this time!" He hangs up the phone with a sigh. "This is crazy! They say all our hope lies in today's young generation! Well, I say we should ship them all off to work in Alaska!"

"Time to eat," Harvey announces a little coldly, given that he can't help considering himself part of today's young generation.

His father grumbles something about the time and picks the green book up from his desk.

"What's that?"

"Nothing that would interest you," he replies dryly.

"*The Life of Charles Darwin . . .* ," Harvey reads from the spine of the book.

"Have you already studied him at school?"

"Of course," the boy replies. "He's the one who thought we descended from the apes."

The professor walks halfway around his desk. "Amazing."

"What?"

"That such a complex theory as the one regarding the origin of the species could be summarized like that."

"Did I get something wrong?"

"No. Actually . . . it's the essence of the problem," he replies, switching off his desk lamp. "Darwin said that today we can find only one percent of the animals that have lived on the Earth since the beginning of life itself."

"We've lost ninety-nine percent of the animals?"

"We haven't lost them. They've changed. And man has changed as well." Professor Miller picks up a black folder and walks out of the study with Harvey.

"But what if the apes were the ones who evolved from man?" his son asks him as they make their way into the kitchen.

"Possible, but improbable."

In the kitchen, Mrs. Miller is already serving up the broccoli soup. "What are you two chatting about?"

"Apes and bigger apes."

"Don't you have anything better to do?"

Her husband hands her the folder. "Take a look at this, if you like."

"What is it?"

"A catalog from an antiques dealer. He came to see me, passing himself off as a student. An odd fellow, but definitely cultivated. Kind of like a skeleton with a Russian accent. Mmm . . . ," he adds, sitting down at the table. "This smells delicious."

"Broccoli and lentils."

"Lentil soup in March?" grumbles Harvey, whose training at the gym has left him starving. "Isn't that a winter dish?"

"Technically, it's still winter," his father points out. "It will be until March twentieth, the spring equinox."

"Are we having anything else with this?" Harvey asks, tasting the soup. His mother delves into the pages of the catalog.

"They opened up a new restaurant over on Seventh," Mr. Miller remarks distractedly.

The woman glances up at him. "The Ethiopian restaurant? Terrible. You have to eat everything with your hands."

"So what? It could be fun! And those spicy concoctions are fantastic!" the professor replies.

"Is there anything else, besides the soup?" Harvey asks.

"But still, I'm not going to eat with my hands."

"Can I have a steak?" Harvey says insistently.

The antiques dealer's catalog is removed from the table. Mrs. Miller stands up and takes a brick-shaped steak out of the freezer. "I'll thaw it out for you in the microwave."

"At the dinner table," her husband remarks, raising his fork, "there are those who are evolved and those who aren't."

"What about the Chinese, then?" asks Harvey.

"I hate those ridiculous wooden chopsticks!"

"You should try telling Sheng they're ridiculous."

"Who's Sheng?"

"What do you mean, who's Sheng?"

"Ah, yes," Professor Miller continues, recalling their New Year's in Rome. "Your Chinese friend. The one with the eye affliction."

"What affliction are you talking about?" his wife asks, turning the dial on the microwave all the way up.

"Have you ever seen a Chinese person with blue eyes before?"

The microwave hums for a few minutes and then lets out its high-pitched chime.

"There wouldn't happen to be two steaks, would there?" the professor asks.

"I believe there are, dear."

The man nods, pleased by the news. "Everything all right at school, Harvey?"

36

"Of course."

"Homework?"

"Not much of it, these days."

"No second thoughts?"

"George!" his wife says reproachfully, resting the griddle pan for the steaks on a burner.

"Not yet," replies Harvey.

"Not even just to brush up a little?"

The second it touches the griddle, the meat lets out a rising cloud of steam.

"I think we've already discussed this topic enough. Harvey wants to do it all on his own."

"That's right." The boy gets up from the table and puts his bowl in the sink.

"I'm sorry if I keep going on about this," Professor Miller protests, "but given that I'm not exactly ignorant when it comes to scientific topics, I'd like to give Harvey a hand."

"I don't need you to baby me, Dad."

"I'm not babying you. But if you're having problems at school, I—"

"I'm not having problems at school. Just a few little hiccups. I'll take care of it."

"Little hiccups? Is that how you see it? Your brother—"

"Can't we leave Dwaine out of this, for once?" Mrs. Miller exclaims, her voice shrill.

The meat is sizzling on the stove. Mr. Miller drums his spoon against his bowl. The family's embarrassment hangs awkwardly in the air. Harvey can't stand being compared to Dwaine. Not even over his grades. And he doesn't want tutoring or help from

37

his dad. He wants to do whatever he can manage to do on his own. Without help. All on his own.

Harvey grabs the antiques dealer's catalog simply because it's the closest thing around to read. He thumbs through it without any interest at all.

His father changes the subject. "Today I sent back some findings from the Pacific Ocean, made by some kids from the university. . . ."

"Why's that?" his wife asks, although her mind is actually light-years away.

"They indicated a half-degree rise in the water temperature in only three months. Impossible!"

"Couldn't it be the greenhouse effect?"

"No. It's some incompetent researcher who got the measurements wrong. Either that, or the ocean's planning on flooding the whole globe over the course of a single generation."

"It's happened before," Harvey remarks, still thumbing through the catalog.

"What?" his father asks curiously.

"The Great Flood."

"Those are just legends," his father snorts. "The truth is, it's simply impossible for the temperature of an ocean to go up half a degree in three months."

"The steaks are ready."

Harvey closes the folder while his father continues. "Besides, it's far easier to believe that a group of students used the instrumentation improperly!"

The boy nods. Then he stares down at the platter, stunned. His mother made three steaks. When Dwaine was still around, the "triple-steak platter" had practically become a dinnertime ritual.

"The other one's for me . . . ," Mrs. Miller lies, trying to cover for her mistake. She can't stand meat.

Once they've finished eating, Mr. and Mrs. Miller drink chamomile tea and Harvey clears the table. "Hey!" the boy suddenly exclaims when he catches sight of a page in the antiques catalog. He puts down the water pitcher, grabs the folder and takes a closer look at it. He shakes his head, not believing his eyes. On the page is a photo highlighted in yellow.

"Dad," he says, almost whispering, "who gave you this catalog?"

"I told you. An antiques dealer who looked like a skeleton. His business card must be in there, at the back. . . ."

Gaping at the photo in the catalog, Harvey stops breathing. It's a picture of an old wooden top. On it is engraved a drawing of a bridge, or maybe a rainbow. It's identical to the four tops they found in Rome, together with the map of the Chaldeans, which he hasn't used since.

It's the fifth top.

"The top of the rainbow," Harvey murmurs. Then, out loud, he repeats a thought that popped into his head, as if someone else had just said it. "The others. I've got to call the others."

"What's that, Harvey?"

The boy looks around. *Who said that?* he wonders.

The voice in his head repeats clearly, *The others. You've got to call the others.*

Harvey recognizes the voice. He runs out of the kitchen and into the hallway.

Rome.

New Year's.

The bridge.

The others, the voice repeats.

Harvey runs like crazy to his brother's room, throws open the door and looks inside. "Dwaine!" he cries.

But no one's there.

It's the top of the rainbow, nobody's voice says again inside his head.

Harvey staggers, claps his hands over his ears and stares into the darkness, stunned. Then he turns around and goes back to the kitchen. His parents are silent, their cups of chamomile clenched in their hands.

"Why did he come see you?" Harvey asks his father.

The professor seems confused. "The antiques dealer, you mean?"

"Yeah. Why did he come here?"

"I don't know," his father continues. "He was just a run-of-the-mill antiques dealer. With a Russian accent. I've already told you. . . ."

Harvey grabs the catalog again and flips through it nervously, looking for the business card. "But . . . has this ever happened to you before? I mean, has anybody else ever showed up here, trying to sell you stuff?"

"Oh, that happens practically every week. Paintings, electronic equipment, encyclopedias . . ."

It's a coincidence, Harvey thinks. *It's just a coincidence.* But as he's turning the pages, it's as if his brain shuts down. Was it Dwaine's voice he heard? What did he say, exactly?

It's the top of the rainbow. You've got to call the others.

"Where the heck is the business card?" Harvey shouts, exasperated.

The professor steps over to him. He turns to the last page of the catalog and pulls out a handwritten card:

Vladimir Askenazy
Antique Art
48th Street
Queens, NY

"Vladimir Askenazy . . . ," Harvey whispers. "Can I keep this?" Without waiting for an answer, he walks out of the kitchen and, two at a time, climbs the stairs leading up to the loft. Once he's there, he locks the door, his heart beating wildly.

"The top . . . ," he says, starting to tear the room apart, looking for something. Then he stops in his tracks. *Idiot*, he thinks. He didn't hide the top in his room. He sits down on the bed and forces himself to breathe. He can't tell if he's more scared because of the picture of the top or because of the voice he heard in his head.

"Vladimir Askenazy," he repeats to himself, trying to concentrate. The name doesn't ring a bell. Beatrice, Joe Vinile, Jacob Mahler . . . Harvey goes over the list of names from his Italian New Year.

He can hear zapping on the TV downstairs.

For the millionth time, the boy reads the antiques dealer's name on the business card. He makes sure the door to his room is closed, stands on a chair and opens the ladder door leading up to the attic. He pulls down the ladder and climbs up into the darkness above. Then he walks through the dark, hunched over, using his memory to guide himself through the maze of old junk until he reaches a metal cage beside the skylight. Inside of it is a carrier pigeon, which is cooing softly.

"I never would've believed I'd actually use you," he whispers. Next to the cage are boxes of birdseed that Ermete gave him, an old lamp and some little square slips of paper. Harvey switches on the lamp and grabs a piece of paper and a pen. I found another top, we need to meet up, he writes. He slips the note into a tiny metal cylinder, which he ties to the pigeon's leg.

"Here we go, my friend. It's up to you. I just hope you really know the way there. . . ."

Harvey nudges open the skylight with his elbow and frees the messenger into the dark city sky. He watches it fly off until it's disappeared. Then he shuts the skylight. And he waits.

Later on that same night, Harvey hears a noise coming from the roof. It's a faint but insistent noise followed by a fluttering of wings and something tapping against the glass.

The boy wakes up with a start, emerging from a dream that's both confused and frightening. His throat is dry. He can barely move. Lactic acid has stiffened his muscles. It's raining.

The house is silent. Harvey sits up in bed and when he hears the tapping noise again, he opens up the ladder door and climbs up to the attic.

Outside of the skylight is the pigeon. It's wet and trembling from the cold. Harvey opens the window, scoops it up gently in his hands, rewards it with a little ball of birdseed and tries to detach the tiny cylinder from its leg. Once he's managed to take it off, he puts it down on the table and lets the pigeon back into its cage.

He turns on the lamp, opens the cylinder and reads Ermete's reply:

Tomorrow afternoon at 4. The Montauk Club,
25 Eighth Avenue, Brooklyn.

FIRST STASIMON

"Hello? Vladimir? Any news?"

"I tried to contact Harvey."

"Did you manage?"

"I'll let you know over the next few days. How's it going there?"

"Everything seems fine. I haven't heard from anyone."

"Your niece?"

"She's not talking. I think they're in touch, but I'm not sure."

"Spring's almost here."

"Now comes the hardest part."

"Tell me what's scaring you."

"I don't know how to approach this. I don't know if someone's around . . . trying to track down Alfred."

"You don't know their names?"

"No. Except for Jacob Mahler."

"Forget that name."

"Well, I've got good news and bad news."

"Tell me the good news first."

"Two days ago there was a short article in the regional paper. They found the bodies of two men in a town just outside the city. One of them was a petty criminal from Rome. Joe Vinile, the man who tried to steal the Ring of Fire from my niece."

"And the other man?"

"The article just said it was a middle-aged man with no ID on him. His face couldn't be identified. I thought of Jacob Mahler, but I suggested that Fernando investigate. You know, using his novel as an excuse . . ."

"What's the bad news?"

"If Mahler's dead, too . . . who killed them?"

5
THE PANTHER

A LONG, BLACK, ASCENDING HALLWAY. A PAIR OF STILETTO HEELS click rhythmically on the polished floor. Then they stop. A black hand, the nails painted black, knocks on the gold door three times. It waits. Then it knocks three more times. With an electric groan, the door slides back into the wall.

Beyond it is a room with red upholstery. Massive gold picture frames. A man, his back turned to the doorway, watches the images sliding along inside one of them. It's a television monitor.

The man is wearing a dark blue velvet jacket and an eighteenth-century shirt with long, ruffled cuffs that cover his hands. He's leaning against a cane with a pommel shaped like a bunch of grapes.

"Go ahead and tell me, Panther," he orders, still peering at the images. The woman walks into the room, her heels sinking down into the leopard-skin carpeting. She's very tall, with a dancer's body. She's wearing a tight black catsuit with a white fur-trimmed collar and a wig glimmering silver. She doesn't say a word.

The man continues to observe the monitor. The images are showing the inside of a nightclub. It's called Lucifer. It's his club.

The owner is old, even though no one could say how old, exactly. Some claim he opened his first nightclub back when New York was founded. Others say he's even older than that.

His name is Egon Nose, also called Dr. Nose because of his incredible nose for business. And because of his enormous, pockmarked nose. But he hates it when people talk about his nose.

The man heaves a sigh and switches off the monitor. Then he turns around.

In her hand, Panther is holding the body of a sleeping pigeon.

"Ah, good. You got it," he remarks wearily. Clutching his cane, he moves toward her a few steps. His eyes are glittering with excitement, but his neck is hunched forward, as if the weight of his nose has become unbearable. "Hmm . . . of course . . . Very good. Put it right here."

Panther lays the pigeon on the majestic baroque desk in the middle of the room. Four massive legs shaped like lion's paws. Cherubs and floral inlays. On its front panel, a cornucopia brimming with animals and baskets of flowers.

"Go ahead and move the tray, my dear," Egon Nose suggests, rapping the tip of his cane on a large silver platter piled high with bananas and red apples. "I'm not hungry tonight."

Panther still hasn't spoken.

"Did it have anything on it?" the old man asks, stroking the pigeon's chest with his right index finger. He has long, sharp nails the color of alabaster.

The girl reaches into the top of her catsuit, pulls out a note and hands it to her boss.

Egon reads it avidly. "Excellent, excellent," he remarks, nodding. "This is the news we've been waiting for. Heh, heh, of

47

course . . ." He makes the note disappear into his jacket pocket and leans against his cane with all his weight. "Now one of you needs to get to work. . . ."

Panther steps over to him. She slides her hand down his arm, then strokes his neck with her fingers, their nails polished black. The old man lets out an unusually childish laugh, which makes his fleshy, undulated nose quiver. "All right, all right, Panther . . . Choose another one of the girls. You'll both be going to that dreadful Montauk Club tomorrow."

Panther steps back and sits down on the wooden desk.

Egon Nose taps his cane against a cart beside him, making the crystal wineglass on it clink. "Go ahead and help yourself," the old man adds. Next to the glass is a decanter half-full with a ruby-colored liquid. "I need to make a phone call."

The girl's gaze follows her boss as he goes to sit down in a damask armchair. Behind him, the giant gold frames. Above him, a Venetian glass chandelier. Its light is too faint to illuminate the walls. Egon Nose lets out a long sigh. "You can go, my dear," he says. His eyes are two desolate, rocky reefs.

The woman obediently withdraws. She slides off the desk and points at the pigeon's body.

"No, leave it there. I'll set it free myself later on. Or I might get my appetite back."

She strides out of the office, her hips swaying, the heels of her boots clicking on the hallway's polished floor. The gold door slides shut behind her.

Now alone, Dr. Nose pulls open the heavy desk drawers, one after the other. In the third one he finds a cell phone. He rests it on the table. He rifles through the right pocket in his tartan trousers, pulls out a gold lighter, flicks open its hinged top and stares at his office in the light of the flame.

"Heh, heh, heh," he repeats, waiting for the phone to switch on. Then he tosses the lighter on the desk. He dials a number very carefully, because any other combination would make the cell phone explode: 666.

He hears a crackling noise.

Egon Nose puts the telephone up to his head, almost making it disappear into his ear.

It's still crackling.

"Heh, heh, heh," the man repeats, raising his cane to prod the pigeon's limp body. "Traditional methods are best!"

The crackling suddenly stops.

It's ringing now.

Nose rests his cane on the floor. He fiddles with the note in his hand. And then . . .

"Heremit," a voice replies from the other side of the world. It's piercing, surreal.

"Cheer up, old friend!" Egon chimes, his nose quivering. "Or perhaps I called you at a bad moment? What time is it over there? Oh, may Zeus strike me down with his thunderbolts if I called you in the middle of the night again! The problem is that I can't even remember what daytime is like anymore. Is it still so ridiculously . . . sunny?"

From the other end of the line comes an eerie noise. And then: "No."

"What a pleasure to hear you speak again. It's been quite a while since we last had a nice little chat. How long has it been? Months? Years? Oh, I'll get straight to the point. . . . I know you're

49

obsessed with time. But there's nothing you can do about it. You're aging, too, even if you've found a way to alter the process. In any case, I have news for you. And since I can't call it *fresh* news . . . heh, heh, heh . . ." Egon Nose's cane prods the pigeon another time. "I'll call it 'new news.' Our man has made a move. Tomorrow at four. At the Montauk Club. Does that mean anything to you?" Not waiting for an answer, the lord of New York nightlife lets out yet another prolonged sigh. "Oh, how could you know about it, since you never leave that skyscraper of yours? The Montauk is a historic club in Brooklyn. An old, decadent Italian American club."

"Send someone," the voice on the other side of the world replies.

"Oh, it's a pleasure to know you're still alive. In any case, that's exactly what I intended to do. Send someone. Of course, it might be rather . . . costly."

"No limits."

"Good. I like it that way. While we're talking, I wanted to give you a second piece of news. It has to do with the first task you entrusted to me. Remember? I had to take care of a two-bit criminal in Rome and your musician friend. . . . Would you like to know how it went?"

"I already do."

"Heh, heh, heh," chuckles Egon Nose. "So it's true that news travels fast! I'm sorry about your friend! I wanted to plan a nice little evening for him at the club, violin included. In any case, it's done. Tomorrow, I'll authorize my girls to—"

"No."

"I understand. I'll tell them to look but not eat. . . ."

On the other end of the line is perceptible hesitation, second thoughts. It only lasts a fraction of a second, and then the voice says, "Only if they see the tops."

"What's that, old friend?"

"If the tops are there," Heremit Devil repeats, as if it were a strain for him to utter each word, "then your girls can intervene."

Twelve days is a long time. Twelve winter nights is even longer. But that's how long Jacob Mahler has stayed perfectly still in the woods. He's sucked up the last traces of snow. He's eaten chestnuts. Raw mushrooms. Roots. Practically without ever moving.

His greatest enemies have been the cold and his broken arm. The only way to defeat them is to stop thinking, to stay there, as motionless as a statue. Like the statues in the garden he escaped from.

Those women were hunters.

And they came for him.

They got out of Joe Vinile's car, already knowing what they were supposed to do: kill. They had a plan, a mission, an objective. But there was one little detail they lacked: They'd never seen his face.

Twelve days and twelve nights ago, Jacob Mahler was being treated in a private clinic in a little town near Rome. Few people. Few questions. He saw Joe Vinile come out into the courtyard, accompanied by the hunter women. *You idiot, Vinile!* Mahler thought, moving as quickly as possible. It hadn't dawned on Joe that he was invited to the feast, too. . . .

Then Mahler removed the bandages covering his face, which had been burned in the explosion, and wrapped them around the face of the man in the bed next to his. As the hunter women's heels were bewitching the clinic's staff members, Jacob Mahler slipped out through a back door. And he hid in the woods.

Once the hunter women reached the room, the man in the bed next to his started shrieking, and Joe Vinile realized what a fool he'd been.

Motionless in the woods, Mahler waits, ignoring the pain.

One more day. Then he'll move.

6

THE CLUB

THE MONTAUK CLUB IS A STRANGE MIX OF GILDED SIXTEENTH-century Venetian and American country styles. Little white tables separated by wooden dividers, mirrors on the walls and sparkling chandeliers. Waiters wearing tuxedos gracefully gliding across the marble floor.

At four o'clock on the dot, Harvey walks in. Hesitating, he looks around for Ermete but doesn't see him. He chooses a booth in the corner and tosses his gym bag under the seat. He starts to flip through the menu.

A hand rests on his shoulder. "Hey, kid."

Harvey leaps to his feet. He doesn't recognize the man in front of him. A cream-colored raincoat, a wool turtleneck sweater and, most noticeable of all, a cascade of long, blond hair. The man smiles.

"Ermete?" Harvey whispers uncertainly.

"Shhh!" the engineer warns him, brushing the hair out of his eyes. "It's a wig. Brilliant, isn't it?"

Ermete wedges himself in between the table and the stiff back-rest, dragging a battered old briefcase behind him. He blows the hair out of his eyes and holds out his hand to Harvey like a suave businessman. "It's a pleasure to see you again, Harvey. I mean it. I was about to give up hope. My pigeons work like a charm, don't they?"

The boy smiles. "They're great. Like real spies."

"This calls for the utmost attention," Ermete confides in him, looking around. The raincoat and wig are making him sweat. "How do you like this place, huh? Doesn't it make you think of Hitchcock movies?"

"*Hao*, awesome!" Harvey approves, quoting Sheng.

"Most importantly, it's nowhere near my house. The only New York street written in code."

"Which would be . . . ?"

"A1 V4 E1 N1 U1 E1 14."

"Meaning . . . ?"

"The value of the letters in the word 'avenue' in the board game Scrabble. You know it, right? The man who invented it lived there, and the street sign was written like that in his honor."

"Seriously?"

"Seriously."

The two of them crack up and order some fruit juice. Then Ermete lies down on the booth and scans the room. "Wow," he remarks at the end of his reconnaissance.

"Wow what?"

"Don't turn around, but there are two drop-dead gorgeous women behind you. Oh, do I love America!"

"You're looking good yourself."

"What about you? You look . . . bigger. What's up with that duffel bag of yours?"

"I'm going to a gym. I signed up for boxing lessons."

"Boxing lessons?"

Harvey brushes the hair out of his eyes. "Yeah. And my trainer's a woman."

"Whoa! It must be fun to get slapped around by a girl." Ermete smiles at the waiter.

Harvey turns around to take a look at the women. "They sure are something," he admits a second later.

"Head-spinning."

"Speaking of spinning . . ."

"The top! Explain it to me, from the start."

Harvey shows him the catalog and the card with the antiques dealer's address.

"That's not far from my place," Ermete remarks, turning it over in his fingers.

"But don't you think it's strange?"

"Very strange. Every time I look for something in this city, it's always at least three hours away."

"No, I mean, don't you find it strange that this catalog just turned up right in front of me?"

"Not in front of you. In front of your father."

"But the antiques dealer highlighted the picture of the top."

"That's true. But why?"

"My dad doesn't know exactly, but from what he remembers, it had already been sold."

Ermete holds the photo of the top up in the light to take a better look. "A rainbow?"

"You got it."

"A passageway. The end of a storm . . ." Ermete rests the sheet of paper on the table and drums his fingers on the edge of his glass.

55

"If you ask me, we'd better hurry up and see this . . . this Vladimir Askenazy."

"Have you heard from the others?"

"I sent an encrypted e-mail to all three of them. Reply: They're fine, they say hi and they're happy to hear about the top in the catalog. They say they want to see us again."

"Me too. This might be our chance to get together. . . ."

Ermete rests his hands on his briefcase. "Yeah, but we need to be careful."

"What are you lugging around in that thing?"

Ermete's fingers fly away from the briefcase. "Summer homework. All human knowledge on Mithra, the Chaldeans, ancient religions, mirrors and comets."

"Find out anything new about the Ring of Fire?"

"Nothing solid, actually. . . ." The engineer leans on his elbows and lowers his voice. "I found a few leads. For example, the word 'Mithra' means 'the pact.' And naturally, the pact with this ancient god of the sun and light is a secret pact. Remember what was engraved on the back of the mirror?"

" 'There is an invisible purpose behind the visible world . . . ,' " Harvey repeats by heart.

"Exactly. I figure that, sooner or later, invisible purposes will become visible."

"Anything else?"

"I could bore you with details about the Mysteries of Mithra convention held in Rome on March 28, 1978, about the Iranian Magi and their relationship with the cult of light, the goddess Isis . . . but actually I haven't come up with very much. Only legends."

"Like what?"

Ermete hoists the briefcase onto his lap and opens it up, revealing a mass of papers. "I decided to call the Ring of Fire 'Prometheus's Mirror,' because it was through a mirror that the Titan stole fire from the gods. But the story of Prometheus is complicated. Not only did he steal fire from the gods, but he also created man, by mixing together rainwater and clay." The engineer sips his fruit juice. "And I discovered that there's another figure in Greek mythology who has something to do with mirrors. His name is Hephaestus, and he's the god of blacksmiths. He also used fire to forge Hercules' shield and Achilles' weapons. Depicted on Achilles' shield, in particular, are the Pleiades and the seven stars of Ursa Major. The Greeks were convinced that the end of the world depended on Ursa Major. Stars, you see?"

"The professor was obsessed with stars," Harvey recalls.

"Exactly." Ermete clasps his hands together in front of his face. "It's all connected, but I still can't put my finger on how. Anyway, you know what happens when Prometheus steals fire from the gods? Zeus goes to Hephaestus and together they come up with the most horrible punishment imaginable. Prometheus is chained to a mountainside and a vulture gnaws away at his liver. As for mankind, which he created . . ." He shows Harvey the statue of a woman holding a vase. "Hephaestus fashions Pandora, the first woman." He plops back against the backrest. "Could you have come up with a nastier punishment?"

Having left the Montauk Club, Harvey and the engineer slip into the subway, heading for the antiques shop in Queens. "What I still don't get," Ermete admits, "is what I should be looking for, and where. Everything's hazy, blending together, getting all jumbled up. Legends and the real world. Mythology and history . . ."

"Anything in the professor's books?"

Ermete shrugs his shoulders. "There's one thing I found. Among the ancient Persians was a caste of learned astronomers called the Magi. They were very familiar with the sun god Mithra. A part of their secret doctrine reached the Western world during the time of the Greco-Persian wars, and it became the basis of the Egyptian dogmas. The Romans conquered both Greece and Egypt—"

"And took it all over."

"They rediscovered an incredible heritage of secret knowledge . . . including the map of the Chaldeans and its tops. The Ring of Fire. Or all three things."

"What a big, confusing mess," Harvey summarizes.

"You have no idea. This calls for a serious scholar, not a dilettante like me."

"But only a dilettante like you would be crazy enough to keep going."

Ermete stops and stares at the boy. "I can't tell whether or not that's a compliment."

7

THE ANTIQUES DEALER

THE ANTIQUES SHOP DOESN'T HAVE A SIGN. THERE'S ONLY A POORLY lit, anonymous-looking picture window facing the street. Behind the glass, a board reads OLD THINGS FROM ALL OVER THE WORLD. There are also a few dusty items displayed on three different stands. Two wooden statuettes, a piece of coral jewelry, a couple of desk lamps, a little inlaid case with the profile of a heron and two vases with orange and black stripes.

Ermete and Harvey push open the shop's metal door, making a little bell jingle. A narrow opening between the walnut furniture leads into an open space dimly lit by a crooked neon ceiling light. Everything is cramped and chaotic, with dozens of old things piled up haphazardly, filling every inch of the room. Étagères and shelves lining the walls are crammed full of books; paintings and picture frames are stacked up against each other; wardrobes brim with colorful fabrics and rag dolls; African masks hang from the ceiling by festoonlike cords.

On the opposite side of the room, Harvey and Ermete see a microscopic desk buried beneath a mountain of papers. Behind it is a little doorway with a curtain of rattling jade bead strings hanging over it.

"Anybody here?" asks Ermete. He moves almost on tiptoe, worried he'll knock something over.

A long, bony hand slides out through the beads, gathering the strings of the curtain into a single cluster.

"Hello," croaks Vladimir Askenazy's hoarse voice. Tall and thin, the antiques dealer creeps through the doorway like a spider and takes his place behind the desk. His face is gaunt, his hair sparse, light gray and disheveled. His eyes are the color of acacia honey. His mouth is wide and thin, his teeth small, closely set and frail looking. His nose is slender and measured. His dragonfly-like hands are so pale they look like they're covered with talcum powder. He's dressed completely in black. "What can I do for you?"

Harvey looks at him carefully and lets Ermete do the talking.

"Oh! Hello there!" the engineer begins. "We saw your catalog and we thought we'd come see you." He hands the folder to Vladimir.

The man looks at it with a certain curiosity and remarks, "Oh, of course."

"You gave it to my father," Harvey explains.

"Of course, of course." The antiques dealer nods and doesn't even bother to glance at the boy. He pulls out a pair of round-framed spectacles that glitter in the light and perches them on the tip of his nose. "I was working on promotion a bit yesterday. So . . . which of these items are you interested in?"

"The wooden top," Ermete replies without hesitating.

Vladimir's spectacles gleam in the light. For the first time, the antiques dealer turns to scrutinize Harvey. "Oh," he says.

"Have you already sold it?"

"I haven't exactly sold it, no. . . . But I can't sell it to you." Vladimir rests the folder atop the thousand others on his desk and turns to look through the beaded curtain, as if he's heard a noise. Then he goes back to concentrating on his clients. "The fact is . . . Listen, let's do this . . . if I may . . ."

Stepping around the desk, Vladimir slips between Ermete and Harvey, flips over the little sign on the front door from OPEN to CLOSED and turns the key in the lock a couple of times.

"Please, follow me," he suggests, retracing his steps and pushing aside the beads in the little doorway leading into the back of the shop.

"Watch your head," the antiques dealer warns them, leading them down a dark, narrow hallway. "I've never gotten around to having this light fixed, but right here, halfway across, there's a beam in the ceiling that—"

A barely muffled thud tells them that Ermete's forehead just found it. Behind him, Harvey tries to keep from laughing.

"Are you hurt?" Vladimir asks, although he shows no signs of stopping.

"No, it's nothing! Don't worry! I'm a hard-headed guy."

"We're there," the antiques dealer announces a second later. Now his face is lit up by daylight. They're inside a large room with glass walls, quite like a greenhouse. Twelve metal supports are holding up its clear ceiling. The whole back of the shop looks like a transparent party tent set up in a courtyard. With its full view of the sky above, the room is well illuminated by the outdoor light. Warm and dusty, it shines down on the furniture, statues, paintings and other antiques.

"This is my kingdom," explains Vladimir, whose body seems to have lost a bit of its frailness as he makes his way through his favorite objects.

Harvey clutches his gym bag tighter and looks up at the silhouettes of the buildings looming overhead on the other side of the glass ceiling. "Awesome," he remarks.

The antiques dealer mutters something unintelligible, opens an old cabinet and pulls out some cases. "The item you're looking for should be right here . . . ," he says softly, resting one of the cases on a workbench cluttered with picture frames and stuccos to be restored.

"Do you have any others, by chance?" Ermete asks, staring nervously at the antiques dealer's long fingers as they fiddle with the case.

Vladimir shakes his head. "No, no. That would be a true stroke of luck, given their value."

"Oh, are they worth a lot?" Ermete inquires.

"I should say so," the man replies, finally pulling out the wooden top. He holds it firmly in his fingertips for a moment and then hands it to Harvey. "I presume you were the one who noticed it."

Harvey lets his gym bag slide to the floor. He takes the top and peers at it. His heart has started to beat faster. He turns it over and over in his fingers, admiring the engraving of the rainbow and its metal tip. There's no doubt about it. It's one of their tops. The fifth one.

Although he senses the same thing, Ermete feigns indifference and remarks, "I don't get what's so valuable about it. It just looks like an old toy to me."

"Ah!" Vladimir exclaims, raising a finger. "You've managed to make two mistakes in a single sentence."

"I'm an expert in—"

"That top isn't old. It's *ancient*. And it isn't a toy. It's a theurgic instrument."

"Theur . . . what?"

"Theurgic. It's a derivative of a Greek word describing the ability to accomplish things thanks to the intercession of the gods. That top, my friend, was used in a complex series of rituals. It served to put people in contact with the gods and obtain their response. It was an oracular top."

"Did you hear that? It's an instrument of the gods!" Ermete says to Harvey, who's always been more reluctant than the others to accept how the tops work and how they can be used on the wooden map.

"A mysterious oracle, to say the least," Vladimir Askenazy adds. He looks around for something on the workbench, then picks up a small tattered booklet and thumbs through a few pages. "Michael Psellos, an ancient Byzantine scholar gifted with encyclopedic knowledge, wrote something about these very tops. Here's his treatise on the Chaldean oracles. . . ."

"Chaldean oracles?" Ermete repeats with a start.

"You've heard of them?"

"Of course! Who hasn't?" The engineer smiles.

Vladimir chuckles. Then he grabs an old ring set with a ruby. "You know," he says, holding it up, "all women should know about the Chaldeans. They're the ones who had the idea of wearing engagement rings on the fourth finger of the left hand. They believed that a line of energy began at that finger and was connected directly to the heart."

Ermete makes a face.

The antiques dealer walks halfway around the workbench and points at the face of a clock hanging on the wall. "They also introduced the system of calculation based on the number twelve. As well as the sixty-minute hour. And the signs of the zodiac and a great deal of the names of the stars."

"We know that," Ermete interjects, a hint of pride in his voice. "Just like we know about the Magi . . ."

"Knowledgeable priests, but not exactly Chaldeans," Vladimir Askenazy begins again. "They were keepers of ancient traditions. They knew . . . they knew *something,* which they passed down through oral tradition to those who came after them. Something that might even be lost to us today." The man sighs. "Poor Magi! The only thing people remember about them now are the three who went to Bethlehem following a star. Soon enough, children will even forget about them . . . and about the most important of the three gifts they brought with them."

"Gold?" Ermete asks.

"Frankincense?" says Harvey.

Vladimir Askenazy shakes his head. "Myrrh, naturally."

"I was just about to say that!" Ermete groans.

"I don't think anyone these days knows what myrrh was once used for," the antiques dealer goes on. Wanting to avoid embarrassing themselves, Harvey and Ermete stay silent.

Behind the thick lenses of his spectacles, the antiques dealer's eyes look huge. "We've lost everything," he continues. "Meanings, symbols, traditions . . . we're even losing the gods themselves."

"Maybe we just came up with new ones," Harvey suggests. "Internet, oil, cell phones, TV . . ."

"And what knowledge do we receive from these new gods?" Vladimir shakes his head. Then he returns to the topic he'd begun before. "In any case, these aren't tops. Their real name is *iynges*."

"*Iynges?*"

Vladimir begins to paraphrase from the book by the Byzantine scholar. "Within each top is a golden sphere with a precious gem inside of it. Once cast, the top mimics the bellowing of the primordial bull and is influenced by the rotation of the celestial orbs."

"Golden spheres? Precious gems?" Ermete asks.

"Bellowing of the primordial bull? Celestial orbs?" Harvey says.

The antiques dealer rests the book on the workbench and stares at the top, which is still in Harvey's hands. "Inside the wood, which represents the cosmos, is a gold sphere, which represents the Earth, and a precious gem . . . the heart of the Earth."

"Then it must cost a fortune," Ermete murmurs, worried.

On hearing this, Vladimir Askenazy frowns. "I never said it had a price. Nor that it was for sale. I only explained why it's so precious: because it's one of a kind."

"I'm not so sure about that," Ermete shoots back. "Who knows? We might have another four or five of them. . . ."

"Now it's my turn to doubt you. Such items are impossible to find."

"Then how'd you get this one?" Harvey asks.

"I have my friends."

"So why aren't you selling it?" Ermete demands.

"Because it was put on hold months ago by a client of mine."

"And there's no way to . . . ?" Harvey's voice trails off.

"Not any longer."

"Can't you even tell us . . . ?" says Ermete.

The antiques dealer shakes his head. "I'm sorry. All I can do is let you see it." Vladimir Askenazy takes the top out of Harvey's hands and rests it back in its case. Then he looks up. A crow with one blind eye is perched on top of the roof. Its feet are clicking rhythmically against the glass.

"Did you know that the great Homer studied with the Magi?" he asks distractedly. "As did Pythagoras, the master of numbers?"

But Harvey and Ermete don't reply. All their attention is focused on the wooden top as it slowly disappears into its case. Harvey sighs. Ermete scratches his head, forgetting about his blond wig for a moment.

"The thing is . . . ," Harvey starts out.

Vladimir Askenazy stretches his lean, bony neck farther over the table. "What?"

"We . . ." Ermete gulps and struggles to continue.

"We need to know who put the top on hold," Harvey blurts out. "We really need to."

"I can't tell you that. . . . Not yet," Vladimir replies, shaking his head.

Nevertheless, it doesn't sound like a refusal to Harvey. There's something left unspoken in the man's tone of voice. Besides, what he's said about the Chaldeans, the Magi and the gods of antiquity was like a tacit invitation, as if he's given them information and now, before going any farther, he wants something in exchange.

"We've already seen other tops like yours," Harvey ventures to say.

"Where?" Vladimir Askenazy asks, as if he already knows the answer.

Ten feet above them, the crow's claws are clicking against the glass ceiling. Then comes the sound of someone banging on the door in the front room of the shop. Startled, the crow takes wing.

"I think I should go open up," says Vladimir. He's only taken a couple of steps when he's stopped by the deafening clang of a metal cable striking the glass, the violent thud of something heavier . . . and an entire section of the ceiling shattering into a thousand pieces.

A figure plummets to the ground in a shower of glass. Vladimir cries out, stunned, while Ermete throws himself down, trying to shield his head from the shards of glass raining on top of him. Harvey dives under the table.

In a flash, a second figure plunges down from above, clinging to a rope, and lands athletically on the floor a few steps away from the first one.

"What's going on? Who are you? What do you want?" Vladimir shouts. There's a fluttering of wings and the crow flies down into the room, too, circling madly around Vladimir and Ermete.

There's more banging on the front door, and this time it's even louder.

From his place beneath the table, Harvey watches as four legs clad in jeans draw closer. The floor is covered with broken glass.

"Stop! Who are you?" the antiques dealer groans a few yards away from him. The two figures ignore him. Women's boots crush shard after shard with their every step.

Harvey's heart is beating wildly. He waits for the mysterious women to move even closer and then springs to his feet, trying to overturn the table right on top of them. The two leap back. Among the countless objects that crash to the ground, they spot the case containing the top and grab it at once.

Harvey bares his fists and then, suddenly, he recognizes them. They're the two women from the club. One white and one black, with geometrical faces and sparkling white teeth, like predators.

He takes a swing at the one closest to him but misses. An instant later, a hand grabs his wrist, stopping him. Panther whirls him around, twisting his arm behind his back. Then she moves her lips up to his ear and lets out a long, threatening hiss. Finally, she shoves him away.

Harvey stumbles and falls down onto the broken glass. He hears Vladimir let out a final shout: "Stop, thief!" When he looks up again, he sees the two women climb swiftly up the rope and disappear.

"Dammit!" Harvey shouts, getting to his feet. One of his palms has a cut on it. "They stole the top!"

Once he's sure the danger is over, Ermete pulls himself to his feet and shakes his fist at the hole in the ceiling. "Lucky for them they got away. Otherwise I would've . . ."

Vladimir Askenazy coughs, looking around in a daze. His eyes are wide open, his pupils dilated.

"You okay?" Harvey asks him.

"Just a few scratches."

"We need to call the police. . . ."

The man checks the little wooden cases and the other items that have tumbled to the floor. He's in shock. "Yes . . . I think . . .

I think that would be best." He can't make heads or tails of what's happened. "You . . . you two . . . they . . . ," he says to the boy, trying to understand.

Ermete is searching the floor for the blond wig he's lost.

"Yeah, it's our fault," Harvey confesses. "They followed us."

"What do you mean they . . . they followed you?" Vladimir gasps.

The boy points up at the shattered ceiling. "I should've realized it the moment I saw that crow."

"What does the crow have to do with it?"

"Aha!" Ermete exclaims. He's just slipped his wig back on, even though it still has a few pieces of glass caught in it.

Harvey shrugs. "Let's just say that for a while now I've felt like . . . like I was being followed. And those two women were at the club where Ermete and I met today."

The engineer is walking around the room with long strides. "They swiped that top from right under our noses!"

"The two women from the club," Harvey repeats.

Ermete helps the antiques dealer turn the table right-side up. "Yeah. This is the first time in my life that two women have followed me . . . and look how it ended up."

"I'm the one they were following," Harvey points out.

Vladimir doesn't ask any questions. He's bewildered, devastated.

"We've got to warn the others," Harvey says.

"We aren't safe," Ermete says.

"We never have been." Harvey clenches his fists angrily. The memory of the woman's hiss in his ear is still vivid. "I didn't even manage to hit her."

69

8

THE DEBATE

AUNT IRENE'S BEDROOM IS FILLED WITH PERFECT SILENCE. THE elderly woman is sitting in her wheelchair, a plaid blanket covering her lap. Sitting on the floor facing her are Elettra and Sheng.

"Well?" Irene asks her sister, Linda, who's standing rigidly behind the kids.

"Well what? It's sheer nonsense!" the latter blurts out, her hands on her hips.

Elettra rolls her eyes, nudging Sheng with her elbow. "What did I tell you? It's no use."

"Linda, please be reasonable!" Irene begs.

"I *am* being reasonable! Can't Fernando go?"

"It seems that a mystery publisher liked his novel. They made him a good offer and—"

"Let's not talk about that novel of his, please!"

"In any case, Fernando can't leave town right now."

"Neither can I. Or maybe you want the Domus Quintilia to fall to pieces?"

"It's been standing for four hundred years, Linda." Irene sighs. "I don't think it's going to collapse over the course of a week."

"I wouldn't be so sure about that. Besides, the Olfaddestens will be checking in on Wednesday, and they—"

"They're two of our oldest clients who'll be coming back to stay with us for fifteen more years even if they happen to find a speck of dust on a nightstand this time," Irene insists.

"So what? Have you forgotten that the curtains need to be laundered? That the wardrobes are packed full of clothes that need to be aired out? Heavens! You all buy far too many things! Things I need to miraculously straighten out . . ."

"Auntie! Don't you understand how important it is for us to go? Sheng's father needs us," Elettra breaks in, jumping to her feet.

"I can't help you with that, not this week. Nor next week, for that matter. I have spring-cleaning to do. . . ."

"Linda, for goodness' sake!" her older sister interjects. "All the kids are asking is that you go with them to New York for one week. The plane tickets have already been paid for. So has the hotel." Irene rolls her wheelchair forward slightly. "As I see it, Sheng's father is offering the kids a wonderful opportunity, and they're offering to share it with you."

"But isn't there anyone else who can go with them?" Linda Melodia suggests, staring stubbornly at the ceiling. "Mistral's mother, for instance?"

"She's away on business."

Linda glances at the kids and points at a tiny patch of dampness in one corner of the ceiling. "Do you two see that? If I go to New York with you, once we're back it'll be twice as big as it is now!"

"We have three rooms booked on the top floor of the Mandarin Oriental Hotel. . . ."

"There's a spa. . . ."

"A view of Central Park . . ."

"It's only a short walk away from the boutiques on Fifth Avenue. . . ." Irene notices a glimmer of interest in her eyes and seizes the opportunity. "Linda, when's the last time you bought yourself a nice pair of shoes?"

"Oh, don't be ridiculous. What would I do with new shoes?"

"That's my line, little sister. You can still use your legs."

"I wasn't saying that, Irene." But the woman's eyes have grown sweet and understanding.

"I know perfectly well what you meant. But just imagine, a vacation, at long last, after all these years! In the world's most beautiful city. Besides, the kids will behave like little angels."

"We'll be on our best behavior," Elettra agrees for both of them. "You won't even notice we're there."

"The truth is that . . . well, there's nothing I'm interested in seeing in New York," Linda bursts out.

"Not even the skyscrapers?" Elettra asks.

"The museums?" says Sheng.

"The Brooklyn Bridge?" Irene offers.

"The Statue of Liberty?" says Elettra.

When Linda hears mention of the Statue of Liberty, her eyes sparkle. The woman looks like she's about to give in. But suddenly, she raises her head and emphatically exclaims, "I can't."

"Auntie!"

"I can't, I can't, I can't," she repeats obsessively, waving her hands in front of her. "I don't have that optical thing."

"Huh?"

"To enter the United States these days, you need that special

72

doodad. The passport, I mean. The electronic one. I've read that it takes them almost two months to issue one. Which means I can't go."

"So that's the problem, is it?" Irene asks her.

"Isn't that reason enough? Without the right passport, they arrest you. And what about the children? What will they do?"

"I've already got an electronic passport," says Sheng.

"Me too," adds Elettra.

"But I haven't!" Linda Melodia retorts triumphantly.

"Fernando!" Irene calls out.

The bedroom door opens slightly and in steps a grinning Fernando Melodia. The man winks at the kids. Linda peers at him suspiciously.

"It just so happens," her older sister explains, "that one of Fernando's friends works over at the police headquarters."

"I don't understand," grumbles Linda, who now clearly smells a rat.

"With friends in the right places, instead of it taking the customary two months, your passport was renewed in only—"

"Six hours!" Fernando says, finishing her sentence and handing Linda a brand-new biometric passport. Then he adds sheepishly, "Sheng took your picture."

"With a telephoto lens, ma'am," the boy specifies.

Linda Melodia takes the passport, making no further protests. "Rascals," she remarks. "You were all in on this, were you?"

Irene, Fernando and the kids cast knowing glances at each other.

"Actually, yes," Elettra says, grinning.

* * *

73

Later on, Sheng locks himself in his room. He leans against the wall and sighs. On the other side of the door, the three daughters of the family hosting him are dancing nonstop to "You Make Me Crazy," which is turned up full blast. The floor is even trembling. The Chinese boy claps his hands over his ears and tries to think straight. He soon realizes it's no use.

He pulls his biggest wheeled suitcase out from under his bed, unzips it, opens the dresser drawers and throws in everything he can fit into it. He grabs his toothbrush, toothpaste and floss from the bathroom, thinks it over for a moment and adds a perfectly useless disposable razor. Then he looks in the mirror hopefully. "Maybe I'll start growing a beard in New York," he muses.

Trying to ignore the commotion the three young girls are making, Sheng walks over to the shoe cabinet, detaches the bottom of the lowest shelf and gropes around the gap beneath it. He pulls out a small wooden object and says, "You're coming with me, little top."

Now it's time for his ever-present backpack. He takes it off its hook, hides the top in an inside pocket and slings it over his shoulder. Then, wheeling the suitcase behind him, he goes back to the door. A second before he walks out, he freezes. "Oh, man! The tickets!" he exclaims. He rushes back, opens the desk drawer and grabs the hotel vouchers and the open-ended plane tickets that his father gave him. Then he walks out of his room. The music hits him like a blast of air from a hair dryer.

"Hey, guys!" he hollers to the three hyperactive girls. "Can you hear me? Tell your folks I'm leaving! Got that? I'm going to New York for a week!"

They nod, but Sheng doubts they hear a single word. He waves to them and hurries out of the apartment.

"It's eight-nineteen! We're late!" Linda Melodia says fussily from the backseat of the minibus. They're in the Domus Quintilia courtyard, waiting to go.

"Just a sec!" Elettra shouts, shoving in her suitcase and running back into the house.

Fernando plops into his seat. Behind him, Sheng pats his bulky carry-on bag, as if to make sure it's really zipped up. Linda's yellow suitcases, all lined up by height like Russian nesting dolls, have taken up every square inch of the luggage compartment.

Meanwhile, Elettra climbs the stairs two at a time and reaches Aunt Irene's room. "We're leaving!" she cries, saying goodbye for the hundredth time.

The woman wraps her feeble arms around the girl and strokes her black, black tangle of hair. "Be careful, you hear me?"

"Of course, Auntie."

"Don't do anything crazy, under any circumstances."

"You can count on me."

"And—"

A horn honks down in the courtyard.

"What?" Elettra says, breaking away from the hug.

"Nothing. Go on. Have fun. And say hello to the other kids for me."

Irene listens to her niece going down the stairs, the minibus door slamming shut and the engine starting up with a sputter.

"Make sure you come back, my dear," she whispers to the old furniture in her bedroom. Then she clasps her hands together on her lap and adds, "And you, Nature, protect her."

* * *

Mistral reaches the front door of her apartment. She glances around again. The note for her mother is there on the table. She's rewritten it five times. She never managed to get through to her on the phone to say goodbye. She bites her lip. Maybe she's being a little too cold? She walks back, rereads what she wrote and, at the bottom of the note, draws her profile and writes I love you. Then she pulls a lilac-colored hat with a cloth flower onto her head and shuts the door behind her.

The taxi is waiting outside. It's noisy and looks like a big beetle.

"Charles de Gaulle airport," Mistral says, getting into the backseat.

Ermete stops a few houses down from his place on Thirty-fifth Avenue in Queens. Something's not right. Something's wrong with his house.

The light.

He didn't leave the kitchen light on.

He leans against a lamppost and waits. For ten long, long minutes, nothing happens. *What if I actually did leave it on?* the engineer wonders, riddled with doubt.

Just to be on the safe side, he waits ten more minutes. Then, once he's convinced everything's okay, he crosses the street and opens the front door.

His doubts are confirmed.

"There you go," he says under his breath as he walks inside. "They were here."

His apartment is a total wreck. Scattered all over the floor are papers and notebooks. Suits, socks, shirts. His comforter ripped off the bed and slashed in two, the pillows gutted. Foam rubber everywhere. The drawers dumped upside down. The closet doors wide open.

Ermete shuts the door behind him. He's unusually calm. If the robbers found what they were looking for, it's over. It's all over.

He steps over his things strewn around on the floor and walks into the bathroom. His toiletries have been opened and dumped into the sink. His toothbrush is on the floor. The shower mat is crumpled up. He looks at his reflection in the mirror and smiles, immediately reassured.

Then he leaves his apartment, goes out onto the street and keeps walking until he finds a pay phone. He checks the time. "They should be here by now," he mumbles. He slides a coin into the slot and dials the number.

"Mandarin Oriental Hotel, good evening."

"I have a message for Elettra Melodia, Sheng Young Wan Ho and Mistral Blanchard," says Ermete, listing them. "Tell them it's a bad idea for us to meet. A *very* bad idea. My apartment is a wreck. A *total* wreck. Tell them I'll be in touch. Good night. And good luck," he concludes before hanging up.

To be on the safe side, he calls Harvey's house and leaves a brief message: "Ciao, Harvey! It's me! I know we were supposed to meet, but believe me, we better not! I'll call you as soon as I can! Bye-bye!"

Suddenly nervous, he stares at the lights glowing in his apartment, not sure what to do. Should he check into a hotel or stay here? The people who trashed his place might come back. If they came back, how would he handle them?

He tries to calm down. In gangster movies, this kind of break-in is almost always meant only to scare someone. It's intimidation, a way to say, "We know who you are and where you live."

"What the hell!" Ermete grumbles, heading back home. "I'm not leaving!"

Sitting in the lobby of the Mandarin Oriental, Harvey checks for the millionth time the notes he jotted down on a piece of paper:

> They know Ermete.
> They're following me.
> Clues: the crow and the two women.
> Can Vladimir Askenazy be trusted?
> What does the Ring of Fire do?
> Did I really hear Dwaine's voice?

A bit of commotion by the reception desk makes him look up. The first thing he recognizes is Elettra's black hair, then Sheng's colorful gym shoes, and finally Mistral's graceful, heronlike profile. With them is the lady from the Domus Quintilia, who's arguing with the bellhop. Actually, more than arguing; she's waving her hands around and pointing at a canary yellow suitcase that's fallen to the floor.

Harvey smiles. He crosses off the last line of his notes and then, just to be on the safe side, he rips it off and tosses it into a wastepaper basket.

He heads toward the reception desk, feeling unusually cheerful.

He can't wait to hug his friends again.

It's the fifteenth of March. And all four of them are together again.

9
THE BUYER

"THIS IS THE PLACE," HARVEY EXPLAINS, LEADING ELETTRA, SHENG and Mistral to the door of the antiques shop. It's the morning of March sixteenth, and they're on a dark street lined with grim-looking cement and brick buildings. The little sign in the window shows that the shop is open.

"My aunt's going to the top of the Empire State Building," Elettra tells them, reading a message on her cell phone. "She says there's even a sign on the ground floor that tells you what the visibility is like."

"*Hao!* Cool! Why don't we go up in the Empire State Building, too?" Sheng suggests, a hopeful look on his face. "Just like King Kong!"

"Maybe later on. I think we should do some interviews for your father," Elettra reminds him. "Otherwise, he won't be very happy he sent us all here, don't you think?"

"No, no, he'd be happy anyway," Sheng jokes.

"How many families do we need to meet?"

"Around ten, at least."

"This isn't going to be quick."

"No," Sheng replies sheepishly. "But it won't be so bad, either. We can split up."

"I'm afraid we can't," Elettra says. "Your father wants to know if the families on the list are okay for Chinese kids. And I don't see many Chinese kids among us."

"Oh, thanks for the help!" Sheng bursts out. "Well, that means that once we get out of here, if there aren't any problems . . ."

"Exactly. You said it. If! *If* there aren't any problems," Harvey grumbles.

"One thing at a time. First let's try to learn something about this top," Mistral says, following Harvey into the shop. "Then we can do some sightseeing."

The moment the bell over the entrance jingles, Vladimir comes out through the little doorway with the bead curtain. "We're closed," he says before recognizing Harvey. "Oh, it's you."

"These are the friends I told you about," the boy replies, making three brief introductions.

The antiques dealer clasps his hands together hesitantly. His fingers are bandaged. Then he flips the sign in the window from OPEN to CLOSED and turns the key in the lock a couple of times.

"Come with me, please. And be careful," he says, stepping back to the beaded curtain. He escorts the kids down the hallway into what remains of the back room. The glass ceiling has been sealed up with a tarp held in place with duct tape. Vladimir points at the shards of glass and the objects that are still strewn on the floor. "I was trying to put everything back in its place, but it's not easy all alone. Watch your step and don't touch anything. There's glass everywhere."

"Any news from the police?" Harvey inquires.

"I didn't call them."

"Why not?"

"I haven't had the time. Come . . . let's sit down back here. These chairs are still in one piece. At least, I hope so." He accompanies them to a little makeshift sitting room amid the furniture in the back of the shop.

Resting on Harvey's chair is a terra-cotta flowerpot with a small, withered primrose plant. The boy distractedly strokes it with his finger, moves it to a shelf beside him and takes a seat.

Sinking down into the armchair facing the kids, Vladimir looks like a giant hunched-over grasshopper. His honey-colored eyes peer at Elettra, Sheng and Mistral, one by one. He looks for his spectacles and perches them on his nose. "Harvey told me that you . . . well . . ."

"I told Mr. Askenazy that each of us has a top identical to the one stolen from him," Harvey explains. "And I described the symbols engraved on ours."

"Do you have them here with you?" the antiques dealer asks.

"We brought pictures of them," Elettra replies, handing him photos of three tops.

"Magnificent," Vladimir remarks, looking them over slowly. "May I ask how they came into your possession?"

"They . . . they aren't exactly ours," Elettra says.

"Somebody gave them to us," Mistral explains.

"To take care of," Sheng finishes.

"What about yours, Mr. Askenazy?" Elettra asks him.

"It was in a crate of items from Iraq. That's where the ancient Chaldeans lived."

82

"Have you already told the person who asked for it that it was stolen?"

The man shakes his head. "No. That's another thing I haven't managed to do. Actually, to tell you the truth, it's been a long time since I heard from him."

"Then how'd he reserve it?" Sheng asks.

"I have a file with the names of various collectors. There are those who want to be notified whenever I receive a Russian icon. Some are interested only in vases from the nineteen-thirties, others in ancient Assyro-Babylonian relics. . . ."

Vladimir wearily gets up from his chair and begins to rummage through a series of containers piled high with file folders, shuffling through them with his long, skeletal hands. "Here we are," he finally says, pulling out a sheet of paper. "Mr. Alfred Van Der Berger."

On hearing that name, the kids jump in their seats.

"Do you know him?" asks Vladimir.

The four exchange uncertain glances. They've already had a long discussion about what tactics to use with the shop owner, and they've come to the conclusion that they should try trusting him, at least partially, as long as they're very careful and avoid telling him too much.

"Not really . . . ," Harvey replies slowly, sensing what everyone wants him to say. "But he's the one who gave us the tops."

"When was that?"

"A few months ago, in Rome. He asked us to keep them for him, but then . . ."

After a moment of awkward silence, the antiques dealer adds encouragingly, "But then?"

83

"Then . . . let's just say he never came to get them back."

Vladimir Askenazy sits down again. "I don't understand."

"He died," Mistral explains.

"He didn't just die," Sheng says. "They killed him."

The man shakes his head, feigning disbelief. "For what reason?"

"Maybe for the same reason those women broke into your shop. Somebody wants to get their hands on these tops. At any cost," Elettra says.

"Do you have any idea who that might be?"

"We were hoping you could tell us," Elettra says.

"But how?" asks Vladimir, a helpless look on his face.

Elettra wrings her hands. "Alfred Van Der Berger might have told you about someone or something that . . . that he was terrified of. When he gave us the tops, the professor was running away from someone."

Vladimir rests his right index finger on his temple, still looking shocked. "As far as I remember, he was a perfectly calm person. He would talk about the most unbelievable topics, and you might even say he had his head in the clouds, but . . . no, he never spoke to me about any danger or anything that frightened him."

"We think the tops can be used to discover something really important," Harvey ventures to say. "We just haven't figured out what."

Vladimir Askenazy shakes his head slowly. "In any case, it's strange that you met him in Rome, of all places. Alfred Van Der Berger wasn't Italian."

"But he'd lived in Rome for years," Elettra explains. "He had an apartment there."

84

"Actually, he had two of them," Sheng points out.

"One-twenty-two East Forty-second Street, Chanin Building, apartment fifty-seven," Vladimir Askenazy reads from his file.

"What's that?"

"It's his address," the antiques dealer explains, showing the kids Professor Van Der Berger's sharp, angular handwriting. "Here in New York. In Manhattan."

The moment the four friends have left, the antiques dealer returns to the back room, picks up the pot of primroses that Harvey moved off the chair and goes back to the little desk in the front of the shop. Both impressed and amazed, he brushes his pale fingers over the two little yellow flowers that have sprung up among the leaves.

He bends over, sinks down into a chair, rests both the vase and his elbows on the desk and cradles his head in his hands. He sits there, motionless, his head pounding, not seeing or thinking anything. When he finally catches his breath, he releases his grip on his head and grabs the phone. He mechanically dials the country code for Italy, the area code for Rome and a phone number he knows by heart.

10

AGATHA

THE SKYSCRAPERS ARE DISAPPEARING INTO THE CLOUDY SKY LIKE endless towers. The kids walk along, their eyes turned upward, staring at the thousands of windows overlooking the streets. Each intersection they come across is like an intricate puzzle made of mirrors. Manhattan is a city of glass that rises up, connecting heaven and earth.

Talking nonstop, Harvey, Sheng, Elettra and Mistral are walking briskly among the hundreds of other people who are walking briskly. They tell each other details of what's happened over the last few months and share their ideas, suggestions and fears.

Finally, they reach a towering, narrow building with two friezes running across its facade. Bronze birds and fish are frolicking among geometric terra-cotta designs in a lush patch of stylized blossoms. The entrance of Grand Central can be seen nearby, as well as a Starbucks.

The kids pull open the large front door and find themselves walking on marble flooring. On the walls are big clocks, futuristic mailboxes and bronze decorations depicting the life of the man who built the building. The elevator doors are the color of the sea at sunset. The kids breathlessly sneak past a bored-looking doorman and go up to the seventeenth floor.

"This seems a little different from the professor's apartment in Rome," Mistral says, almost whispering, amazed by so much opulence.

"*Hao!* Let's hope it doesn't meet the same fate," Sheng adds with a nervous giggle.

It only takes the elevator a few seconds to reach their floor. On the ground is the same marble flooring as in the lobby. Elegant wall lamps line the hallway.

Apartment fifty-seven.

"This is it," says Harvey, stepping up to the door. No name is written beside the doorbell. The kids look around.

Silence. No one. Just other closed doors.

Elettra reads the names on the other doorbells. "Whisper, Allmond, R.G."

"Then somebody lives here."

"What do we do?"

"Easy. Let's see if anybody's home," Sheng suggests. Before the others have the chance to stop him, he rings the bell.

"It's no use," Harvey jeers, pointing at the closed door. "It's empty."

"Why do you say that?"

"The professor died in Rome," the boy shoots back. "It isn't very likely he'll come open the door, do you think?"

"Who is it?" asks a delicate female voice just then, as the door opens slightly. A blue eye scrutinizes the kids from right below the door chain.

"Hello there!" Sheng cries, shoving Harvey away. "Sorry to bother you, ma'am. We're looking for Professor Van Der Berger."

"Oh, you don't say!" the woman exclaims, peeking out from behind the door. "Might I know why?"

"I'm . . . I'm his nephew!" Sheng replies, saying the first thing that comes to his mind: the excuse he already used in Rome.

The woman looks him up and down for a long moment through the crack in the door. Then she concludes, "I don't believe you." With this, she slams the door in his face.

"Hey!" protests the Chinese boy, who barely manages to save his nose.

Mistral rests her hand on his shoulder. " 'I'm his nephew'? What a brilliant idea!"

"Maybe that's his wife," Harvey guesses.

"His wife?" Sheng exclaims, stunned.

From inside the apartment, they can hear the door chain rattling as it's slid through its frame and then the door being unlocked. A moment of silence. And then, finally, the door opens wide.

Standing before the kids is an elderly woman wearing a pair of big tortoiseshell glasses and a cream-colored dressing gown, beneath which are black-and-white polka-dot leggings. She leans against the doorframe and stares at the four friends with a mix of skepticism and amusement.

"In any case, since I've had a lot of free time on my hands lately, you might as well go ahead and explain to me exactly what it is you're doing here." She steps away from the door and waves them into the apartment. "If you want, I can make you some tea. Do people still drink tea these days?"

"That would be very nice, ma'am," Mistral says gratefully, gesturing to the others to behave just as politely.

Inside, the apartment looks like a picture frame shop. Every square inch of the walls is covered with black-and-white photos and framed newspaper clippings. There are frames in silver, gold, dark wood and light wood, frames in crystal, ivory and coral. Ethnic frames and frames covered with synthetic fiber.

The lady of the house walks the kids into a living room with spectacular picture windows looking out over the street and the other buildings. The view is breathtakingly beautiful. The furnishings in the room, on the other hand, look like they've seen better days. A worn-out zebra-skin rug is laid out between a peach-colored sofa and two sunken-in armchairs with striped upholstery and ripped fringe. Lampshades sagging under the weight of time cast eerie glows on a vast array of crystal knickknacks.

"Please, make yourselves comfortable," the woman says hospitably.

A cat statue is sitting in the center of a low, octagonal coffee table. The kids take a seat around it hesitantly while the lady of the house disappears into the kitchen, shuffling her feet. "So you'd be Alfred's nephew, then," she says to Sheng as she bustles about at the stove. "What about the rest of you?"

"I'm sorry. I lied. It was only a joke," Sheng apologizes at once, trying to make amends. "I just told you the first thing that popped into my mind."

"Interesting," the woman replies from the kitchen as she takes out the teacups.

"Can I help you?" Mistral offers, getting up from her seat and leaning in through the doorway.

"Oh, no, thank you! On second thought, yes. You could clear off the coffee table for me. Would you bring me the tray that's on it?"

Mistral looks over at the octagonal table. "The tray?"

"You'll need to move Paco."

Sheng reaches out his hand toward the cat statue in the center of the coffee table. Only then does he realize it's an animal in flesh and blood. "Oh, man!" he cries when his fingers submerge in the ball of fur, the cat not even budging a fraction of an inch.

Paco is gently lifted up and rested on an empty armchair, which he sinks down into without making a noise. Elettra picks up the tray he was snoozing on and hands it to Mistral, who takes it into the kitchen.

"As I was saying, it's interesting," the elderly woman continues, rinsing the tray, then lining up five unmatched, saucerless teacups on it, "that the first thing that came to your mind was to say you were the nephew of someone I haven't seen for five years."

"Five years?"

"Unless I'm counting wrong . . . yes," the lady of the house confirms. "How old do you think I am, kid?"

Sheng holds back a groan. "Please, don't make me guess! I'm terrible at guessing people's ages."

"What about you guys?" the woman insists.

"Fifty?" Elettra ventures. Harvey hangs his head. From the kitchen, the woman bursts out laughing. "That's overdoing it, young lady. Thank you, but that's really overdoing it. I'm eighty-two."

"*Hao!*" exclaims Sheng.

"Congratulations." Mistral smiles. "You don't show it at all."

"I bet you're the woman in all these pictures," Elettra adds, looking around at the walls.

The woman comes out from the kitchen for a moment and follows the girl's gaze. "Yep. Quite a few years ago." She nods, pleased. "When it still meant something to be young and to work as an actress."

"You were an actress?" Sheng asks, surprised.

"Technically, I still am," the woman points out, propping her tortoiseshell glasses up on her forehead to take a better look at him.

"I'm sorry. I just meant that—"

"No need to apologize. Life is too short for that. I've never apologized to anyone."

Elettra and Harvey peer at the photos with renewed curiosity. In some of them, Harvey recognizes the names of famous New York theaters.

"Were you a Hollywood actress or the to-be-or-not-to-be-that-is-the-question kind?" Sheng wonders admiringly.

"Even better." The woman grins. "An actress in Greek tragedies."

"Cool!" Sheng exclaims.

"What's your name?" Elettra finally asks, her gaze lost in the pictures of years gone by, with their long, black gowns, little hats with ostrich feathers sticking out of them and cream-colored cars with round headlights.

"I'm Agatha."

"Nice to meet you, Agatha. I'm Elettra."

"Mistral."

"Harvey."

"It's a pleasure, Agatha Van Der Berger. My name is Sheng."

The water kettle on the stove lets out a long, satisfied whistle. Agatha turns around with an affected laugh, shakes her head and says, "You sure put your foot in your mouth a lot, kid. What were you thinking? I'm not his wife."

The tea is served, boiling hot. Sitting on the sofa between Elettra and Harvey, Agatha starts to tell them her tale. "I met Alfred at the opening of *Medea*, a Greek tragedy. I loved those frightening plays full of blood and ruthlessness. It was an autumn evening and we were making our debut at the Lyceum on Broadway, the oldest theater in New York that's still open. Naturally, it was raining cats and dogs." Agatha sips her tea and pauses for a long moment.

"Just to be clear, kids, I've never been a famous actress. I gave it a shot, but after taking a few dives in the world of show business, I settled for small parts here and there when they came along. My brilliant career is all around you. Some black-and-white photos, a few short critiques in the papers, a dinner or two with celebrities of some sort and lots and lots of gossip. That's it.

"In *Medea*, I was playing the nurse. It's a minor role but an important one, because I was the one who had to get up onstage first, when the whole theater was perfectly silent. I had to start things out by saying, 'Oh, if only the *Argo* had never set sail for its long journey beyond Colchis. . . .' I wasn't a girl anymore, but I can assure you I was so nervous, I felt like it was my very first time onstage. I'd acted here and there all over the world, kids, but the Lyceum . . . Oh, the Lyceum is the Lyceum. It's something totally different."

Agatha pauses again for another sip of tea. When she begins to tell her tale again, her gaze is locked onto the kids, gaining their total attention. "Our *Medea* was a major success, and when the performance was over, the other cast members came to see if I felt like going out to dinner with them. But I didn't feel up to listening to their dreams and hearing the words I'd already heard so many times before, so I turned them down. I wanted to enjoy the dressing room in peace and quiet. After a play, the theater is a world full of whispers and mysteries. It's as if in your mind you could hear the voices of all the actors who've come before you."

Harvey's ears perk up.

"I took off my makeup in no hurry at all," Agatha continues, "and when I walked out, the only people left were the cleaning staff and the doorman. Outside, it was pouring down rain. And on the other side of the street was Alfred."

The woman smiles. She puts her teacup down and emphasizes the words that follow with the movement of her hands. "He was standing there, stock still, in the rain, as if it weren't even coming down. He'd waited for me out there for such a long time that he was sopping wet. He was very, very thin, almost gaunt, and he wore a long, brown raincoat. He clearly hadn't shaved for a few days. In one hand he was holding a bouquet of flowers that were dripping wet, and in the other he had an umbrella that had been completely torn apart by the wind. I didn't realize he was there for me. Then, when he saw me come out, he walked up and congratulated me. I burst out laughing, thinking he was just joking. But his face turned perfectly serious . . . and he invited me to dinner."

"And you said yes?" Elettra asks, growing a little impatient.

"Of course not," Agatha replies. "I'd never seen him before and I had no idea who he was. Besides, he didn't have what I would

93

call compelling charm. That night, I took a taxi back to my hotel, but the next evening, Alfred was there outside the theater again. He did that for a whole month. If he saw me all alone, he'd walk up and congratulate me again. Otherwise, he'd stand there discreetly in the distance. He never followed me or forced me to talk to him. He simply waited for me there outside the Lyceum.

"After a month, our theater company went to put on *Medea* in another, smaller theater off Broadway. And when I came out of this other theater, I found Alfred there waiting for me again. He walked up to me as if it were for the very first time and invited me to dinner again. It was so sweet that this time I accepted.

"During that one, single dinner, Alfred won me over. He'd reserved a table at Bacco, but it wasn't because of what we ate or drank. It was all because of him. He turned out to be an excellent conversationalist, although a rather sad one. He claimed he couldn't find anyone to have the pleasure of talking to. Talking for the joy of talking, filling the air with notions, ideas and theories. He said younger people would rather *do* things, but they didn't have the foggiest idea why they were even doing them. He felt that no one was interested in words anymore, that instead of cultivating them, everyone just let them wither away in silence. And that because of it, words didn't grow, didn't bear new fruit . . . I listened to him and thought he was perfectly right. Words are so important! Just the right words at just the right moment. They're the only things capable of really changing the world!"

"*Hao* . . . cool!" Sheng exclaims, suddenly realizing he's been holding his breath for a long time.

"My world changed after all that talking. We started seeing each other more and more seriously, and after a few months,

94

he invited me to come live with him in this apartment, which is his. I accepted. I accepted him and his words for many years, little by little abandoning the theater and Greek tragedies so I could concentrate on the most wonderful show of all: my life with him. But don't get me wrong. I have no regrets. Alfred spent a good deal of his time in his study, down there, engrossed in writing, reading and researching. I would sit here, on this sofa, waiting for him to finish. But it was a full life. I never needed anyone else's company. Not even Paco's."

Agatha strokes the cat without getting any appreciable reaction, then picks up her tea, which is now cold. "Finally, one fine day, just as unexpectedly as he'd appeared in my life, that man dressed in words left."

"Did you have an argument?"

"Oh, no. Never. In fact, our life together was perfect. We were growing old together. Actually, I was growing old, but he wasn't. At least that's what it seemed like to me. While my face was getting covered with wrinkles, he stayed the same thin, gaunt Alfred I'd seen that very first day. But no, there was no argument between us."

"So what happened?"

"He just up and walked out on me one day five years ago, without any explanation. I haven't even heard a single word about him since. Not until you kids showed up, that is." Agatha smiles. Her tortoiseshell glasses look like two dark wells. "Now that you know my half of the story, I think I can ask how it is you ended up here."

"We got this address from an antiques dealer," explains Harvey. "We wanted to buy something the professor had on hold, so we thought we'd come talk to him in person."

95

Agatha lets out a bleak little laugh. "An antiques dealer? And here I was, letting my imagination go wild! For a moment, I thought Alfred was too ashamed to come back here and had sent some kids on a reconnaissance mission. But instead . . . an antiques dealer! One here in New York?"

"Yes."

She shrugs. "If nothing else, given that he ordered something from an antiques dealer, that must mean he's still alive."

The kids don't reply. All they do is uncomfortably stare at the picture frames on the walls.

"So what's the antique, anyway?"

"A toy top."

"That's just like Alfred." Agatha nods. "He'd spend all his money on books and bizarre objects. Not that he ever had money problems, or left me with any. In fact, still today, money is put into my bank account every month by an anonymous depositor. But I don't ask any questions. Alfred and I never talked about money, and in all the years I lived with him, I never knew what he did for a living. All I know is that antiques were his passion. He was in constant contact with shops all around the world, finding books and knickknacks that were older and older and, from what he said, more and more fascinating. He was constantly buying them, trading them, selling entire shelves of them from his study to make room for new purchases."

"He must've had a lot of them," Mistral comments.

"Oh, yes," Agatha confirms. "During our last years together, he started traveling to go hunting for books. Before then, he'd barely even leave the house. He'd travel so far away in his imagination that the idea of physically going somewhere never

96

even crossed his mind. But to track down a special book, he might be out of town one, two, even three days at a time. And then, finally . . . five years," Agatha concludes, a bitter smile on her face. Then she slaps her hands on her knees, making Paco flinch. "But now, enough with the whining from the poor, abandoned old maid."

"You aren't a poor, abandoned old maid at all!" Mistral protests. "Say it out loud: 'I'm not a poor, abandoned old maid.' After all, words have the power to change the world, don't they?"

Agatha welcomes her remark with a warm laugh. "Alfred would be proud of you, young lady."

"I'm sorry, Agatha," Elettra cuts in hastily. "Could I ask to see Alfred's study?"

"Why not? Nothing's left in there."

"What about all the books and knickknacks he bought?"

"They disappeared with him. If he'd left them here, I might have even entertained the notion I'd see him come back one day. Not for me, but to look up something really important in his beloved collection."

A long moment of silence follows, which is broken by the lady of the house. "You might be wondering why I never went looking for him, or why I don't want to know the name of the antiques dealer who sent you here."

"Actually . . . ," Sheng says softly.

"It's because I was seventy-four years old when he left, and today I'm seventy-nine," the actress continues. "Once you get to a certain age, take my word for it, there's only one question on your mind, one that no book can give a reasonable answer to.

In any case, come on. . . ." Agatha wearily rises to her feet. "I'll show you what I have left of him."

The door at the end of the hall leads into an empty room. The empty skeleton of a bookshelf covered with dust. A table with a green banker-style desk lamp. A window looking out over the city. Four chairs with velvet upholstery sitting on an old rug worn with age. That's all there is. Not a book, a relic, a diary. Not a notebook or a clue that could be of any use.

"This is my last memento of him," Agatha says wistfully, picking up a tiny silver frame from the back of a shelf and handing it to Mistral. It's an old black-and-white photo of three smiling men, one beside the other.

"That's Alfred in the middle," the woman explains to the kids, who've already recognized him. Compared to the frightened man they met in Rome, he looks far more reassuring. A young man with a satisfied smile on his face, he's clearly pleased to be there with the other two people in the picture.

"Who are the others?"

"I never knew. Or maybe I did, but I've forgotten. Classmates, I think."

Their clothes are old. Very old. The picture was shot from fairly close up and very little can be seen of the background. The light is casting the long shadow of a fourth man onto the sidewalk: the photographer.

"May I take it out of the frame?" Mistral asks Agatha. "Maybe there's something written on the back of it."

"Certainly," she replies.

Mistral rests the frame upside down and undoes the three clasps, keeping it pressed up against its wooden backing. She gently lifts it up and discovers that on the back of the photo are a dedication and a small swatch of cloth with a label on it.

"What did you find?" the others ask when they see her hesitate.

"There's a fabric sample," the French girl replies. It's a black, glossy swatch not much bigger than a postage stamp. The label is from a tailor's shop and is held in place by three gold needles. It reads:

HELIOS, CUSTOM-MADE SUITS

"Does that mean anything to you?" the kids ask the actress.

She shakes her head. "I don't remember that being there. And no . . . I'm not familiar with that tailor. I think it's Greek. 'Helios' means 'sun.' But I have no idea how that piece of cloth ended up in there. Of course, Alfred loved to have suits tailor-made for him. He never liked mass-produced things, and he had worlds of fun spending his days at the tailor's. He'd stand up tall and proud, stare into the mirror and spend whole afternoons deciding what kind of fabric he wanted for his new suit. He was very vain when it came to that. I think he was quite pleased with his appearance."

"The sample . . . may we keep it?" asks Mistral.

"Sure, why not?"

Mistral slips the piece of black cloth into her pocket, being careful not to prick herself with the three needles. Then she picks up the photograph and reads the dedication written on the back of it. " 'To Paul, Alfred and Robert' . . . Have you ever heard of these men, Paul and Robert?"

Agatha shakes her head a second time.

"Do you happen to know when this picture was taken?"

"Thirty years ago? Fifty? Alfred already had it when we met. He used it as a bookmark until he decided to have it framed."

"So you didn't put the piece of cloth in there?" Elettra insists.

"No! Why would I have done that?"

"Which means," Sheng whispers to Harvey, "this piece of cloth might be important."

Agatha lets out a laugh. "So tell me: Why are you all so interested in Alfred?"

"Could we ask you another favor?" Harvey asks instead of answering her.

"Of course."

"Have you got a phone book?"

A few minutes later and seventeen floors below, over at Starbucks, Harvey finally manages to thumb through a phone book. Not only did Agatha not have one, but she didn't even have a telephone anymore.

"Here it is!" he tells the others. "Near Little Italy there's a tailor's by that name: 'Helios, custom-made suits since 1893.'"

"What do you say, guys?" asks Elettra. "Should we go?"

Sheng is sprawled out in an armchair, biting into a giant blueberry muffin. "When are we going to meet up with Ermete, anyway?"

"He said he'd be in touch," Harvey remembers. "Maybe tomorrow, at this point."

"Perfect," Mistral murmurs. She's drawing Agatha's face in her notebook.

"Not exactly perfect," Elettra groans, checking the display on her cell phone. "Tomorrow I've got to spend at least half the day with Aunt Linda. Otherwise, I'm done for."

"Is she getting mad?" Harvey inquires.

"She just bought a bronze replica of the Statue of Liberty and she wants to go see the real one with me."

SECOND STASIMON

"Hi."

"How did it go?"

"I gave them Agatha's address."

"They're asking a lot fewer questions than we did."

"I think that's a point in their favor."

"I think so, too."

"I could feel your niece's energy from a yard away. She could've set fire to my documents if she'd known how."

"What about the others?"

"Sheng hasn't discovered his abilities yet. His instinct is still dormant. And just to think that those eyes . . ."

"Eerie, isn't it?"

"He has a disarming smile."

"What was your impression of Mistral?"

"She's like a breath of hope."

"Which was the very last thing at the bottom of Pandora's box . . . Hope is woman. . . ."

"And courage is man."

"What do you think of Harvey?"

"I had him pick up a vase of withered primroses."

"Did anything happen?"

"After he touched them, they blossomed again. The Earth is reawakening, Irene."

11
THE TAILOR

THE HELIOS TAILOR SHOP'S LOGO IS A GOLDEN SUN, THE TIPS OF ITS rays forming tiny hands. The name is written in angular Greek characters over a tiny shop partially hidden behind some Dumpsters. The pouring rain and the almost total lack of light are making everything look rather abandoned. Standing on the opposite side of the street, the four kids look around, discouraged.

"What do you say? Should we go in?"

"To do what?" Elettra groans.

"I don't know. We could ask if they knew the professor. . . ."

Harvey turns the piece of cloth over in his fingers. "Maybe these three needles mean something."

"Oh, yeah. Sure," Elettra grumbles skeptically. "It's easier for a camel to pass through the eye of a needle than for us to make sense of anything that's going on."

"We're on the right track," Mistral states, pointing at the sign. "We're always chasing after the sun. In Rome it was the sun of Mithra, and here . . ."

"The sign at a tailor's shop." Sheng smiles, crossing the street. "*Hao*, cool!"

"Maybe we shouldn't all go inside," Elettra insists.

"Why not?" Mistral asks.

"I don't know. I've got a bad feeling about this. . . ."

"A bad feeling, like the ones you had in Rome? Are your fingers tingling? Do you feel hot? Are you going to make the streetlights explode?" Harvey asks.

"Something like that, yeah."

"Would you rather wait out here?" says Harvey.

"I'll stay with you, if you want," Mistral offers.

"No, no. You guys go on in," the girl replies. "Meanwhile, I'll call my aunt."

"But don't you think you might be useful in there? Maybe you'll feel something," Harvey insists.

"All I feel is that I don't want to go in there. Isn't that enough?"

"We'll be in and out in no time," Mistral replies as she and Harvey catch up with Sheng at the door to the shop.

Standing there alone, Elettra sighs as she looks around, disoriented. She lied. She doesn't feel anything in particular. In fact, she feels completely empty, maybe because of jet lag, maybe because she's so far from home. But still, it's as if her energy has disappeared. In the electric city surrounding her, among the windows reflecting images of the streets, before the giant picture windows revealing crowds of people, she feels stifled. Every street in Manhattan makes her uneasy. She feels like she can't breathe. But it isn't air she's lacking. That's fresh and crisp, full of the smell of the sea. She's even seen seagulls with their white wings flying among the skyscrapers. It's the earth that she's lacking. It's as though it were constantly trembling beneath her feet, as though it, too, were uneasy, agitated. Or in the never-ending expectation of reawakening.

The sun is hidden behind the clouds. Elettra feels drained. She can't describe what's going on inside her, but she's learned to trust her feelings. And they aren't all negative.

When she sees Harvey's silhouette through the tailor shop's window, she cheers up.

Then she hears a noise beside her.

An ugly black crow is pecking at the bags of garbage in the Dumpster.

The tailor's shop is small and dark, filled with the smell of wool and other scents difficult to make out: old wood, steam, vanilla, cotton yarn and buttons. Two people are working there: an old man with sparse gray hair and a pair of thick reading glasses who's staring at a crossword puzzle, and a woman with bowed legs who's sewing the sleeve onto a jacket that has been fitted over a mannequin covered with pins.

"Hello, kids," the old man greets them, pulling his nose out of the puzzle. Two tufts of long, graying hairs are sticking out of his nostrils like antennas. "What can I do for you?"

"Hello," Harvey replies. "Actually . . . we aren't sure, exactly."

"Excellent," the man replies good-naturedly. "That's just the kind of answer one expects from someone who walks into a tailor's shop, of all places!"

The woman makes an impatient gesture as she tugs on the sleeve on the mannequin. It doesn't escape the man's notice. "Can't a man make a joke, Trittolema? Please!" he exclaims, pushing the newspaper on the counter away from him. "You're always so serious! Always sewing and cutting, sewing and cutting . . ."

The woman says something in Greek, but her tone is universal.

"Don't mind her," the old man begins again. "She's been this way for fifty years, but she's never been one to bite. Isn't that right, Trittolema?" He rests his fists on the table, his thumbs tucked inside of them. "In any case, as we were saying, you don't know exactly what you're doing here. Well, this is a tailor's shop. We offer custom-made clothing. Pardon me for saying so, but it doesn't look like that's anything for you. Not that I have any objection to your jeans or to your sweatshirt with the pig on it . . ."

"It isn't a pig!" Sheng protests immediately. "It's a hippo. It's really famous in China."

"That's my point. In here, the only thing famous is our Prince of Wales."

"I don't even know what that is."

"It's the name of a black-and-white fabric," Mistral explains.

"Very good, young lady. Fortunately, there's still someone in this world who remembers such things."

"My mother works in fashion. She makes perfumes, actually."

"That's wonderful. Hear that, Trittolema? Perfume!" Then, in a hushed voice, to make the kids laugh, he says, "I've never managed to convince her to buy any for herself."

Harvey reaches into his pocket and pulls out the swatch of black fabric with the three gold needles. "Actually, we came here because of this. Does it mean anything to you?"

The old man rests the snippet of cloth on the workbench and takes a deep breath, making the hairs in his nostrils quiver. "Outstanding-quality English wool, fourteen stitch . . . heavens!

106

It must be twenty years since I've seen one of these samples, but it's definitely one of ours. Not only because of the label, of course."

"What about the needles?"

"Three *excellent* needles. May I?"

"Please."

The tailor pulls the arm lamp toward him and turns over the tapered shapes of the three gold needles directly under the light. "Oh, yes. Of course. These are ours, too. Or better, I bet they're my father's old gold needles, imported directly from Holland. Let me check. . . . Hmm . . . yes, yes, just as I imagined. They're three different needles for three different kinds of fabric. A New York needle, long and sturdy, for sleeves and buttonholes. The Paris needle for lapels. And finally, the London needle, the thinnest one of all, for the lining. What a trip down memory lane, kids! We haven't used these since back in my father's day, rest his soul. . . . Anyway, it's been a long, long time, you see. Where did you find them?"

"In an old house."

"Oh, Father's needles! He'd only give them to important customers, together with swatches of cloth and thread from their suits. That way, even if they were somewhere on the other side of the world and they needed a patch or a little darning, the suit would already have its own needles and spare pieces of the original cloth. I'm sure these things don't mean anything to you, but once, a good suit was a thousand times more precious than a nice car. In any case, I'll buy these back from you, if you like."

The seamstress grumbles something in Greek, which perfectly infuriates her husband.

"Yes, I *do* want to buy them! They're Father's needles, and these kids just brought them back to me. They're a part of my past, which, if I may point out, is far more interesting than my future." The old man clears his throat and goes back to focusing on the three kids. "How much do you want for them?"

"Actually, we didn't come here to sell them," Harvey explains, a little embarrassed.

"Oh, you didn't? Then what is it you want?"

"Like we told you before, we're not exactly sure," says Harvey.

"Do you know a man named Alfred Van Der Berger?" Sheng asks.

"Van Der Berger? Hmm . . . And why should I know him?"

"We thought he was a customer of yours," Harvey says.

"The cloth and the needles were his," Mistral explains.

"Van Der Berger, Van Der Berger . . . no, it doesn't ring a bell. Trittolema!" the tailor shouts. Then he starts rambling on and on in Greek, the only intelligible thing being the professor's last name. At the end of their question-and-answer session, the tailor is even more bewildered.

"Is something the matter?" Mistral asks him, seeing him increasingly lost in thought.

"No, it's just that . . . this is absurd . . . ," he replies, straightening his thick glasses on his nose. "Truly absurd. But Trittolema is never wrong about these things. She's got a remarkable memory."

The kids turn toward the woman, who's concentrating on fitting a jacket and some cloth over another mannequin, her back turned to them.

The elderly tailor leans down behind the counter and pulls out a cookie tin with a sticker on it labeled UNCLAIMED.

"Are you relatives of his?" he asks the kids, opening up the tin. Inside of it are lots of square slips of paper stacked one on top of the other.

"I'm his nephew," Sheng replies right off the bat, beaming at his two friends.

The tailor looks up at him for a second with glittering eyes. Enlarged by his thick glasses, they look like two giant jellyfish. "You?"

"That's right," replies Sheng. "Would you like to see some ID?"

"What would I do with ID?" the tailor replies, starting to riffle through the slips of paper.

The kids watch him anxiously. Harvey glances through the shop window and smiles when he sees Elettra outside, pacing on the sidewalk.

After spending a few minutes shaking his head, the tailor freezes. In his fingers is a slip of paper that's so thin and worn that it's almost transparent. "Naturally, it was the very last one in the box. As always, Trittolema was right. Five years ago. Alfred Van Der Berger. A black tuxedo that needed mending on the right elbow. Hmm . . . you're lucky," he adds.

"Why's that?"

"He paid in advance."

12
THE POSTCARD

Elettra sees Harvey, Sheng and Mistral walk out in single file. First Harvey, then Sheng with a gigantic package wrapped in brown paper tucked under his arm and finally Mistral, who's still saying goodbye to the people inside.

"What's that?" she asks Harvey, pointing at the bulky package.

"Professor Van Der Berger's tuxedo, which he left here for mending five years ago."

"You're kidding!"

"Nope."

"You mean they kept it here this whole time?"

"Sure looks that way."

"Instead of standing there chatting, would you give me a hand?" Sheng groans, hidden behind the paper wrapper from the tailor's shop.

"You're his nephew. You carry it!" Harvey snaps.

"So this is the thanks I get! If it hadn't been for me, we never would've been able to claim it."

"I'll help you, Sheng," Mistral says, grabbing the other end of the bundle.

"No thanks," he retorts testily. "I wanted Mr. Grumpy to help."

Harvey whirls around. "You got something to say to me, Sheng? Because it just so happens that you've had this attitude all morning long."

"What attitude? Being happy despite everything? When we showed up at the hotel, you barely even said hello to us! It's like everything we say ticks you off—"

"That's enough," Elettra says, cutting him off. "Both of you, stop it."

Harvey's eyes are hidden behind his hair. He turns to stare at the street and stands there, stock still. Behind him, Sheng lets Elettra pull him away and he follows Mistral down the sidewalk, carrying the package with the tuxedo along with her.

"Harvey?" Elettra asks.

"Forget about it. I'm already over it."

"No, I won't forget about it! Sheng's right."

"Then go on with him and leave me alone."

"We're friends, aren't we?"

Harvey doesn't answer her. He just clenches his fists in his pockets.

"We're all doing the best we can," Elettra continues, "and we only managed to come here because of Sheng's father."

"Then let's run off and thank him!" Harvey snaps sarcastically.

"Would you mind telling me why you're mad at him?"

"I'm not mad at him. I'm not mad at him at all!"

"Then what's wrong? Are you mad at all of us?"

"Don't be stupid!"

Elettra tries to get him to look her in the eye. The air reeks of the garbage in the nearby Dumpsters. "You picked a really nice place to get all huffy."

"I'm not getting huffy."

"Then what's up with you?"

Harvey bites the inside of his lip and shakes his messy hair. "Okay. All right. I know I'm not being very nice. Maybe I was wrong to get on his case. . . ."

"You were way wrong."

"It's just that . . . he . . ." Harvey watches Sheng and Mistral walking away. "He takes everything so casually, like he doesn't care at all. Like it isn't real."

"What's wrong with that?"

"It's that . . . I can't."

"You can't what?"

"I can't take things casually. And he . . . Sheng, he . . . he acts just like . . . oh, forget I said it."

"No, tell me!"

"The thing is, the farther we get into this whole thing, the worse I feel. Inside. I feel . . . oh, how can I explain to you what I'm feeling?"

"Are you scared of the people following us?"

"No, I'm not scared."

Elettra looks at him, waiting for an explanation.

"It's because of . . . because of my brother," Harvey says, caving in. "My brother died a year ago, more or less to the day."

"Oh . . . I understand."

"No, I don't think you understand at all. It isn't just because it happened a year ago. Although it's tough. I mean, at my place these days, every single day, all we do is think about him. Because . . . because it happened right at this time of year . . . in March."

"How did it happen?"

"I don't feel like talking about it."

"Maybe you should."

"He fell. Underground. On a construction site. He used to walk around on the scaffolding like . . . like he wasn't running any risk at all. Like he was taking a stroll through the countryside. Carefree . . . and then, suddenly, one day . . ."

"What was his name?"

"Dwaine."

"So what does Sheng have to do with Dwaine?"

"Every time I talk to him, I feel like I'm talking to my brother. They're . . . happy. Happy, carefree . . . careless, even. And Dwaine sure paid the price for being careless."

"Then we'll make sure Sheng doesn't pay the same price."

"That isn't going to be easy, you know."

"Well, sometimes it's good to take things a little casually." Elettra waves her hand in the air.

"What are you doing?" Harvey asks her.

"I'm saying hi to the crow," she replies, pointing at a crow that takes wing and flies off.

Harvey's face darkens. "That bird again . . . ," he murmurs, looking around.

"What's wrong with the crow?"

"It's a sign that they're following me."

"How do you know that?"

"I just do, that's all. Come on. Let's go, quick."

Elettra nods. "We'd better not leave Mistral at the mercy of Sheng's sense of direction. If he managed to get lost on the buses in Rome, I don't even want to think what he might do in New York."

Harvey takes Elettra by the arm and heads after the other two. "I think I should apologize to him."

"I think you're right."

"Olympia says I've got a lot of anger inside me."

"That's no reason to take it out on us."

Sitting in the subway car, Harvey and Elettra on one side, Mistral and Sheng on the other, they move westward. The tuxedo that belonged to Professor Van Der Berger resting on his lap, Sheng lifts up a corner of the brown paper wrapper and peeks inside.

"It looks really nice," remarks Mistral beside him.

"It's black."

"Tuxedos are always black."

"How come?"

"They're just made that way."

"I've never even seen a tuxedo before."

"Doesn't your father have one? What does he wear when he goes to a formal event?"

"His red tunic and babouche slippers!" Sheng replies, beaming.

"Okay, forget I asked. . . ."

The train car starts to slow down.

"Don't you think we should give it back to Agatha?" Elettra asks.

"I say we take a look at it over at my place first," says Harvey.

The others think it's a good idea. The train stops, the doors slide open and the voice over the loudspeaker announces the next stop. People get in and out of the train car, which soon continues on its way.

"I think we should cast the tops," Mistral suggests as the underground rails squeal on the other side of the windows.

"To look for what?" asks Harvey.

"The top they stole from Vladimir," Mistral replies.

"Yeah. Who knows where it is right now?" Harvey sighs.

"Each one of those tops is worth a fortune. Gold, precious gems . . ."

A woman sitting nearby turns to stare at them. The kids lower their voices.

"Do you think they might've killed Alfred and tried to scare you, Ermete and Vladimir just to get their hands on something they can sell?" Mistral whispers.

Harvey throws his hands up. "They obviously did, wouldn't you say?"

"But don't you think," Elettra interjects, "that they want to use the tops on the map, too?"

"I don't think so," Harvey shoots back.

"I say Elettra's right," Sheng bursts out. "If they could, I bet they'd use the map. I mean, come on! What the professor left us belonged to the Three Wise Men, Marco Polo and Christopher Columbus! It isn't just *any* map!"

Around them, a rare silence has fallen. But it's only a matter of a second. After that, the other passengers' superficial attention moves on to other things. At the next station, people get on and off, and the episode is immediately forgotten by everyone.

*   *   *

In Harvey's kitchen, Mistral is the first one to notice there's something in the tuxedo. "It's something really thin . . . in the inside pocket." She pulls out an old black-and-white postcard with rounded corners. Depicted on it are workers setting up scaffolding for a railway.

Harvey kicks the fridge door shut. "What is it?"

"Take a wild guess."

"An old postcard of New York."

"We got a lead, guys," Sheng says in a low voice, rubbing his hands together.

Mistral turns it over. "It's addressed to Agatha!"

"But he never mailed it."

Harvey walks over to the table and hands Elettra a carton of milk. "That looks like construction being done on the subway," he remarks, looking at the picture. "This guy here looks like the director of the construction work."

"Maybe that's the man who made that . . . that bridge," Sheng guesses.

"Brooklyn?"

"Yeah, him. Brooklyn."

"Brooklyn didn't make the bridge," Harvey points out. "It was a guy by the name of Roebling."

"Then why didn't they call it the Roebling Bridge?"

"Because it goes to Brooklyn."

"Shh!" Elettra interrupts them. "Can't we talk about that later, please? Mistral, what's written on the postcard?"

"If I got this in the mail, guys," she says, "I think I'd have a little problem understanding it."

"Let me see." Elettra groans, starting to read. " '129, 90, 172, 113, 112, 213, 25, 73, 248, 11, 247, 71, 168, 142, 168, 128, 82, 82, 84, 140, 162, 81, 208, 27, 1, 25, 102, 212, 124, 172, 84, 212, 168, 171, 97, 75, 1, 107, 132, 15, 168, 186, 1, 233, 162, 212, 1, 162, 88. Star of Stone, two of four.' "

"And then?" asks Sheng.

"That's it," Elettra says.

Mistral takes back the postcard and double-checks it. "There's nothing else," she confirms.

"Should we call Ermete?" Elettra asks.

"This is right up his alley." Harvey nods. "I'd say these numbers are some kind of code. A cipher, to be precise."

"Meaning . . . ?" Mistral prompts.

"Each number stands for a letter."

"It's easy, then!" Sheng exclaims. "One stands for A, two stands for B and so on. . . ." They try it out, but the string of letters they come up with is incomprehensible.

"Maybe it's not the right code." Sheng tries again, but it's no use.

"What do you guys think 'Star of Stone' means?"

"A meteorite," Mistral replies without even thinking it over. When she notices the others gaping at her, she adds, "A shooting star, a bolide. What do you call it?"

"Yeah, it's called a meteorite," Elettra confirms, "but why'd you think of a meteorite, of all things?"

"I don't know. It just seemed obvious to me."

"It could be anything," Sheng objects.

"Such as . . . ?"

Nothing else comes to the Chinese boy's mind. He twists his lips, thinking, and then gives up. "I guess you're right."

"In Rome, the professor left us clues on how to track down the Ring of Fire," Mistral says calmly, "and it turned out to be a mirror. Now he's telling us about a star of stone. . . ."

"Which could be a meteorite," Elettra says, finishing her sentence for her. "Why not? Harvey, are there any meteorites here in New York?"

"There's a massive one over at the American Museum of Natural History," he replies. "But, please, let's not jump the gun, here! We still don't know what the Ring of Fire actually is or what it's supposed to do. Or what really happened when Elettra looked into it. Besides, we've got a top to look for. Maybe we shouldn't be trying to track down the Star of Stone just yet."

"I agree," Sheng says. Then, noticing the amazed look on Harvey's face, he adds, "No, really. Let's move cautiously this time instead of throwing ourselves into this headfirst, risking our necks. Also because we aren't alone, and they know about Ermete . . . and maybe about Harvey, too, at this point."

"So what do you say we should do?" asks Mistral.

"Let's try working with Ermete to figure out what's written on this postcard. But most importantly, let's get ourselves a New York street plan and . . ."

Use the map, a voice says in Harvey's head. The moment he hears it, the boy's eyes grow wide and he looks around, scared.

"What did you say?" he asks the others. "Did you say we should use the map?"

Sheng shakes his head. "No, but I was just about to suggest we do whatever the tops tell us to."

Harvey rushes out of the kitchen.

"What's up with him?" Sheng asks the two girls.

CENTURY

MAP

OF THE

NEW YORK CITY

My dear Irene,

As you can see from the material I'm
sending you, the challenge continues.
But I've grown terribly afraid of being
discovered, and I need to protect
myself. They've learned about Century,
and they're beating us to it. I think
they even know our names. If that's
true, please be careful, because it
would mean that we've been betrayed and
that the secret has been revealed.
    I still don't understand what the
kids' real objective might be. What are
all those things we gave them supposed
to be used for? Why can't we tell them
everything we know? We were told to
honor the pact, but for what reason?
And how much longer will we be able to?
    Giant hugs, and I hope to see you
one more time before all of this comes
to an end.

Vladimir

THE BRONX

OLYMPIA GYM

①

Boxing and Greco-Roman Wrestling

FIGHT II
JOE FRAZIER vs MUHAMMAD ALI
MONDAY EVENING
JAN. 28, 1974
8:30 P. M.
2nd PROMENADE
$50.00

MADISON SQUARE GARDEN
PENNSYLVANIA PLAZA, N.Y.
FIGHT II
JOE FRAZIER vs MUHAMMAD ALI
2nd PROMENADE
$50.00
N. Y. State Law - Children Under 14 Yrs of Age
NOT ADMITTED

P 6 2132

2nd PROMENADE $50.00
232 D 14
SEC. ROW SEAT
FRAZIER MON. EVE.
vs ALI JAN. 28
1974

②

③

Card and Paper Trimm
School and Kindergart

Springfield, Mass.
November 15

Mr. Alfred M. Butts
Park Avenue
New York City

 After giving your game our very careful
consideration, wo do not feel we would be interste
this item to our line.
We are returning the model under separate

Very truly yours,

The doctor of Scrabble

6

7

OLD THINGS
OF ALL THE WORLD

OPEN

9

8

10

City Hall
Subway Station
New York

11

UPPER WEST SIDE

CENTRAL PARK

UPPER EAST SIDE

W 84TH ST

W 82ND ST

W 81ST ST

W 80TH ST

79TH ST

W 78TH ST

W 77TH ST

W 75TH ST

W 74TH ST

W 73RD ST

AMERICAN MUSEUM OF NATURAL HISTORY

W 86TH TRANSVERSE

TURTLE POND

W 79ST TRANSVERSE

THE LAKE

CONSERVATORY WATER

E 85TH ST

E 83RD ST

E 81ST ST

E 79TH ST

E 78TH ST

E 76TH ST

E 74TH ST

E 84

E 82

E 80

E 7

E 75

BROA

COLL

5TH AVE

MADISON A

LE

METROPOLITAN MUSEUM OF ART

WHITNEY MUSEUM

THE AMERICAN MVSEVM OF NATVRAL HISTORY

FOVNDED 1869

20

21

22

(23)

(24)

(25)

26

27

28

29

32

33

34

W 51ST ST
AVE
W 51ST ST
ST PAT'S
E 51ST
E 50TH ST
ROCKEFELLER
CENTER
PARK AVE
E 49TH
TH ST
E 48TH ST
W 48TH ST
5TH AVE
W 47TH ST
6TH AVE
MADISON AVE
E 46TH ST
3RD AVE
W 45TH ST
TIMES
SQUARE
MIDTO
43RD ST
BROADWAY
GRAND
CENTRAL
CHRYSLER
BLDG
E 42ND ST
BRYANT
PARK
NY PUBLIC
LIBRARY
40TH ST
E 40TH ST
5TH AVE
PARK AVE
3RD AVE
38TH ST
6TH AVE
E 38TH ST
BROADWAY
GARMENT
DISTRICT
E 36TH ST
MURRA
36TH ST
5TH AVE
E 34TH ST
EMPIRE
STATE BLDG

35

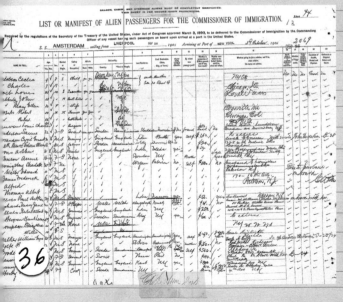

LIST OR MANIFEST OF ALIEN PASSENGERS FOR THE COMMISSIONER OF IMMIGRATION.

36

37

38

INDEX

Ellis Island 1905

Alfred Van Der Bergen

SHORAKKOPOCH

Inwood (Indian Road)

They hear him run up to his room, rifle through his dresser drawers and come back downstairs, his gym bag slung over his shoulder. He's sweating, a haunted look in his eyes. "Sorry," he says, "but I've got to go."

"Hold on a second," Elettra says, stopping him. "What are we going to do with the tops? Where's the map, Harvey?"

"I don't have it," he replies, heading toward the door. He passes by the grandfather clock and stops in his tracks, as if in a trance. "But here's what we can do: I'll stop by and pick it up after I go to the gym. We can use it tonight. At the hotel."

Everyone agrees with his plan. They quickly walk out of his house, leaving Harvey behind to lock the door. Sheng and Mistral walk out ahead, while Elettra waits for him to pocket his keys.

"What's up with you?"

"I'd rather not talk about it."

"Maybe you should've left a note about the tuxedo for your mom."

"Too late now."

They make their way through the garden. The first leaves have appeared on the highest branches, and the little path that crosses through it, heading toward the gate, is lined by patches of little light blue flowers. Spring is in the air. Once they're out on the street, Elettra turns to look at Harvey. "Can I come with you to the gym?"

"If you want."

13

THE LOCKER

"Your trainer's really nice . . . ," Elettra comments a couple of hours later. She's walking southbound with Harvey among the hordes of cold, shivering people on Church Street. The skyscrapers in lower Manhattan tower around them like the glass pipes of a massive underground organ. The air is filled with the smell of dirt and gasoline. The trees are dark skeletons. The grass in the flowerbeds is scrubby.

Harvey grimaces, feeling his rib cage.

"Does it hurt?"

"Not as much as my pride."

"You landed a few punches yourself. How long have you been training?"

"Two months."

"That's a little early to consider yourself a real boxer, don't you think?"

Harvey doesn't answer her. They reach Barclay Street and keep going straight, walking slowly.

"Olympia said you weren't concentrating," Elettra continues. In her mind, she can still see Harvey's very brief match in the ring.

Him against Olympia, a woman made of muscles, swiftness and intelligence. A legend. "She hit you hard to make that clear to you. In fact, she did more than just hit you. I'd say she gave you a real pummeling."

"I didn't see it coming."

"Olympia says whoever lowers their guard gets hit."

"That happens to lots of people," Harvey replies, stopping beside a large open area.

Elettra looks straight in front of her and is left speechless. A sudden silence overwhelms her thoughts and squelches all her enthusiasm. She feels as if she were walking on eggshells or, better, on tissue paper. "Is this it?"

"Yeah, this is it." Harvey nods.

Ground Zero, the empty expanse of the World Trade Center, the place where the Twin Towers once stood. Bulldozers are working below street level like big mechanical worms. A tall metal fence surrounds the entire block. The names of the people who lost their lives are written there in white lettering.

"Do you feel that, too?" Harvey asks, starting to walk around Ground Zero.

"What?"

"The earth below all this."

Elettra nods. "It feels thin, like it isn't even there. Like it's incredibly fragile."

"It isn't fragile. To me, it's like it's constantly talking. There's something I need to tell you. It may sound crazy, but I heard a voice talking to me before, back at home. I think it was Dwaine's. But here, there are hundreds of voices."

"What are they saying?"

"Nothing," Harvey replies. "They're crying."

The two kids walk around the perimeter of Ground Zero, heading toward Battery Park, at the southern tip of the city. Toward the sea. Once they spot the first age-old trees, they turn left, heading over to a big square building whose granite facade is protected by four colossal female statues.

"We're there," Harvey points out, crossing the street.

"What is this place?"

"The National Museum of the American Indian."

"And who are they?" Elettra asks, nodding at the statues.

"The four continents. America looking ahead, Europe surrounded by its old symbols, Asia in meditation and Africa still sleeping."

"Four women." Elettra smiles. "Some cultures believe that everything connected to the Earth is female."

"You bet. But then, what are we guys here to do?" Harvey asks, walking into the museum.

Inside, the building is imposing and majestic, with large columns and tall, tall ceilings. Whirling around the marble rotunda are murals of ships crossing the bay. Harvey doesn't stop to look at them. He doesn't even slow down. He makes his way across the atrium, turns into a hallway that leads to a guarded office and waves.

"Hey, Miller," the guard on the other side of the window says. "Need a hand with something?"

"I just wanted my key."

The guard pulls open a drawer, finds a key with an orange tag on it and hands it to him. Then he glances over at Elettra, who's standing a few feet behind him, looking up. "Your friend's cute."

Harvey jingles his key and goes back to Elettra.

"Why did we come here?"

"To get the map," the boy replies.

"It's in a museum?"

"A good friend of my father's works at the museum. I love coming here. It's so peaceful. Besides, they've got lockers, and they're guarded. It was the best place to leave it."

They reach a row of metal lockers. Inside the one Harvey opens up is the professor's briefcase. Seeing it gives both of them a strange sensation.

"I haven't even touched it since I got back here."

"That feels like years ago."

Not sure who should take it, they both reach out a hand at the same time. They start laughing. They're standing very close to each other. Elettra's hair smells like shampoo. Harvey's fingers are still covered with the acrid smell of his boxing gloves.

They kiss.

It's only an instant, and neither of them could say who closed their eyes first or who it was that kissed the other one. But they kiss, barely touching their lips together. Lips that will be tingling for hours.

They don't say a single word until they've walked out of the museum. Harvey smiles. Elettra's quiet. Both of them knew that sooner or later it was bound to happen. Ever since Rome. Ever since the first time they saw each other in the snowy courtyard of the Domus Quintilia.

Their hearts are racing.

It's one more secret they'll need to keep.

*   *   *

123

Later on, Harvey and Elettra meet up with Sheng and Mistral in the lobby of the Mandarin Oriental. They choose two isolated tables beside an enormous picture window looking out over Columbus Circle and Central Park. Linda Melodia hovers around them, suspiciously eying the room before resolving to go upstairs to sleep. "Don't stay up late, understood?" she reminds them for the millionth time.

"We'll just play a game for a while and be right up, Auntie."

Linda's face is red from the wind. "I went up in the Empire State Building!" she says, which she has already told them.

"Auntie . . ." Elettra tries to cut her short.

"And tomorrow we're visiting the Statue of Liberty together, aren't we?"

"Yes, I promise," her niece replies. "Tomorrow morning. But now, would you please just let us play?"

Linda Melodia lets out an exaggerated yawn. "How long is your little game going to last?"

"You don't have to guard over us like we're on a field trip," Elettra says.

"Who's guarding over you?" Aunt Linda asks with a fake tone of innocence. Then she yawns a second time. But instead of turning around and heading toward the elevators, she spots a free armchair nearby, sinks down into it and nods off instantly.

"Now what do we do?" exclaims Sheng, worried about Elettra's aunt being only a few yards away from them.

"Let's cast the tops anyway," Mistral suggests.

Sheng nods. "You're right. The best way to hide something from someone is to do it right under their nose."

"Let's use the map," Harvey repeats aloud.

They place the ancient map of the Chaldeans on the table. It's a wooden rectangle with an endless series of lines, its outside marked with dozens of inscriptions. One can only imagine the meaning behind all the symbols, the scribbles, the markings, like those left on desks at school. It's thanks only to Ermete's patience and knowledge that the kids were able to give any of those letters a specific meaning. They're the names of the important people who owned it before them: the Magi kings, Christopher Columbus, Marco Polo. But also the mathematician Pythagoras, the philosopher Plato, the historian Seneca and the legendary Leonardo da Vinci. A perfectly simple object, but the map irradiates energy even through the cloth protecting it. It's both light and extremely heavy at the same time.

"Something dawned on me while I was in the shower," Mistral says, pulling out her wooden top.

"You finally figured out how to adjust the showerhead, too?" Sheng jokes, rifling through his ever-present backpack in search of his own top.

"It's about Agatha's photo . . . ," the French girl continues.

"What's that?" asks Harvey, unusually involved in the conversation.

Sitting on the opposite side of the table, Elettra looks at him while trying not to look at him. She can sense he's playing the same game. They wish they could spend some more time alone together. But they listen to Mistral and try to focus on the topic at hand.

"The three men were all different ages, and if you ask me, I don't think they could've been classmates." Mistral makes a quick sketch of the photo and then points her pencil at the man in the center. "Alfred's in the middle, the second of the three, but on the bottom left you can see the shadow of the photographer with his hand raised."

"Yeah, I remember," Harvey says.

"Judging from the shadow, the photographer was a man, too," Mistral continues without missing a beat. "So there were four of them, and written at the bottom of the postcard was 'two of four.' What came to my mind was that there might be four postcards."

The kids exchange excited glances. "That's a good idea. We need to go back to Agatha's place and have her give us the photo," Elettra says.

"I can go there early tomorrow morning," Harvey proposes.

Mistral stares at the map, fascinated. She's the only one of them who wasn't at the Regno del Dado, because she was being held prisoner in the Coppedè district, kidnapped by Jacob Mahler. "So how does it work?"

"It's crazy, actually," Harvey replies.

"That's not true," Sheng protests. "All you need to do is think and concentrate."

"In Rome, we were thinking about you," Elettra adds. "About how to find you."

"So while you were thinking about me, the tops showed you the place where I was locked up?"

"Not all of them did. Only the one with the dog and the one with the whirlpool," Sheng specifies.

"On the other hand, the top with the eye led me to the gypsy woman and then to the Ring of Fire," says Elettra.

"But why?" asks Mistral.

" 'What difference does it make which road you follow as you seek the truth? Such a great secret is not to be reached by a single path,' " Sheng says, quoting the professor's notebooks. "But what's the secret we're talking about now?"

Mistral nods. "More specifically, what I'm wondering is . . . what is it we're looking for now? The stolen top? A way to decipher the numbers on the postcard? The other postcards? The Star of Stone? Or the two men the professor was friends with before he ran off?"

"I don't think he ran off," Elettra interjects. "I think he was forced to run away from someone. Maybe he'd already discovered the existence of the Ring of Fire, or this . . . this Star of Stone. Maybe the star led him to Rome . . . and now we're taking the same trip backward."

"He left us some clues: a picture and a postcard," says Mistral.

"Remember what he said?" Elettra asks. "If you find a secret, you need to guard it and protect it. And maybe . . . maybe he tried but failed. Maybe he got something wrong or betrayed himself."

"Or someone betrayed him," Sheng adds.

"So he ended up crossing paths with . . . them," Elettra concludes.

"Yeah," Harvey says bleakly, spelling it out, "the people who are following us now, searching for the very same secret. That must be it."

Just then, a man dressed in black appears behind them.

14
THE STRANGER

HARVEY, SHENG, ELETTRA AND MISTRAL WHIRL AROUND. OF average height, the man is wearing round glasses and a Sherlock Holmes hat. He has a long beard. He's wearing a nineteenth-century coal-gray trench coat and has a pipe clenched between his lips.

"So who's she?" he asks with a guttural voice, pointing at Linda Melodia, who's curled up in the armchair.

The kids take a closer look at him. Sprawled out over the table to protect the map of the Chaldeans, Sheng notices that one part of the man's beard is coming detached from his chin. "Ermete? Is that you?"

The man raises his pipe as a greeting. "Who else would it be, kid?"

Elettra starts to run over to him, but the engineer stops her with a flick of his hand. "No. No signs of affection. Let's pretend we barely know each other." His eyes dart around the lobby. Then, with skillful slowness, he grabs a chair from a nearby table and drags it over by the kids' seats.

"What on earth are you wearing?" Mistral exclaims, almost at a loss for words.

"Nice, isn't it?" the engineer/radio ham/archaeologist/comics reader/gaming master Ermete De Panfilis says, proud as a peacock. "I found it all on eBay, and at a bargain, too."

"You look like a cross between Sherlock Holmes and Lieutenant Columbo." Elettra smirks, her leg slung over the arm of her chair.

Ermete grimaces with disappointment. "I was hoping that one of you would recognize my tribute to 'The Raven,' the poem by Edgar Allan Poe. He wrote it in this city. . . ."

"Never heard of him," replies Sheng.

"What the heck do you read back in China?"

"I just finished the latest Ulysses Moore book," replies Sheng. "*Hao*, it's wild! Basically, you find out that Ulysses Moore is actually—"

"In any case, you didn't answer me," Ermete says, cutting him off and turning back toward the nearby armchair. "That woman. Who is she?"

"My aunt," Elettra explains. "She can be trusted. She beat the daylights out of Jacob Mahler when she caught him over at the Domus Quintilia."

"I trust her completely, then!" Ermete snickers, resting his elbows on the table. "Have I missed any spins?"

"Actually, we were just deciding what to ask the tops," says Elettra.

"What are the options?"

Mistral hands him the old postcard they found in the inside pocket of the tuxedo. Meanwhile, Elettra tells him how they found it.

"Holy moly. These look like . . . like numbers in a matrix cipher!"

Ermete has never heard about Agatha or about the professor's former life in New York, but when they tell him about his abandoning the Chanin Building, he's stunned. "He left an apartment in the middle of Manhattan for that dump on the outskirts of Rome?"

The Star of Stone is even more of a mystery to him. "The minute I get home, I'll check Alfred's notes to see if he mentions the Star."

"Try looking in the book by Seneca, in his treatise *On Comets,*" Mistral suggests.

"Good idea. I'll check out the legends of Mithra, too. If I remember correctly, that particular sun god was born from a rock. The Star of Stone could be a star that was born from a rock. . . . Does that make sense to you guys?"

"Actually, not really," Harvey remarks. "I mean, it wouldn't make any sense here in New York. The religion of Mithra never came here to the New World. It's a really ancient religion from Asia and Europe. . . ."

"Which officially came to an end in AD 392, when the Roman emperor Theodosius prohibited the worship of the ancient pagan gods under force of arms," Ermete continues encyclopedically.

"Exactly. In 392, there weren't any Romans in America. There were the people that Columbus called the Indians, who had other gods," Harvey explains.

"Let's not forget that Columbus was one of the people who used this map," Sheng reminds them.

"I think we should use the tops now," Elettra interjects, holding up hers.

The five spread a street plan of Manhattan over the wooden

map, holding the corners down taut. Then they deliberate on who should go first.

"I've never spun mine before . . . ," Mistral says in a hushed voice, awed by all their preparations.

"It's easy! You just do this," Sheng explains, casting his top, the one with the eye, onto the map. "This one shows a detail you need to watch for or discover," he continues as the top begins to whirl around, moving along the chaotic grooves below to intersect the gridline streets of Manhattan.

"New York and Rome have something in common," Ermete says in a low voice, staring at the map. "Manhattan was built just like a Roman encampment. See the streets? They intersect at right angles."

The top of the eye begins to move around in smaller circles and finally stops. The corner of Sixth Street and Avenue B in the East Village.

"What's there?" everyone asks Harvey.

He shakes his head, baffled. "Nothing that comes to mind." He reflects a minute. "Tompkins Square Park, I think . . ."

Elettra casts the top of the tower. It spins around with its distinctive rhythm, different from the one before it. It's slower, more deliberate. It stops in the very center of the East River, at the lower tip of Roosevelt Island. "This should be a safe place," the girl says.

"But that can't be," Harvey sneers.

"Why? What's on the island?"

"An old, abandoned smallpox hospital."

"So much for a safe place. . . ."

Ermete looks at Mistral. "It's your turn."

"What about Harvey?" the French girl asks.

"He always goes after the rest of us," explains Sheng. "He likes to be a copycat."

Mistral stands up. Then she leans over the table, gently rests her top with the dog on the map and sends it spinning, almost sad to see it leave her fingertips. This top moves differently, too, swirling around restlessly, furiously. It indicates the guard to get past.

"This one's easy," Harvey remarks when the top finally stops. "And it's definitely a well-guarded place: Rockefeller Center."

"The place with the ice-skating rink?" asks Mistral, who's seen it in lots of movies.

"Yeah. That's where they put the city's tallest Christmas tree, too. It's one of the most famous attractions in New York. And now, check this out!" Harvey rests the last top on the surface, and rather than just casting it, he hurls it onto the map. It's the whirlwind, the place of danger. The top darts around with a threatening hiss until, exhausted, it stops in the center of Hell's Kitchen, the heart of New York's Irish community.

"Oh, great . . ." He groans. "Now of all times. Unless I'm mistaken, tomorrow's the seventeenth, St. Patrick's Day." Harvey points his finger at the neighborhood west of Broadway. "Tomorrow there are going to be tons of people dressed in green parading down Fifth Avenue."

Tons of people.

The danger is a celebration.

15

THE MISSION

It's perfectly silent in Egon Nose's office. As silent as the grave. All the outside noise is muffled by the rosewood panels lining the walls. Soundproofing blocks out the surrounding world, as well as the partying going on in the club. One needs silence to think.

The gold picture frames are gleaming. Dr. Nose is surrounded by a spiral of bluish smoke that drifts up toward the low ceiling lights like a trapped angel.

He's holding a wooden top in front of him and inhaling deep puffs of smoke. Depicted on the wooden top is a bridge. Or a rainbow. Nothing else. Just old wood hardened by the centuries, perfectly conserved by the warm, dry environment in which it was discovered. It's desert wood.

"There was only one tree in the middle of the desert," Egon Nose says aloud. "It was a giant black sycamore. They called it the Judas Tree." He lets out a little cough, his throat tickling. His cigar glows with red cinders. "The Judas Tree had deep, deep roots. All the merchants along the Silk Road gathered around it. For hundreds of years, it marked the passage bridging the East and the West."

"It's gone now," an icy voice replies.

Egon Nose is on the phone. One of the screens in his study shows an urban skyline that isn't Manhattan's. There are tall sky-scrapers, different lights, different swarms of human insects trapped in a megalopolis. It's Shanghai. The icy voice is coming from there.

Dr. Nose balances his cigar on the rim of a crystal ashtray, which breaks the light down into ten oddly shaped prisms. "Yes. They cut it down hundreds of years ago. It's still a shame when a tree dies, don't you think?" He rests his fingertips on the surface of the ancient top and turns it upside down. "So, this is it? An old wooden toy? You sure it's worth what you're paying me to have gotten it for you? I don't think—"

"You aren't paid to think," the voice snaps icily.

"Heh, heh, heh . . . I'm sorry if I doubted you, sir," the owner of the club replies sarcastically, "and if I was lacking respect for your little toy."

"I don't like to play."

"I'm not surprised, Heremit. You don't like anything. Except for yourself, naturally."

A shadow passes across the screen showing the city of Shanghai. It's moving too swiftly to be captured in the image. "I want the map. And the other tops," the shadow says.

"It's only a matter of hours. All we need to do is wait," Dr. Nose replies.

"Tomorrow is March seventeenth," Heremit Devil reminds him.

"It's already March seventeenth," Dr. Nose remarks, checking his watch. "Can't you hear how quiet it is? It's St. Patrick's Day.

Time for the pagan spirits to hide in the shadows, waiting for it to be over. It isn't a good day to come out into the open. Heh, heh, heh . . . But that doesn't mean it isn't a good time to move around *below*."

"I have five days left."

"Before what?"

"Before the next appointment." The shadow reappears on the screen with the image of Shanghai. His back is turned toward the camera, facing the window. He's staring outside, his hands clasped behind his back. "I can almost see it now."

"See what? Your city being crushed by your devastating power?"

"The star," Heremit Devil replies without turning around. "But that's none of your concern."

Egon Nose picks up his cigar again and lets himself be surrounded by its smoke. "There aren't any stars in Hell's Kitchen. And you're right. That's none of my concern. I don't even care. Stars are all useless. They're too small, too distant. Besides, this sky moving around makes me nauseous. What good are stars if you can't even touch them?"

16

THE ISLAND

THE WIND IN NEW YORK HARBOR IS WHIRLING THROUGH ELETTRA'S long, long hair and the rail at the side of the ferryboat. The girl has her eyes closed and is letting her thoughts fly free. Her mood has changed so much since the day before! She feels good, at peace with the world and full of volcanic energy again. Her kiss with Harvey, the way they didn't say anything about it, their stolen glances at the museum . . . it made her feel incredibly pretty. And wanted.

"You look like an octopus," Linda Melodia remarks, snapping her back to reality.

"Thanks, Auntie," Elettra grumbles in reply.

The woman's hands delve into her niece's curls with expert skill. "You didn't use any conditioner," she declares. Linda takes one of her niece's locks between her fingers and studies it like an entomologist would examine a rare tropical butterfly. "Would you look at this! A sea of split ends. You need a haircut!"

Elettra feels a surge of anger rise up inside of her, but it's one of those mild kinds of anger, one that's easy to push back down. She smiles. "Auntie, what man could ever put up with you?"

"Well, see here! When I was your age, boys were lining up at the door. . . ."

"I've never doubted it. This jacket is yours, you know."

"Yes, I know. Capri, 1979." After all the years, Linda Melodia's clothes still look brand-new. "I remember who gave it to me, too," Linda continues, pleased as punch. "A nice, dark-haired young man whom I had to send packing."

"Why's that?" Elettra laughs, imagining the scene.

"Why? Why? First they give you a gift, and then they start calling you, taking you out to places with crowds of screaming people, walking into your house tracking mud because they can't help but play with a soccer ball that's being kicked around on the street . . . and so, simply because you accepted a gift, you find yourself working for them."

"But it's nice," Elettra concludes.

"Heavens, is it nice!" sighs Linda, staring, mesmerized, at the Statue of Liberty, which is now in front of them. "Do we get off here?"

"Isn't there another island first?"

Aunt Linda opens the boat tour program and reads. "Ellis Island. Oh, yes. The one all the immigrants entering the United States would pass through. Imagine that! Millions of people who waited there for their entrance visas . . ."

Who knows how many life stories were trapped in there? thinks Elettra as the ferryboat makes its way around Liberty Island. *And who knows what Harvey's thinking? Who knows where he is right now? . . .*

* * *

Harvey has just come out of the Chanin Building. Agatha's place. His gym bag is slung over his shoulder. Sheng is trotting along beside him, toting his backpack, his camera hanging around his neck. They took a picture of the professor's photograph and its frame. But their day has only just begun.

"Where to now?" Sheng asks.

The sidewalks are packed with people, policemen are everywhere and the streets have been taped off.

"The old Irish part of town," Harvey proposes. "Hell's Kitchen."

"Why's it called that?"

"I don't know. I think it's because the Irish who moved here in the mid-1800s left their country because of a famine. They were desperate for food."

"In any case, Hell's Kitchen must be like my mom's kitchen," jokes Sheng. "Pure hell! Millennia of Chinese culinary traditions mysteriously vanishing without a trace."

The two walk toward Fifth Avenue and soon find themselves surrounded by a chaotic world of music and people. The entire street looks like a sea of green. White and green festoons are draped across the windows, lampposts and traffic lights, while thousands of little flags are fluttering in the sunshine. The cheerful sounds of fiddles and tambourines are echoing from every corner.

"Have they all gone crazy?" Sheng shouts to Harvey, trying to make his way through the crowd. They're surrounded by party horns, green and white checkered hats, clouds of confetti and streamers as long as jungle vines.

They smell the aroma of all kinds of fried foods and beer wafting through the air. The beer is green, naturally. The national color of Ireland.

"Here in New York, St. Patrick is the patron saint of Irishmen, and the police, too," Harvey explains, pointing at the numerous officers lining the sidewalks, "given that most of the city's cops were once Irish."

"Oh, man!" Sheng yells when he's almost knocked over by a procession of kids with painted faces. "I can't move!"

"It's the parade!" Harvey shouts.

They manage to push their way through the crowd to a stand selling fritters. Hanging down from its canopy as decorations are rubber snakes.

"What have snakes got to do with it?" Sheng asks, surprised.

"It's St. Patrick's Day, son!" the owner of the stand says, chuckling. "All the snakes get driven away! Fritter?"

Among the crowd, there's one person who doesn't look at all cheerful. He's so tall, massive and grim-looking that even the confetti seems to shy away from him. He stares at Harvey from a distance, trying not to lose sight of him in the sea of people, studying Harvey's new friend, the Chinese one, all the while.

When the two kids stop to buy a fritter, the man leans against a lamppost covered with decorations, pulls out a notebook and jots down a few quick notes. Then he starts moving again, indifferent and stern-looking.

"Party with us, Indian dude!" a group of kids shout at him. But he doesn't slow down. He tries to figure out where Harvey Miller is going.

Perched on the lamppost, a crow blind in one eye lets out a shrill caw.

17
THE PHONE CALL

"YOUR VOICE IS ALL GARBLED!" ERMETE SAYS ON THE PHONE. "No! It isn't your fault, Mom. It's the connection. I don't have time to call you back. I've got to go now. Yeah, sure, I go out. It's only natural. I'm in New York! Huh? What do you care if I'm keeping my room clean? I'm not expecting any company. Besides, how could it be clean, after the burglars tore it apart?"

Ermete immediately bites his lip. Too late. He let it slip.

"Mom! Wait . . . I . . . no . . . they didn't steal anything. Don't worry! They didn't steal a single penny from me! There wasn't anything valuable here. . . . Sure, they broke a few things. A couple pieces of furniture, but I'm renting the place furnished! It isn't my stuff! Americans all have property insurance! They even get *insurance* insurance! Besides, they came here once, and they certainly won't come here a second time! I . . . Mom, listen, I've really got to go! I . . . Mom . . . I've got to . . . AAAAAAAAHHH!"

With a slam dunk worthy of a basketball champion, Ermete slams the phone down. Then, just to be sure, he yanks the cord out of the wall jack. He stands there, contemplating the mess he's just made, on top of the mess caused by the robbers' search. He takes a deep breath, checks his watch and leaves. He's supposed to meet Mistral in Rockefeller Center, and he already risks showing up late.

He grabs his briefcase and walks to the door but then has second thoughts. He goes back, steps over some big clumps of the couch padding and walks into the bathroom.

"The best way to hide something," he murmurs to himself, looking at his poorly reflected image in the mirror, "is to hide it right in front of everyone's eyes."

Ermete takes the Ring of Fire down from the bathroom wall and tucks it into his briefcase. "Perfect," he says under his breath, checking out his reflection in the only other mirror in the apartment. "Just perfect." He's dressed as a bank manager, in a pinstriped suit and shiny black shoes; no one could ever recognize him.

He walks out of the house, whistling.

Sheng and Harvey climb up onto a stoop to get out of the crowd. There are even people climbing up the lampposts. Sheng keeps on taking snapshots. Then he asks, "What do you think the top was showing us, exactly?"

"This whirlpool of people?"

"In Rome, it led us to Mistral's kidnapper."

"I don't know, Sheng, really. . . ." Harvey stares out at the river of people in the street. "It could mean anything." Then, suddenly, his hand darts out and he grabs Sheng's shoulder. "Come on!" he cries, bounding down the steps. "I saw them!"

"Saw who?" Sheng asks, running after him.

"The two women! The ones who stole the top!" Harvey shouts, diving into the sea of many shades of green.

"I don't think I've ever seen so many people together in one place!" Mistral shouts to Ermete. They're on Fifth Avenue. The people are crowded together on the sidewalks, waiting for the St. Patrick's Day parade to pass by.

"I've heard a lot about it, but this is the first time I'm actually seeing it," Ermete replies, chuckling. "It's fantastic!"

Ermete takes Mistral by the hand and leads her into one of the buildings in Rockefeller Center, the square in the heart of the city. It isn't so crowded here.

"I can breathe again!" Mistral exclaims, looking out at the square, which in winter is turned into an ice-skating rink. Ermete smooths down the lapels of his elegant jacket.

"You look good dressed like that! Very professional . . ."

They walk down the stairway leading inside the concourse, the flags of many different nations flapping in the wind. Mistral looks around, fascinated. Before them are the picture windows and little tables of a big restaurant and then one of the buildings' majestic facade, with a grand entranceway in gold. Behind it, two arched staircases are hugging a fountain, in front of which rises up a gold statue.

"What is it we're looking for?" Mistral asks Ermete the moment they walk through the doorway.

"A dog guarding something," he replies, looking around in search of the elevators. "Should we try going upstairs?"

* * *

The moment she steps foot on Ellis Island, Elettra starts to feel hot. The kind of heat she didn't think she'd ever feel in New York, the kind that builds up because of her ability to absorb the energy around her. A tingling heat. By now, she knows perfectly well what it means: Something's about to happen.

Ellis Island is a flat, skeletal expanse still at the mercy of winter. In addition to the cement pier is a glass and metal canopy leading inside a large redbrick building with windows trimmed in white. Four tall towers mark the confines of the building. Elettra grabs on to her aunt's arm and lets herself be pulled inside.

"We could visit the dormitory where immigrants had to spend the night while waiting for their visas, and . . . the Great Hall . . . then . . . on this side . . . no, on that side"—Linda Melodia turns the map of the building around in all possible directions—"there's the place where the luggage was inspected, plus the vaccine infirmary. Only once the immigrants had gone through all these steps were they given a train ticket." The two continue on until they reach the large waiting hall.

"May I help you?" asks a mustachioed man with an Italian accent.

Linda Melodia lowers her gaze just enough to inspect him: well-groomed mustache, well-combed hair, a presentable overcoat, nice shirt, elegant trousers, well-shined shoes. Her smile instantly broadens. "Yes, would you, please?"

The man slicks back his mustache, delighted. Elettra pulls off her scarf from around her neck. It's boiling hot in the Great Hall.

* * *

Harvey runs through the crowd on Fifth Avenue and heads west, following the women he saw a minute before. He turns around and spots Sheng panting behind him, banging into the people around him and accidentally hitting them with his camera. Then, looking in front of him again, Harvey pushes his way through with his gym bag. After a few blocks, the two women slow down their pace. They're in Hell's Kitchen.

Sheng swings his backpack around in an attempt to avoid being trampled. He slips through and tries to gain his bearings. Harvey waves him over.

Just then, the two women stop. Harvey ducks his head and walks back a few steps. When he turns back to look in their direction again, he sees that they've gone up to the closed door of a nightclub. A place called Lucifer.

Harvey forces himself to stand perfectly still so he can keep them in his sights. The two don't say a word to each other. They ring the doorbell and wait for someone to answer.

Sheng catches up with his friend, panting, and Harvey points at the club on the other side of the street. "It's them."

"H-hao!" Sheng stammers, struck by how beautiful the women are. He pulls out his camera. Click. Click.

Harvey manages to cover the camera just in time. As though they've heard the noise of the shutter, the two women turn around to scrutinize the crowd.

The door to the club opens slightly. A man's hand comes out and caresses one of the women's faces.

"They're going in," Sheng remarks. The two boys start walking and pass by Lucifer. Fifty steps later, the street ends at yet another chaotic intersection.

"You sure it was them?" asks Sheng.

"No doubt about it."

"The top wasn't lying, then."

"Looks that way," Harvey agrees.

"So, what do you want to do? Should we wait or should we tell the others?"

"Tell who?" Harvey says in a low voice. "Elettra's with her aunt, and Ermete doesn't have his cell phone."

"We could call Mistral. He and she are supposed to be together right now."

Harvey wrings his hands nervously. "Let's wait." A flapping of wings over their heads makes him look up toward the sun. It's already low in the sky and is beginning to set.

"The club will be open tonight," says Sheng.

"I suppose so."

Gray clouds are hanging over the river. Harvey and Sheng lean back against a brick wall. Around them, people are celebrating. Then the door to Lucifer opens up a second time.

18
PROMETHEUS

ROCKEFELLER CENTER IS A LABYRINTH OF MARBLE HALLWAYS. Ermete and Mistral search every square inch of the public part, staring at their reflections in the shiny black walls. They go up to the top floors and do a complete round of the shops inside. They search every single corridor with a fine-tooth comb. At least they think they do.

Three hours later, they're back where they started out, sitting at a little table in the café looking over the square with the gold statue. Not even a trace of any guard dogs.

Spread out in front of Ermete is a map of Rockefeller Center, which he picked up at an information desk. He moves his finger over the areas they've visited and shakes his head. "I don't know where else we should look," he says, discouraged. "Especially because we don't even know what we're looking for. In Rome, the guard dog was Jacob Mahler. . . ."

Mistral tries to catch the waiter's eye.

"A person in flesh and blood . . ." Ermete groans, deep in thought. "But there are thousands of people here at Rockefeller

Center. How could we know who the guardian is? Not to mention what he's guarding!"

"A postcard, maybe?" Mistral guesses. "Or the top they stole right in front of your eyes?"

"Maybe we should cast the tops on the map of the complex," Ermete suggests. "That way we could narrow down our search."

Mistral nods and stares at the fountain on the other side of the glass walls. "What a shame," she murmurs.

"Don't give up hope. It's just our first reconnaissance mission," Ermete says encouragingly. "We'll find it."

Mistral sighs. "Actually, I was thinking of the ice-skating rink. It's a shame they've already taken it down. I'd gladly have gone on it."

"You can skate?"

"A little. I saw this movie where a guy and a girl met on that rink. They danced there on the ice with the snow coming down and all the lights sparkling around them. They stopped and kissed right there . . . in front of that statue."

Ermete smiled. "A giant golden eyesore."

The waiter comes up from behind them. Mistral orders a hot tea, Ermete a fruit juice cocktail with a slice of orange. "A businessman's kind of drink," he explains. They sit there for a while in silence, thinking.

"Ermete?" Mistral asks when the waiter brings their order. "What's that statue of, anyway?"

The engineer twists his lips. "Beats me." He turns to the waiter. "Do you know who that guy is, by any chance?"

"That's Prometheus," the man replies with a smile.

Ermete sits up straight in his chair. "Prometheus . . . Prometheus? The one who stole fire from the gods?"

"That's him," the waiter continues. "It's from 1934 and—"

"Keep the change!" Ermete says, almost shouting, as he rushes out of the café together with Mistral.

"Why didn't it dawn on us before?" the engineer asks the girl, who's standing beside him in front of the colossal gold statue. "He's right here, at the entrance . . . guarding the door! Look at him! He's just a kid! And there's the Ring of Fire, too!" The gold carving of Prometheus really does look like a boy. He's holding a ball of fire as he escapes down a mountainside.

"It sure is something . . . ," Mistral agrees.

Written in golden letters on the copper-colored panels behind the statue are the words PROMETHEUS, TEACHER IN EVERY ART, BROUGHT THE FIRE THAT HATH PROVED TO MORTALS A MEANS TO MIGHTY ENDS.

Ermete's head is awhirl with ideas. Prometheus, the Titan who stole fire from the gods to give it to mankind, whom he himself had created by mixing together clay and water . . . a boy.

Mistral looks doubtful. "Could he be the guardian we're looking for?"

"I'll bet he is." The engineer nods.

"So how do we . . . get past him?" the girl asks.

"I think I have an idea . . . a crazy idea," Ermete answers. He reaches down into his briefcase and strokes the Ring of Fire, the mirror they found in Rome beneath the *mitreo* in San Clemente Church.

Prometheus's mirror.

"Mistral, I . . . ," Ermete grumbles. "I don't know if this makes any sense, but . . ." He pulls the ancient mirror out of his brief-case. "If Prometheus is the guard . . . and this is his mirror, maybe we need to . . ."

"To what?"

"I don't know," Ermete admits, getting as close to the statue as possible.

Prometheus has one hand free. It's open. The fountain is gurgling up in front of him. Ermete looks around to see if there's a policeman, a guard or an alarm system.

"It's too tall and too far away," Mistral whispers to him, walking around the fountain until she's reached the bronze panels.

"You may be right, but . . ." The engineer looks carefully at the golden ring surrounding Prometheus's body. Engraved on it are the signs of the zodiac. The constellations devised by the ancient Chaldeans. They've always been right there, in front of everyone's eyes. The Ring of Fire. And the constellations. The young Titan who tricked all the gods.

"I'm going to try it!" Ermete exclaims. With this, he steps into the fountain. He wades a few steps through the ice-cold water, until he can almost reach up and touch Prometheus. Then some-one behind him starts yelling.

"Don't worry!" he shouts, raising his hands. "I'm not doing anything bad to it." He can see parchments engraved on the in-side of the ring. The parchments on the side where he's standing form a sort of indentation. A gap. A niche.

"Ermete!" Mistral calls to him, begging him to come out.

But he doesn't listen to her. What's done is done. He can hear other people shouting with surprise, while a few others are laughing, but he couldn't care less. They can't kill him just because he stuck his feet in a fountain. . . .

Click. Someone decided to photograph him.

"Here goes nothing!" he exclaims, rising up on his tiptoes. He lifts up the mirror and places it inside the gold ring. The mirror slides in, slips over and then, just when Ermete is about to give up, it clicks perfectly into place between the two parchments in relief.

Clack! goes one of the fountain's lowest panels, revealing a tiny secret compartment. Two streams of water begin to lower, allowing him to reach out to it. Ermete turns around, triumphant. But his smile vanishes instantly. A swarm of security guards is running toward him. Big, angry-looking security guards.

"Uh-oh . . . ," he groans, looking over at Mistral. She, too, noticed the secret compartment behind the fountain. She's really close to it. She needs a diversion. The guards need to focus all their attention on him, and *only* on him. Ermete can't think of anything better to do than plop down into the water, shouting, "Help! I'm drowning!"

A moment later, the guards are on top of him. They grab him by the shirt and pick him up like a bird with sopping-wet feathers. "What's the big idea, huh?"

"Thank you! You saved my life!" Ermete exclaims. Meanwhile, he peeks around, looking for Mistral. Not seeing her anywhere, he smiles.

"This is no laughing matter, you know!" A security guard yanks him away before the eyes of the curious onlookers. "What'd you do to the statue?"

"Nothing. I just added its missing piece," Ermete replies, grinning from ear to ear.

Elettra's fingers hurt. It's a sharp pain, as if her skin weren't thick enough to protect them. Just like when she crossed the Quattro Capi bridge back in Rome the night they met the professor.

In the giant lobby of the immigration building on Ellis Island, she feels suffocated, as if she were inside a tiny prison cell. The laughter of her aunt and the man with the mustache aren't doing anything to help her understand why she feels this sudden surge of energy.

There's someone here . . . , she thinks, trying to follow her instincts. *Or maybe something's happening to the others. Maybe they've found something. Maybe Harvey . . . with the whirlpool . . .*

She doesn't even want to think about it. She tries dialing Harvey's number. Straight to voice mail. She tosses her phone back into the pocket of her white ski jacket. Then she looks down at her hands angrily. "Why do you hurt so much?" she asks them.

There's nothing electrical around, except for the lights. And there aren't any mirrors. Who's there? Who is she about to meet? Is someone watching her? If so, why? Could it be the man with the mustache? The woman dressed in blue? The three kids with the heart-shaped balloons?

A drop of perspiration rolls off her eyebrow and splashes down onto the tip of her shoe. Elettra takes off her jacket. She ignores her aunt Linda's protests, as if they were coming from a different planet, and peers around. Rows of wooden benches. The white toweringly high vaulting holding up the American flag on the back wall. The windows that the pale sunshine is streaming in through. The computers with records of the immigrants. Irish, Italian, Dutch, Spanish, Russian.

Elettra can feel someone's stare piercing the back of her neck. When she turns around, she sees a man leaning against a brass railing. He's a Native American dressed in old-fashioned clothing. He's standing so still that he looks like a statue. But he isn't. Why is he staring at her? There are lots of people there in the lobby. All around them is the shuffling of feet and a low murmur of voices.

The Native American casts one last glance in her direction before he steps back from the railing and starts to walk away.

That's him, thinks Elettra. She doesn't know who he is and she doesn't know why, but she knows she needs to follow him.

She starts running.

19

THE APPOINTMENT

"Well, Mistral," Sheng says on the cell phone. "Find any-thing?" A moment later, he's gaping. "What do you mean, a secret compartment? You lost the Ring of Fire? In a statue? Hold on, hold on! I'm not following you. . . . What angel are you talking about?"

Harvey isn't even listening to him. He starts walking. The two women have just come out of Lucifer. "Let's go!"

Sheng glances at him and whispers into the phone, "Mistral! We've got to . . . I'll call you in a bit. Really, otherwise they'll get away. I don't know! Oh, man! Why'd they beat him up?" Without taking the phone away from his ear, he dashes after Harvey, who's following the women from Lucifer. "Okay! See you. Where? I don't know! So who is it that beat up Ermete? Okay. Half an hour and we're there . . . wherever 'there' is. I've got to go now or I might get lost forever!"

Sheng tosses his phone into his backpack and starts pushing his way through the crowd, trying not to lose sight of his friend's messy head of hair. When Harvey stops, Sheng is panting, feeling like he's just spent hours struggling to chop open a path through the jungle. "I want to learn boxing, too!" he grumbles, almost clinging to his friend.

Harvey has a serious look on his face. Sheng tries to figure out what he's looking at, but the crowd is blocking his view. "What's up?"

"They're handing out something . . . ," Harvey says, keeping his voice down.

"That is . . . ?"

"Flyers."

"Flyers?"

"Looks like it." Harvey takes a few steps forward and picks up one that a man just dropped to the ground.

"What's it for?" Sheng asks him.

"A party," he replies. "A rave, in fact."

"One of those wild parties that last all night long?"

"At the City Hall subway station," Harvey continues. "But look at the drawing. . . ." Written on the flyer is:

THE UNDERGROUND SPIN
AROUND THE OLD CITY HALL STATION
MARCH 19TH, AFTER MIDNIGHT

"This might come in handy," Harvey says, worried.

The two quickly walk off. A tall, brawny Indian picks up another one of the flyers from the ground and slips it into his pocket.

"The R stops at City Hall," Harvey points out, reading over a map of the subway hanging near the train door.

"The flyer calls it the *old* City Hall station. . . ."

"Well, I don't know where that is," Harvey admits.

Having gotten off at the second stop, they reach the street level when the sun is practically only a memory. They walk into the Time Warner Center and head toward the café inside Whole Foods, the enormous supermarket at Columbus Circle. Once they're off the escalators, Sheng spots Mistral sitting at a table off to the side.

"You alone?" he asks her the moment he's beside her.

"Yes," she answers, "and you have no idea how happy I am that you're here!"

"Ermete?" Harvey asks, sitting down next to her.

"He went to buy a sweat suit and a ski jacket. It was incredible! You can't even imagine. . . ." Mistral rests a brown wooden box on the table and slides it over to Sheng.

"Where'd this come from?"

"It was being watched over by the guard dog."

"What is it?"

"Go ahead. Take a look."

Sheng clicks open the lock and the box opens up. Inside of it are two golden objects: a key with the number thirty-two written on it and a little statue of an angel with its wings unfurled, its right hand stretched out, as if it were pointing at something.

"*Hao!* So what are they?"

"Pick up the angel," Mistral says encouragingly.

Sheng does what she says. The statue is really heavy. On its base is the artist's signature: Paul Manship.

"I don't get it."

Mistral is so excited, she's almost babbling. "I went to an Internet café and discovered that Paul Manship is the sculptor who made the Prometheus at Rockefeller Center!"

"So what?"

Mistral takes a deep breath and gives them a recap of their day. "The ring around Prometheus had a sort of niche in it, and the Ring of Fire we found in Rome fit perfectly into that niche . . . opening up a secret compartment."

"No way!" Harvey exclaims.

Mistral continues. "While the guards were busy yelling at Ermete, I went over to the secret compartment, looked inside and found this box."

"You *stole* it?" Harvey gasps.

Mistral's angelic face turns bright red.

Sheng slaps her on the shoulder. "Way to go! You're fantastic!"

"What about our mirror? The Ring of Fire?" Harvey asks.

Mistral shrugs. "No problem there. Luckily, after roughing him up a bit, the guards at Rockefeller Center told Ermete to take it with him, so he went back into the fountain and got it. With everyone around him laughing the whole time."

"*Hao!*" Sheng exclaims. "I wish I'd been there."

"You could've taken a nice snapshot of him, too."

The angel statue is handed to Harvey, who turns it over with a suspicious look on his face. "I'm not sure why, but this looks familiar. . . ."

"You're the only one it might mean anything to."

After a long while of thought, the boy shakes his head. "Vladimir Askenazy," he concludes.

"What does Vladimir have to do with it?"

"We've got three old things now: a postcard, a key and a statue. On top of that, Sheng and I discovered the place where the two robbers hang out," Harvey explains, then tells her about their trip to Hell's Kitchen and shows her the flyer.

"Maybe an antiques dealer can explain how an object that's supposed to be thousands of years old, like the Ring of Fire, could fit into a statue from . . ."

"Nineteen thirty-four," says Mistral, finishing his sentence.

"That's really strange, don't you think?" Harvey's cell phone lets out a series of high-pitched beeps. It's Elettra. Harvey jumps up and walks off, leaving Sheng and Mistral all alone.

"I know who that is," the Chinese boy says. "Wanna bet?"

The phone call only lasts a few minutes. Then Harvey comes back to the table, clearly troubled. He doesn't even sit down. He hides his cell phone in his pocket, but he can't hide the fact that he's a little shaken. "Elettra's on her way back from Ellis Island," he says. "She . . . she met someone in the museum . . . someone who showed her the immigration registers. She says she found an Alfred Van Der Berger who came to the United States from Amsterdam."

"Great!" Sheng exclaims. Then he hesitates. "How's that going to help us?"

"Well, a little extra information can't hurt," says Mistral. Noticing that Harvey isn't showing any signs of sitting down, she asks him, "Are you leaving?"

"Yeah. I'm going to pick her up at the ferryboat terminal. What are you guys going to do?" His question makes it clear that they aren't invited.

"I could use a bite to eat," Sheng says, looking at the mountains of food surrounding them.

"Okay." Harvey raps on the table and sheepishly waves goodbye.

"What's wrong, Harvey?" Mistral asks him.

"It's nothing."

"You sure?"

Harvey rolls his eyes and dumps his gym bag on the floor. "Listen," he starts out, resting his hands on the table. "Something dawned on me, but I'm warning you, it's actually impossible. . . ."

"Shoot."

"If I'm right, we'd have another little problem to solve. A problem that doesn't seem to have any logical explanation."

"Which would be . . . ?"

"The photograph at Agatha's house. The three men. The names written on the back."

Mistral reads from her notes. "Paul, Alfred and Robert."

Harvey points at the signature on the base of the angel statue. "Paul Manship."

"No way!" Mistral exclaims. "He was alive a hundred years ago!"

"Exactly," Harvey insists, unusually grim. "That's exactly the problem."

20

THE REGISTER

◯

EVENING HAS FALLEN IN BATTERY PARK. ELETTRA AND HARVEY are walking along the seaside at the southernmost tip of Manhattan. The sun has slid down behind the horizon, now a prisoner of the long winter night.

"I thought it was just my imagination," Elettra explains, dragging her feet on the path's fine gravel. "I looked everywhere, but the guy wasn't there. He'd vanished, like he'd never even existed. So I retraced my steps. I was burning up like a furnace. Then, suddenly, I heard someone's voice asking me if they could help me somehow. I whirled around and there he was. The Indian man who'd been staring at me before. I wasn't wrong. He really was wearing old-fashioned clothes. But he had a name tag on his coat."

"What was his name?"

"Washington." Elettra smiles. "The moment I saw the name tag, I calmed down and realized that Washington worked at the museum's help desk. His outfit was a kind of uniform. I asked him a few questions about the history of the city and he told me about the first settlements, the street fights and the skyscrapers, which according to one legend were built entirely by the Indians. In any case," Elettra continues, "while I was talking to him, I kept feeling . . . charged. So I asked him some other questions about immigration and Ellis Island, until he took me to see the computers that have the names of all the immigrants to the United States over the last two hundred years. He asked me if I wanted to try looking someone up . . . and I got the idea of checking for Alfred Van Der Berger."

Harvey stops and stares at her.

"The computer found one," Elettra continues after a long pause. "Then I jammed the system. I short-circuited the entire computer network."

"How do you know it was you?"

"My keyboard caught fire," the girl explains. "It was me. I could feel it."

Harvey and Elettra start walking among the long shadows of the trees. A woman wearing a sweat suit and white earphones passes them, a poodle in tow.

"Among those millions of names, signatures and registered documents, there was only one Alfred Van Der Berger." Elettra stops a short distance from the light-colored trunk of a cedar. An icy breeze is coming in from the sea. The trees are skeletal and perfectly still, as though lifeless. "In 1905, Harvey," whispers Elettra. "In 1905."

"That's impossible."

"It was him, Harvey," the girl insists.

He laughs nervously. "The man we met in Rome wasn't over a hundred years old, Elettra!"

"I know, but I'm telling you, it was him!"

Still skeptical, Harvey doesn't answer her. "You know that's crazy!" Then he stares at her with all the intensity he can summon up. "How can you be so sure it was him? If the computer hadn't short-circuited, maybe you would've found thousands of other Alfred Van Der Bergers."

"The computer short-circuited because I short-circuited it," Elettra objects. "And I short-circuited it because I could tell that it . . . that it was him."

Harvey shakes his head. "It's totally impossible! The average life span for men is eighty years."

"Maybe Alfred Van Der Berger isn't simply . . . a man."

"Then what is he?" No voice, inside or outside Harvey's head, whispers the answer.

Elettra wraps her arms around him gently. "I don't know, Harvey. We've always just called them . . . 'them.' "

Harvey raises his hands and rests them on Elettra's back, drawing her closer protectively.

"If they're our enemies, Harvey . . . maybe Alfred and the other men who were with him in that picture . . . his friends . . ." Elettra's next words are drowned out by the wind, which is making the lowest tree branches groan and their bark grow brittle.

"Friends?" Harvey repeats.

Elettra's eyes are as dark as ink. Full of words to be written. "Isn't there anyone who can help us, Harvey? Can't you hear a voice, one that's telling us what to do?"

"No," he answers with a shudder.

"I'm getting scared."

Harvey's heart is beating stronger and stronger. Elettra's shoulders are tiny and delicate. Her neck long and slender. Her glimmering eyes troubled.

"There's no need for you to be scared," he replies, kissing her.

161

21
THE TOWER

DRESSED AS A VAGRANT, ERMETE ARRIVES AT THE CORNER OF EAST Sixth Street and Avenue B. The East Village is a clump of dirty, narrow streets lined with chaotic homes with peeling facades, much different from the Upper East Side.

Ermete wraps his crumpled coat around himself more tightly. His woolen hat is doing nothing to keep the cold away from his brain. It's early morning, and Ermete hates early mornings and everything that happens before eleven o'clock. The sky is a gray mountain that the sun is struggling to scale.

The kids got there before him. They're waiting for him now on the other side of the street.

"No luck," he says, greeting them. His breath freezes in a puff in front of his lips. "I spent all night trying, but I couldn't understand a thing."

Harvey, Mistral, Elettra and Sheng look over the sheets of paper covered with Ermete's handwriting. Numbers and letters. Numbers and letters.

"There isn't a simple alphabetic code on that postcard," the engineer continues. "No alphanumeric substitutions. Not even a variation of the Caesar cipher."

"Oh, now I get it. . . ." Sheng groans, handing the pages back to him.

"A Caesar cipher with a shift of three, for example, would mean that instead of each letter, you write the one that comes three letters later in the alphabet. You can make a variation of a Caesar cipher using alphanumeric substitution, but . . . no dice. I tried all the possible combinations. None of the recurring numbers let me clearly identify a vowel. There isn't even any kind of logical numeric relationship. I tried with multiplication tables, I applied a few matrices I'm familiar with . . . but I couldn't make heads or tails of it." Ermete sighs. There's an early-morning winter chill, and the city seems shrouded in gloomy sadness.

"So, what now?" Elettra asks.

"There are only two possibilities," the engineer continues. "The first is that the numbers on the postcard don't mean anything. Who knows? It could be an expense report or numbers to play in the lottery. . . ."

"And the second possibility?" Mistral asks encouragingly.

"It could be a cryptogram."

"Oh, wonderful," Sheng remarks, rubbing his arms, trying to warm himself. "Mind telling us what a cryptogram is?"

"The most famous ones are the Beale cryptograms. They contain instructions for finding a treasure, and now, over a hundred years later, not all of them have been solved yet."

"Then it's bound to be a cryptogram," Harvey remarks pessimistically.

"We've only got five days to solve it. After that, we're leaving," Mistral reminds them. "If this cryptogram can be solved, that is."

"A cryptogram is both perfectly simple and perfectly impossible to solve," Ermete explains. "The only way to decipher it is to discover what text it's based on. The only one of Beale's cryptograms that's been solved, for example, was based on the Declaration of Independence. Each word in the Declaration was assigned a progressive number: one, two, three . . . all the way to the end. Then, Beale had simply written down the numbers of the various words whose first letters, one after the other, spelled out the message. That's it."

"So in order to crack the cryptogram on this postcard, we've got to find the writing it's based on?"

"Exactly."

"But couldn't that be anything?"

"Once again, exactly. It could even be a Coca-Cola label." Ermete holds up both hands in front of him. "Just kidding! I already tried that."

"So how are we supposed to find out what it is?" Mistral asks rather skeptically. "The Star of Stone . . . any idea if that's a book?"

"We can look it up. For now, our only clue is that it must be a text that was around five years ago," says Ermete. "A text that's always valid, that can't be changed. Otherwise . . . goodbye, cryptogram!"

The kids look at each other dismally. Every once in a while a car zooms by noisily.

"It's a lousy day for lousy news, if you ask me," Elettra grumbles.

"What are we looking for here, anyway?" Ermete asks, yawning.

"Some strange detail that the top was pointing out to us."

"Something like the cat in Rome."

"Actually, I might have an idea," Harvey says. "Now that I think about it, there is something strange nearby. Over there, in the garden . . ."

It's a wooden tower standing on a little patch of grass beside the paved road.

"*Hao!*" gasps Sheng, pushing open the green gate leading into the garden. "What is it? The world's biggest toy?"

The tower rises up like bizarre scaffolding, with beams and wooden structures piled one atop the other chaotically. Peeking out from the empty spaces, looking like an odd race of creatures from a fairy tale, are all sorts of random objects: giant stuffed animals, fiberglass mannequins, rocking horses, parts from old merry-go-rounds, table legs and lampshades, forgotten dolls and plastic toys.

"It's a monument to consumerism, I think," Harvey explains, stopping with the others at the base of the tower of forgotten things. "It's full of lost, useless stuff that erodes in the rain."

"I've never seen anything like it . . . ," Elettra whispers, fascinated by the mass of decomposing objects.

"It's an eyesore," says Mistral decisively. Still, she can't help staring at the hundreds of curious items crammed into the tower.

"It's definitely strange," Ermete agrees, scratching his head.

"Well, now we need to discover what it is we need to discover. Who knows? Maybe there's a top somewhere in all that junk," Sheng jokes. He pulls out his camera and zooms in on one detail after the other.

Then Elettra points out something on the side opposite the garden entrance. It's a mannequin that seems to have been stuck onto the bottom part of a rocking horse. "Am I wrong, or is there something beneath that mannequin?"

Sheng looks for it through his lens. "There it is!" he cries after a moment. "Yeah, you're right. It's some sort of toy train. . . ."

"It looks like there's something written on its side. What does it say?"

" 'Pneumatic Transit,' " Sheng reads, zooming in as close as he can. "Wait a sec. It isn't a train. It looks more like a string of toy cars. There's a drawing, too: a pyramid, an obelisk . . . No, hold on. . . . Oh, man! It's a comet!"

When she hears Sheng cheer, Mistral walks over to them. "Have you found something?"

"Maybe. I might be all wrong about this," Sheng says in a low voice, adjusting the focus, "but it looks like there's a key chain in the last car." Then he lowers his camera and looks at the two girls, who are peering around, scanning the area. At that time of the morning, there isn't a soul on Avenue B.

"Should I climb up and take a look?" Sheng asks, reading their minds.

Ten minutes later, they're all standing in a circle around a park bench, staring at a bizarre little tin train. The *Pneumatic Transit*.

"We're turning into real delinquents," Mistral remarks, clearly amused by the idea.

"You think anyone saw me?"

"No, nobody. But the real question is this: What do we do now that we've got it?" Harvey groans.

The train is in terrible condition. Eaten away by the humidity and half-covered with rust, it's formed of four cylindrical cars with big, funny-looking side wheels, like the steam trains back in the Old West. A comet is painted on the side of the central car. Tied around the caboose is the chain of a key ring, complete with a plastic tag and a little metal key.

"We've got this," says Sheng, showing the new key to the others. Written on the tag is a number: 181.

"That's a prime number," Ermete remarks. "And on top of that, it's a palindrome." Then, noticing the inquisitive stares of the others, he shrugs his shoulders. "Sorry. I spent all night going crazy with numbers."

22

THE ATTIC

THE DOOR TO THE ANTIQUES SHOP IN QUEENS OPENS WITH A creak.

Hunched over at the doorway, Vladimir takes in deep breaths of the crisp air and checks his watch. Noon. Right on time. He brushes off his black overcoat and waits there until the taxi arrives.

"Grand Central, please," he tells the cabbie.

Once he's there, he reads something from a slip of paper he kept folded up in his pocket. Then he walks into the station, checks the signs on the walls and heads down the hallway leading outdoors. He stops just before the Oyster Bar, steps over to one corner of the crowded room and waits, facing the wall.

He's just about to check his watch when he hears the first whisper. It sounds like it's coming from the very stone in the gallery, which is transmitting a clear male voice to him.

"Hello, Vladimir!" the wall whispers.

"Hello," the elderly antiques dealer replies, rather surprised, moving his mouth closer to the vaulted stone wall, just as the instructions on the slip of paper told him to do.

"*Hao!* It really works!" the voice from the wall cries. Vladimir doesn't even have time to turn and look behind him when the voice adds, "It's me, Sheng, sir."

"Well, it looks like the Whispering Gallery really works," Vladimir agrees.

"You bet it does! It sounds like you're standing right here next to me," exclaims Sheng, who's all the way in the opposite corner of the room.

"And now? What are my instructions?" Vladimir asks, rather curious.

"Ermete said we needed to be really careful."

"I imagine he's the one who told you about this place, then."

"Yeah. He said he saw it in a movie where—"

"Where are you sitting?" the antiques dealer asks, cutting him off.

"At the Oyster Bar. Table eighteen."

"Have you noticed anyone suspicious?"

"No. Have you?"

"No, neither have I. Why don't you go on ahead? I'll join you in a few minutes."

Vladimir counts to a hundred and turns around. To be even safer, before slipping into the Oyster Bar, he heads toward the main hall of the station. Overcoats and hats swarm around him like moths around wool. When he reaches the Main Concourse, Vladimir looks up at the ceiling. The moment he sees all the constellations painted up there, he remembers how much he loves Grand Central. The sky with its stars, the twin staircases in light-colored marble and the old clock over the information booth.

"Every hundred years, it's time to contemplate the stars," he

169

murmurs to himself, staring at the stars on the ceiling. Every day, thousands of people cross through that hall without even glancing up. By now, no one knows the secret of those stars better than Vladimir does.

"This is the secret of Century . . . ," the antiques dealer adds. Then he goes back to the Whispering Gallery. The Oyster Bar overlooks the short side of the hall. Vladimir pulls the door open.

Just then, a black bird flies across the starry sky of Grand Central and perches for a moment on the golden spire atop the old clock. It's a crow with one blind eye.

"Excellent technique, kids!" Vladimir Askenazy says, sitting down at the table in the Oyster Bar. "Just like real spies. Although, I have to admit that when I found this note slipped under my door, for a moment I feared the worst."

No one feels like wasting much time with small talk. By the time they've ordered lunch, the kids have already told Vladimir everything they discovered in Hell's Kitchen.

"Lucifer . . . ," Vladimir grumbles when Sheng mentions the name of the nightclub. "No, I don't know it. But then, I'm not one to frequent late-night establishments."

When Sheng hands him the flyer for the rave, the man's face grows even darker. "This sounds much more worrisome to me," he remarks. "The old City Hall station has been abandoned for years." He rests his long, long alabaster index finger on his lip. "Unless I'm mistaken, it was inaugurated in October 1904 and was closed in December 1945. Lines four, five and six stopped there, heading toward Brooklyn. Today, I think you can see a part of the station loop from the window of the six just before it dives down below the river."

"So it really was a subway station once?"

"Yes, one of the oldest ones on the old IRT line. I stopped there a few times myself. I remember there being big archways, decorated ceilings, plaques on the walls. . . . I imagine it still looks like it did sixty years ago. From what I know, when the station was closed down, the street level entranceways had to be sealed off. That's it."

The kids exchange worried glances.

"In any case," Elettra cuts in, "that isn't the real reason we asked you to meet us here. We'd like to show you something we found. A few things, actually."

"I'm listening." Vladimir smiles, clasping his long, spiderlike hands together on the table.

"The first . . . is this," Mistral starts out, handing him the gold angel they found in the fountain at Rockefeller Center.

Vladimir Askenazy gapes at the little golden angel and turns it over in his hands as if it might shatter at any moment. Then he rests it on the table, stares at it, scratches his eyebrow, looks at it from another angle and remains silent, sitting perfectly still for an endless amount of time.

"Well? Does it mean anything to you?"

"It looks like a replica," the antiques dealer concludes enigmatically. "Paul Manship," he adds, "was one of the most important sculptors in New York during the last century. You might be familiar with his Prometheus over at Rockefeller Center. . . ."

"We sure are," the four kids reply.

"Then at the Western Union building on Broadway is his interpretation of the elements: fire, earth, air and water. Manship spent a great deal of time studying in Europe, particularly in

Rome, where he discovered a passion for ancient art. He studied the most important Roman monuments and then delved back further in time, studying the Greeks, the Egyptians and the Assyrians."

"The Chaldeans, too?" asks Mistral.

"Also," the antiques dealer nods. "Paul loved the symbolic language of legends. In fact, his Prometheus is full of symbols. This angel would be, too, if it weren't a copy. . . ." He's about to go on, but then, as if he's had second thoughts, he stops himself.

"Why do you say this is a copy?" Elettra asks.

"Because with the exception of its raised arm," the antiques dealer explains, "it is."

"But a copy of what?"

"The Angel of the Waters in Central Park," Vladimir Askenazy answers. "It's the angel standing in the fountain at Bethesda Terrace. The original has its hands down at its sides, but in every other respect, this is the same angel."

"Are they both works by Paul Manship?" asks Mistral.

"Oh, no!" the antiques dealer exclaims. "The Angel of the Waters is much older. If I remember correctly, the fountain was inaugurated . . . in 1873. The angel was commissioned to celebrate the opening of the city's first freshwater system, the Croton Aqueduct, the first plumbing in New York. The angel in Bethesda Terrace has watched over their underground aqueduct ever since."

"But why would Manship make a copy of the Angel of the Waters?" Sheng wonders aloud.

"I can't tell you that," the antiques dealer replies. "Maybe you should tell me where you found this statue."

"In an old wardrobe," Harvey answers quickly. "Together with this . . ." He hands him the gold key they found together with the angel. A perfectly ordinary house key with the number thirty-two on it. "And this," Harvey adds, pulling out the toy train they found in the tower in the East Village.

When he sees it, Vladimir smiles. "That's a Beach Railroad model train," he explains, brushing his fingers over it. "In the late 1800s, a fellow by the name of Beach secretly dug a series of tunnels below the city to build a pneumatic transportation system. Imagine it as an ancestor of today's subway system, but with compressed air."

"Cool!" gasps Sheng.

"His plans were coming along well, but it didn't work out in the end, and pneumatic transit was soon forgotten. And this chain? Oh, it's a key ring."

"Do you recognize it?"

"Certainly. It's a key to one of the lockers here in the station."

A strange little group comes out of the Oyster Bar and walks across the Main Concourse of Grand Central Terminal. A tall, skinny man gestures upward, showing four kids the ceiling of the hall, pointing out that it was painted backward. "Those aren't the stars as we see them from Earth, but the artist's interpretation of how you'd see them from the outside, traveling toward our planet."

"Professor Van Der Berger was obsessed with stars," Elettra recalls. "He'd even covered the ceiling of his bedroom with constellations."

"How could anyone not be obsessed with them?" the antiques

dealer says approvingly. Then, before saying goodbye, he points them in the direction of the lockers. "If you need any more advice, you know where to find me."

"You can count on it," the kids remark, saying goodbye.

Once they're alone, Sheng looks for locker 181 and tries to open it. The lock puts up a bit of a fight, but after a moment it finally gives in.

"Rats!" the blue-eyed Chinese boy groans, thinking the locker is empty.

Instead, there's an old postcard at the bottom of it. On it is a cross section of the construction plan for the Brooklyn Bridge. Paul Manship's name is written on it, although there's no mailing address.

The message on the postcard reads:

7, 212, 51, 113, 65, 186, 168, 101, 102, 107, 73, 155, 87, 164, 77, 26, 71, 25, 212, 141, 174, 178, 212, 61, 26, 121, 174, 186, 107, 212, 168, 25, 30, 45, 91, 107, 77, 224, 14, 53, 45, 13, 13, 148, 14, 79, 168, 1, 90, 162, 198, 27, 26. Star of Stone, 3 of 4.

23
THE CENTURY

BETHESDA TERRACE IS IN THE SOUTHERN SECTION OF CENTRAL Park, in a wide, open space that leads to a placid lake. To the left and right begin an array of picturesque paths leading off through the trees.

The fountain is located right by the terrace. Its basin is low, round and dark. Standing in the center of it, on a pedestal resting on little pillars, is the Angel of the Waters, gazing forward confidently, her wings spread open as if in an embrace.

"Vladimir was right," Elettra remarks the moment she sees it. "It's the same angel."

"So what now?" asks Harvey.

The angel's arms are lowered. The water in the fountain is clear and ice-cold. The lake is rippled by a light breeze. Not far away, a homeless man goes over to a stand selling coffee, orders a cup and slowly walks toward the kids. Suddenly, he howls with pain. "I don't know how you can drink this! It's boiling hot!" wails Ermete, who's still wearing that morning's disguise. "Everything okay with the antiques guy?" he asks then, sitting down on a park bench not too far away. "Did he get the note?"

The four nod. A man with two dogs on leashes jogs by the fountain to then disappear along the path to the left. From a branch in one of the age-old trees, a crow lets out a low caw.

They tell Ermete everything. Then Elettra walks halfway around the fountain and comes back to where she started. Ermete sips his coffee. Sheng leans over the edge of the basin to take a better look at the fountain sculpture. Mistral joins him. She rests the copy of the angel on the edge of the fountain and starts to turn it to the left and right. "Maybe this angel is trying to tell us something. . . ."

"So what's around us?" Sheng asks Harvey.

He points toward the trees. "This here behind me is the park's thickest patch of woods. In front of the fountain is all open area. Fifth Avenue is right around there, and if you take this path to the left, you'll end up in Strawberry Fields, which was given its name in memory of John Lennon."

Ermete sighs. "Mistral's right." He gets up from the bench and hands his boiling hot coffee to Sheng. "Hold this." He walks over to Mistral and takes the statue from her. Looking down at the icy water in the fountain, he sighs again. "Any cops around?"

Elettra shakes her head.

"You can't be thinking of—" Mistral says, but it's too late. Ermete's already stepped into the fountain.

Standing there at the edge, the kids watch him wade over quickly, groaning because of the cold, cold water that goes up to his knees. He's almost reached the sculpture's base when the man from the coffee stand spots him and lets out a gruff shout.

Ermete doesn't slow down. He reaches the center of the basin, grabs hold of a pillar with one hand and pulls himself up. In his other hand he's holding the golden angel. He starts circling around the sculpture's base, searching it.

"What do you think he's trying to do, guys?" Sheng asks from the edge of the fountain, discouraged.

"I think he's looking for a place where it might fit in," Mistral replies.

"Like with Prometheus?"

"Something like that."

"Think he'll manage?" asks Elettra.

"Unless they shoot him first, yeah."

"Maybe we should help him."

"But how?"

"By creating a diversion."

"Anything come to mind?"

"Should we try to tackle the guy from the coffee stand?" Sheng suggests sarcastically. Meanwhile, the man in question starts yelling at Ermete, grabbing the attention of a few curious onlookers. Ignoring them completely, Ermete reaches the front part of the angel's base, where he seems to find something.

He leans over, rests the angel between the pillars and leaves it there for a few seconds. Then he looks around, picks up the angel again, jumps back down into the water and starts running toward the edge of the fountain.

"Looks like he doesn't need a diversion after all," Harvey points out.

"More than that, I think he could use some dry pants and shoes."

Worried, the kids look around at the people who are gathering by the fountain. Ermete runs toward them, grinning from ear to ear. "I found it! There's a slot in this statue, too!"

It's the man from the coffee stand who hauls him out of the fountain. He showers Ermete with insults, but they're water off his back. The engineer from Rome makes his way through the curious onlookers and, nodding to the kids, says, "Let's get out of here!"

Once they're far away, Ermete explains what happened. "The angel fit perfectly into the base. It was pointing toward the left, in that direction . . . toward the skyscrapers. That brought to mind the key. . . ."

"The house key?"

"Exactly."

"What are those buildings anyway?" Mistral asks Harvey.

"The one right there with the two towers is the San Remo," Harvey replies.

Ermete shakes his head. "Not that one. The building farther south. Down there . . ."

Harvey freezes. "The Century Building."

The engineer nods. "Yeah, the Century. I think that's what we're looking for."

The doorman at the Century Building doesn't say a word the whole ride up, but the suspicious look on his face speaks worlds about what's going through his mind. He agreed to let the kids in and take them up to apartment 32 only because they were so insistent. After all, they seemed to have the key. Besides, they insisted so much that after a while they made him think of his grandchildren. The kids look honest. Although their request sounded crazy and he was a little suspicious, he decided to go up and check with them.

The elevator ascends swiftly. Standing next to the doorman and still dressed as a homeless man, Ermete tries to drip as little as possible, but a puddle has already formed around his feet. Harvey, Sheng, Elettra and Mistral are staring at the floor indicator, which is climbing dizzyingly fast up to number 32.

Then, with a ding and a sigh, the elevator reaches its destination. The doorman ceremoniously leads the way down the corridor. They can practically see their reflections in the marble floor. "This way, please," he grumbles, disgusted. Behind him, Ermete's shoes splosh with water.

The door he leads them to is made of light, shiny wood. There are no plaques or names on it. After pointing to it, the doorman stands there, stock still.

"Do you mind?" Ermete asks him, trying to get by. "Oh, right," he mumbles after a second, rifling through his pockets in search of a couple of dollars to tip him. He finds a five-dollar bill and hands it to him. "Thank you. Very kind of you."

The man pockets the bill with professional swiftness and then, with another suspicious sneer, goes back to where he came from, staring at the wet tracks left behind by the tramp.

"Don't worry about it!" Ermete calls after him. "I'll clean that up myself."

The golden key turns one, twice, three times. The lock lets out a clack and the door opens.

"*Hao!*" Sheng exclaims. "We guessed right!"

"They don't call me Fountain Man for nothing," Ermete

jokes, pushing them all inside. The apartment is dark and musty smelling. Groping around for the light switches, the kids activate old chandeliers with half the bulbs burned out.

There isn't a single piece of furniture anywhere. The apartment has been abandoned. It's completely empty. Not a chair, a table, a rug . . . nothing.

The five quickly search all the rooms.

Sheng walks over to the picture windows looking out over Central Park and stares, breathless, at the expanse of natural beauty in the middle of the city. "How could anybody own this place and not live in it?" he asks aloud.

"Because they're dead, maybe?" Harvey answers. He's holding something in his hand.

"You found it!" cries Elettra when she realizes it's a postcard. It's an old picture of Rockefeller Center in the thirties. On it is written the name Robert Peary, without a mailing address. Its message looks very familiar:

56, 90, 102, 168, 241, 241, 34, 125, 81, 212, 201, 79,
67, 216, 28, 107, 69, 83, 102, 18, 56, 210, 212, 85, 100,
102, 45, 173, 128, 204, 38, 85, 206, 45, 168, 10, 171,
212, 128, 212, 14. Star of Stone, 4 of 4.

Egon Nose is pacing endlessly in his office. Then, exasperated by the wait, he throws open the door and hobbles down the long, black hallway. From there, he makes his way to the upper floor of his nightclub, Lucifer. It looks like a red cave, with oddly shaped divans, stalactite light fixtures, twisted shadows, fake stalagmites full of air bubbles. Relentless, ear-shattering music is pounding everywhere. People are thrashing around on the dance floor. Some girls are waiting on the tables while others are dancing on the stage, dressed as angels, all in black. Dr. Nose turns to the first one he comes across and screams into her ear, "I want them here. Now!"

The woman runs across the bloodred carpeting and disappears down an aluminum staircase. Fake candles are burning along the mirrored walls.

Egon Nose smiles. He stands there, watching his clients as they drink, dance and forget about the very existence of the outside world. He leans against the handrail and even manages to take his mind off things for a few seconds. Then he goes back to focusing on the present. His girls have arrived. His five predators.

Panther, Wolverine, Ferret, Mink and Mongoose.

Five magnificent, unscrupulous women.

Dr. Nose brought the newspaper clipping with him. He gives it to the woman closest to him. It's from one of those free papers handed out in the subway stations. The article is brief, but there's a color photograph. It's entitled "Another Dive for the Fountain Man?" The picture is of a man being hauled out of the Bethesda Fountain.

"Recognize him?" The newspaper is passed from hand to hand and then returned to Egon Nose. "No? Well, I'll tell you who he is. He's the man you were following. The one who's always calling his mother. Our carrier pigeon."

The women stare at him without saying a word. Their glittering, beady eyes are the size of precious gems.

"Do you know what he's doing? Heh, heh, heh. The article says that over the last few days, this illustrious stranger is said to have gone for a little swim in the fountain at Rockefeller Center and the one in Central Park. No one knows why. Not even us."

The women stare at the old man without speaking. Five drop-dead gorgeous statues, all perfectly silent.

"The question is, why don't we know?" Egon Nose's eyes shoot daggers. "Did we get something wrong? What? I don't know. . . . But I have no intention of getting a phone call from Only-I-Know-Who, asking me what's going on. So there's a change of plans. I . . . I can't stand . . . no . . . I *detest* the very idea of having anything to do with those damned kids. But we know where one of them lives, isn't that right? Miller . . . Harvey Miller?"

The man begins to hobble back and forth, interpreting his girls' silence. "But we don't know anything about the others, because it seems the kids are pretty bright. They split up, they use spy tactics . . . and we aren't following them closely enough. So I say we do a better job and make sure they come to us. How? Heh, heh, heh . . . What man could resist the right female charms? Yes, excellent, excellent plan, my sweet, sweet ladies! Go find me this Fountain Man. I think he'd enjoy a little company. . . ."

24
THE RETURN

NIGHT IS FALLING ONCE AGAIN IN NEW YORK. VLADIMIR ASKENAZY'S tall, bony figure leaves the headquarters of the *New York Times* after an entire day spent reading through old newspaper articles. He's worried. Very worried.

He looked into Lucifer and its shady, mysterious owner, and he tracked down some information he wishes he'd never even seen.

It's worse than he thought.

Much worse.

Now, discouraged and frightened, he ponders what it would be best to do. He goes down to catch the subway to the Village, and as he's waiting for the train, he tries to think of exactly what to say. He can't explain everything. He can only suggest, guide, drop hints, point them in the right direction. But then they'll have to walk that road all on their own. That's part of the Pact.

"What difference does it make which road . . . you get wrong?" he groans, bitterly thinking back to many years before, when he, Alfred, Irene and *that woman* were faced with the same challenge. Without succeeding. Ignoring suggestions. Heading in the wrong direction.

It was 1908.

It was a century ago.

When Vladimir Askenazy gets out of the subway station, his face is painted with a smile. He's always loved this neighborhood of Manhattan, with its low houses, its ailanthus trees, the warmth of its twisting streets.

Vladimir coughs, folds up the lapels on his overcoat and thinks back on the years gone by. They were spent keeping a secret that not even he understood completely: the secret of Century. An ancient pact made between man and Nature. A pact connected to the Earth and its elements, written with the trajectories of the stars and the wooden tops. A pact of silence and secrets to be revealed.

"Revealing means unveiling," murmurs the antiques dealer, who's lived for two centuries and is an expert on ancient philosophy. "And every secret that is unveiled reveals even more secrets. It's like a snake biting its own tail."

When he reaches the corner of Grove Court, Vladimir takes a quick step back. At the gate outside the boy's house, Harvey and Elettra are wrapped in a warm embrace.

No one expected this, naturally, the antiques dealer thinks. *Not even Irene*. In a way, it makes him smile. Here, in the very heart of tragedy, young love has blossomed. One of those hopeless, wonderful loves that's remembered your whole life.

But now what should he do? He looks around uneasily. Manhattan is dark and shadowy. A Native American wearing a mail carrier's uniform crosses the street with his bag of letters to deliver. There's a strange fog in the air and no sign of spring's arrival. Vladimir holds back a shiver.

He finally comes to a decision and turns the corner.

"Mr. Askenazy!" the two kids greet him the moment they notice he's there. "What are you doing here?"

Although they're a little embarrassed about being caught like that, Harvey and Elettra pretend they're perfectly calm. They even manage to confide in the antiques dealer that they found a third postcard.

"Robert Peary?" he asks when they tell him who it was addressed to. "The explorer?"

"You've heard of him?"

"He explored Greenland. He also donated one of the world's largest meteorites to New York's American Museum of Natural History."

"Maybe Mistral was right, then!" Elettra exclaims when she hears meteorites mentioned. "The Star of Stone . . ."

Vladimir frowns slightly. "Maybe you should keep searching. . . ."

"Do you have any suggestions?" Harvey asks him, wrapping his arms around Elettra's waist.

"Actually, no. I came here to warn you."

"Warn us?"

Vladimir looks around, then points at the gate. "Could we . . . ?"

"Only up to the entranceway," answers Harvey. "My folks are home."

"That's better than out here in the dark."

The three cross through the flowery garden, where the air itself seems warmer and the earth more compact. They step into the entranceway of Harvey's building and stop at the bottom of the stairs.

"His name's Egon Nose," the antiques dealer begins. "He's the problem. He's the owner of Lucifer. A criminal. For years he's been running nightclubs here in town and most of them were shut down for problems you can't even begin to imagine. The worst of the worst. Nevertheless"—Vladimir rubs his hands together to warm his long, numb fingers—"he's always gotten off scot-free. Friends in high places, it seems. Some say politicians, others say the police. One club shuts down, another one opens up, and the money starts flowing again. Those in the nightclub circles call him Dr. Nose because of his grotesque appearance. And his nose for business.

"I don't know what it is you're looking for," the antiques dealer continues, "but you should watch out for him and his girls. It seems he's surrounded by women who are just as dangerous as he is."

Elettra shivers, holding on tighter to Harvey.

"Now do you see why I came here at once to tell you? I . . . I'll try to get in touch with a few friends, but in the meantime, I'm asking you to . . . Well, I don't know. Just be careful, promise?" As if he is uncomfortable about having said too much, the antiques dealer turns to leave.

"You be careful, too," Elettra tells him.

The streetlights on Thirty-fifth Avenue are pale, glowing spots that look like they're floating in the gray mist. It isn't unusual for it to be foggy in New York at this time of year, but it's unusual for it to be this thick.

Ermete walks along slowly. His feet are aching. Not only

186

because he dipped them in the icy waters of the fountain, but most of all because he's walked around half the city in search of a way to decipher the numbers on the postcards. Still, he hasn't managed to find a book. No reference text. No further clue as to what the Star of Stone might be. In his pocket is a piece of paper with the twenty-five attempts he's made so far.

All of them are crossed off.

Twenty-five dead ends.

"Maybe I'll have better luck tomorrow," he says, walking up to his house. If even one of them had a real stroke of luck, they could keep going. Otherwise, the only alternative is to cast the tops. A second time.

Ermete notices that someone's there on the sidewalk in front of his house. There are shadows rising up through the fog.

"City by the sea? Gimme a break," he grumbles. "This is like being in London." Not that he's ever been to London.

The first person he sees coming out from the fog surrounding his building is a young woman. He thinks nothing of it. No alarm bells are going off in his head. It's when he sees the second one, and then the third, that he realizes something's wrong.

Three women. Extremely tall, extremely beautiful. They're wearing brightly colored ski jackets, wide scarves that cover their faces, army boots and woolen gloves.

"Oh, boy," Ermete whispers, even more worried. He clenches his fists in his pockets, slows down his pace and checks the address on the building, but there's no doubt about it. The three of them are right in front of his house.

What should I do? he thinks. *Turn and run away, or ignore them and keep walking?* Maybe they won't recognize him. Maybe they'll mistake him for just another tramp.

He hangs his head and keeps walking.

He takes five, ten, twenty steps.

Just when he thinks he's gotten away with it, he hears the sound of the women's boots breaking into a run. He doesn't wait another second. He bolts. As he's running, the engineer makes a mental list of what he has in his pockets: nothing. What did he leave back at home? The mirror. Everything else is in the kids' hands.

He crumples up the sheet of paper with the numbers written on the postcards and throws it to the ground, where it disappears into the fog.

He runs awkwardly, almost staggering. He runs like somebody who's never run before.

But not for long.

He feels something hit him in the back, and then the ground suddenly disappears from beneath his feet. He stumbles and falls forward. He crashes down onto the sidewalk.

Ermete rolls over twice. He's left dazed, his lip and cheek throbbing. He hears footsteps approaching. He sees their boots. He can't move. Something heavy is keeping him pinned down to the ground.

One of the women leans over until her face is a palm's width away from his. She has long, long red hair and eyes as green as emeralds. At any other point in his life, Ermete would've fallen in love with her on the spot. But now, all that face does is scare him. Her perfect mouth looks like it's about to devour him.

"What—what do you want?" he stammers. A thin line of saliva drips down from his mouth. It feels like he's broken a tooth.

He isn't given an answer.

Sheng's in bed, dreaming. He knows perfectly well it's a dream, but he can't wake himself up. He's afraid, because it's that same dream again. The dream that comes back to him from time to time.

He's in the jungle with Harvey, Elettra and Mistral. It's a tropical forest, sweltering hot and perfectly silent. There are no insects, no birds. It's as if it were empty. Here and there, an ancient monument peeks out from behind the plants—a building, a column, an obelisk—as if the forest grew right over a city. Then the tropical vegetation makes way for an expanse of fine, pure white sand that crunches beneath his feet.

On the other side of a narrow inlet of clear, blue water is a tiny island covered with seaweed. All four of them dive down into the silent waves.

Waiting for them on the island is a woman. Her face is covered by a cloak and she's wearing a close-fitting gown with all the world's animals drawn on it.

Sheng can't get out of the water. The woman steps over to him, her dress billowing. She makes him open his right hand. Sheng realizes he's holding the body of a dead pigeon.

With this, Sheng's eyes open wide.

A flutter of wings and the soft tapping on the glass of the roof light are signs that Harvey recognizes now, even when he's fast asleep. He sits up in bed as though he weren't even sleeping and goes up to the attic without switching on the light. He throws open the window. It's one of Ermete's pigeons.

Still groggy, Harvey lets it in, putting it in the cage beside the other bird.

He unfolds the message and reads it:

We'll be expecting you tomorrow night at the party at the old City Hall station. Your friend is here with us. If you want to see him again, bring everything we need.

25
THE PARTY

THE NEXT EVENING ARRIVES IN THE BLINK OF AN EYE.

Sitting in his study, Mr. Miller looks up from his papers. "Come in," he says. It's his wife. As always, she moves cautiously and closes the door gently behind her. "Is he gone?" the professor asks, taking off his glasses and resting them on the desk.

"Yes. He looked so handsome. Unrecognizable," his wife replies. "I think he even combed his hair."

Mr. Miller gets up from his chair and steps around the desk, glancing out the window. "I'm happy to hear that."

His wife walks over to him. She leans against his shoulder and sighs. "You aren't worried?"

"About what?"

"It's after dark and he's going out to dinner all alone."

"He's thirteen. Besides, he isn't alone. He's going with his friends."

"Yes, but . . ."

"But what?" The professor turns around slowly and hugs his wife. "No, don't say it. Don't even think it."

"I try not to be nervous, but it isn't easy. . . ."

"It's difficult for everyone. Even for him. But if he's decided to go out and have fun for once, let's let him do it. Let's trust him. After all, he's our son, right?" he says.

"Dwaine would've been happy to go there with him . . . to keep an eye on him," she says.

"Who says he isn't?"

Mrs. Miller lets out a sob, burying her face in her husband's shirt. "You, of all people, saying that . . ."

"Why wouldn't I?"

"You're the most rational, most logical man on Earth."

Mr. Miller gently frees himself from the hug. "Sometimes being rational isn't enough." He steps back to his desk and picks up a handful of papers. "Do you remember my talking about the ocean temperatures?"

"The research that needed to be redone?"

"It's all been confirmed. A half-degree increase!" Mr. Miller rolls his eyes. "What kind of logic could help anyone understand something like this? The sea is heating up like a giant pressure cooker. It isn't simply the greenhouse effect. It's the mankind effect to the nth degree."

"It is serious?"

"No. It's more than serious. It's disastrous. If the Earth were a patient in the hospital, we'd be sitting down to read his will right now. That's what we adults should be worried about, not about our son going out to dinner."

"But what can we do about it?"

"What's going to happen if we don't do anything? Will there be someone else who could do something for our planet?"

Mrs. Miller is still worried.

"In a few years, we might not even have electricity anymore. Let's let Harvey use it while he still can," her husband says.

"Always the catastrophist."

The professor tosses the papers higgledy-piggledy onto his impeccably organized desk. "It's utter chaos. And I detest chaos theories. There must be an order to things somewhere! There must be something we can do."

"You could have that journalist friend of yours write an article about it."

"Who reads newspapers anymore?"

Sitting on the bed, a towel wrapped around her damp hair like a turban, Linda Melodia peers at her niece, Elettra, with the same critical eye she would use on a roast being given to her at the butcher's. "What kind of party is it?" she asks for the millionth time.

"Auntie!" Elettra cries, exasperated. She doesn't feel like arguing. Not tonight. "It's just a party at Harvey's friend's place."

"And you mean to go to a party at his friend's place wearing that skirt? Or better, where *is* your skirt, exactly?"

Elettra pulls the hem of her miniskirt down until it almost reaches her knees. "This is how they're made these days, Auntie! It's the fashion!"

"Hmm . . . that's what you say!"

"Well, what about *you*, then?" Elettra asks, pointing at the sequined gown hanging out to air beside the closet. "Tonight you're going out with a neckline that reaches down to your belly button. . . ."

"Well, I never!" Linda snaps. "That neckline isn't at all low.

Besides, if I may say, I'm a few years older than you. And I have a rather . . . generous figure."

"I'm not standing here giving you the third degree about where you're going to dinner and who with."

"But you know perfectly well! In any case, let's stop talking about me. The problem here is you and this party. I can't imagine that Mistral will be wearing a skirt like that!"

Elettra grumbles, going back into the bathroom and closing the door. She spends the next ten minutes gussying up, until someone knocks on the front door. It's Harvey, who's wearing a tuxedo that fits him like a glove and a pair of gym shoes. His bow tie is crooked.

"Hello, Harvey," Linda Melodia greets him, trying to keep a straight face. "Elettra will be right here." Still, her nitpicking nature can't pass up the chance to offer some unsolicited advice. "If you like, I could help you fix that. You need to tie it tighter here, right by your neck. . . ."

Harvey's face flushes with embarrassment, but Elettra walks in before it's too late. "Auntie!" she groans, stepping between them. "It's perfect just the way it is, Harvey."

They say a quick goodbye and walk out. Linda closes the door after them and leans back against it. "It looks more than perfect, Harvey," she sighs. "If only I'd met a boy like that back when I was their age."

Sheng's laughter echoes in from the hallway. Familiar with how he matches his clothes, Linda's tempted to go out and give him a once-over, too, but she decides against it. It's only with Mistral that she rests assured.

Sticking out from under the bed is a paper bag that Elettra brought back after shopping. Linda glances at it, pulls it out and puts it in the closet, next to her bronze replica of the Statue of Liberty.

She slides her fingers down her evening gown, unwraps the towel turban from her head and starts planning. "And now for you, my mustachioed friend. You're going to dinner with Miss Melodia!"

"Got everything?" Harvey asks once they're outside the hotel.

Sheng bounces his backpack on his back. "Yeah. We scratched the logo off a wooden chocolate box and added a few mysterious symbols. Then we bought four wooden tops for three fifty at a supermarket and boiled them in water and salt so they'd look old."

"I drew a dog, a tower, a whirlpool and an eye on them," Mistral adds.

"How'd it all turn out?"

"They might fall for it, but they'd have to be really, really stupid."

"Perfect." Harvey steps off the curb and hails a cab. "City Hall," he orders, getting in.

The taxi zooms into the brightly lit street, cuts across Times Square with its giant bright lights and races down Broadway, quickly passing the sleek, shiny cars around it. Elettra looks at her reflection in the cab's glass divider. Mistral double-checks the fake objects they made that afternoon. Her black Lurex flats are glittering beneath her stretch-wool slacks. Even her sleeveless twinset is studded with rhinestones. Sheng doesn't say a word the whole way there, as if hypnotized by the sparkles.

Harvey tries not to think about anything. And not to feel anything.

"What now?" Sheng asks when the taxi drops them off in a square surrounded by obelisks of light. The buildings around City Hall look like luminescent ant farms. The black shadows of a few trees rise up out of the park.

"Now we need to find a way down there," says Harvey. "The abandoned station is right below us."

"I hear something rattling."

"Sheng's teeth, probably."

"It's music. Music coming from right beneath our feet."

Elettra goes up to Harvey and asks him, one last time, "Are we sure this is a good idea?"

"Can you think of an alternative?"

"Not going."

"What about Ermete? He'd do the same thing for us."

"He'd hand over wooden fakes?"

Harvey turns away, annoyed, and starts looking for a way to go down below street level. "If you guys don't want to come, I can't blame you."

Sheng, Elettra and Mistral follow him.

"Are the real map and tops in a safe place?" Sheng asks in a low voice.

"They're in Elettra's room," Mistral replies. "In a shopping bag."

The four continue along without saying another word. As they're heading toward some tall, tall buildings, they hear the music growing louder, even though it's still muffled, thumping, ominous. It's coming from the manholes. From belowground.

Two guys dressed in black leather cross over the sidewalk, striding toward the center of the square. Harvey decides to follow them.

The entrance turns out to be a brick building that looks a lot like a public restroom. In fact, it is a public restroom, but inside, instead of there being stalls, there's a narrow stairway leading down below. The front door is plastered with posters. A stony-faced bouncer with a pierced eyebrow is watching over the clandestine dancers as they arrive.

Harvey doesn't slow his pace, but he doesn't want to just walk downstairs. He heads straight for the bouncer and, with the brazen courage of his thirteen years of age, tells him, "I'm Harvey Miller. Egon Nose is expecting me."

The bouncer's expression makes him look like a long-dead fish. He stares at Harvey like he can't even seen him. Then, when he notices that the boy isn't leaving, he bursts out laughing, as if he's just heard the funniest joke in his life. "Go right in," he says, nodding toward the steep stairway leading down toward the music.

Harvey gestures to the others to follow him downstairs. While he's taking the first steps, the bouncer is still laughing.

At the bottom of the flight of steps is a second door. On the other side of the door they can sense a wall of music full of riveting bass notes. With every step they descend, the volume of the music increases, the percussions sounding more and more like hammers whose blows are making the air tremble.

Once the door is pushed open, the world suddenly changes.

New York is gone. What's before them is something else. With its black-and-white brick vaulting, the old abandoned station is streaked with red lights whirling around, relentlessly slashing through the darkness. A mass of bodies pressed up tightly against one another is dancing, driven by the music and bathed in sweat. The people of the night who dance at all costs.

Harvey, Elettra, Sheng and Mistral stay off to the side, unable to fathom the shape and depth of their surroundings. It looks vast and cramped at the same time. Dark and blinding. It's a world of contradictions. Bass notes so high-pitched they seem silent. Movements so frenetic they seem motionless.

The kids stand side by side, like soldiers, seeking courage in the contact of their shoulders. They can feel evil dancing there right next to them.

Elettra's eyes are big and frightened. Her fingers are sizzling with energy. She clutches on to Harvey like a person tossed overboard clings to the last scrap of floating wood. Mistral has her eyes closed. Sheng isn't laughing anymore. In Alfred Van Der Berger's tuxedo, Harvey tries to make his heart beat more slowly than the rhythm of the music. His fists are clenched, his muscles taut, just like he learned from Olympia. He keeps his head held high. He peers around, anxious to spot the person he's looking for.

"I'm Harvey Miller," he shouts to a young woman who looks vaguely familiar. "Would you tell Mr. Nose I've come to pick up my friend?"

The girl stares down at him with her fashion model's physique. She smiles, a ravenous look on her face. She turns around and walks off. Her long legs look like snakes.

"What'd you tell her?" Sheng shouts into Harvey's ear.

"That we're here."

The dancers shake and thrash around. Their eyes are half-closed, their mouths open as if they were singing, their bodies so flexible they look like they're melting.

Elettra squeezes Mistral's hand. "Everything okay?"

"This place gives me the creeps."

"Me too."

Harvey is standing out in front of them. His back is like rocks protecting a port from the swelling sea. It's blocking out the red lights, damming up the thundering echo of the percussions.

A man wearing a bird's mask passes by a few yards away from them. He turns, lets out a piercing shriek and disappears onto the dance floor.

"Let's get out of here!" Mistral cries. "Let's leave!"

Elettra holds her back. "Nothing's going to happen to us."

Sheng leans in closer to them. "We need to stick together. It's our only hope." His eyes are a man's eyes. His customary smile has disappeared. "Remember what happened when we split up last time?" he asks Mistral, struggling to be heard over the music. "In Rome, at the professor's apartment?"

The girl looks at him, nods and calms down. "Yes. They kidnapped me."

"We need to stick together," Sheng repeats. He holds out his hand. Mistral grabs it. Elettra adds hers. All three of them turn toward Harvey.

"They're coming," he says, even though none of them can hear the sound of his voice. Then his hand clasps all of theirs, as big and strong as a boxer's glove.

26
THE TRADE

THE WOMAN GESTURES TO THE FOUR FRIENDS TO FOLLOW HER. SHE leads them around the dance floor and beyond a divider with the words OFF-LIMITS written on it in black spray paint. Finally, they find themselves beyond a few walls of plasterboard and polystyrene, which are isolating the dance area from the platform running alongside the abandoned train tracks. On the wall, which is still white yet covered with graffiti, is a plaque: CITY HALL—1909.

People are waiting for them on the platform next to the tracks.

A smallish man wearing an electric-blue velvet overcoat and holding a long cane turns around to face them. "Ah, at last!" he sneers.

The woman who led them there goes to stand beside the man. Egon Nose. The master of the night. Behind his enormous nose, two other women are lined up. They're holding Ermete by the arms. The engineer wearily raises his head, revealing two black eyes. He tries to say something, but his mouth has been sealed with tape, so he shakes his head, as if to warn the kids to get out of there, now, as fast as they can.

"What did you do to him?" shouts Elettra the moment she

recognizes him. She takes a step forward, but Harvey stops her. With this simple gesture, the roles on the two sides in this underground confrontation are established: on one side, Harvey and the three kids standing behind him, and on the other side, Egon Nose with his three women, who are eagerly awaiting orders.

"You must be Miller," the man says.

"And you must be Egon Nose."

Nose lets out a little laugh. "Heh, heh, heh . . . Wonderful!" he remarks, twirling his cane around. "So stylish, so formal! A boy from days gone by! And you three, back there? What are your names? Which of you is Mistral?"

"Let our friend go," Harvey replies.

The man's wide nostrils flare. "Why in such a rush, young Miller? Such a rush! Won't you even give me the chance to get acquainted with my new friends? Here, let me introduce you to my three travel companions. My three ladies. Maybe you're still too young to appreciate them, but believe me, they're perfect women, ones who don't need to be taught anything. Not even to keep their mouths shut."

Sheng clenches his teeth, resisting the urge to run away.

"In any case, Miller, they told me you were bright. It seems the others know how to use their young minds, too. Oh, now what do we have here? I see Asian eyes! My client will be pleased. Where are you from?"

"Shanghai," Sheng blurts out.

"You don't say!" Dr. Nose exclaims, raising his cane. "What a small world. It just so happens that it's a man from Shanghai who told me all about you kids. He says you have something that belongs to him."

"And you have something that belongs to us."

"You mean this?" Egon Nose cackles, reaching into his pocket and pulling out the wooden top.

Harvey nods grimly. "That, too."

Dr. Nose slips the top back into his velvet coat and makes a regretful grimace. "Well, there are two sides to every story. And I'm not so good at—how can I put this?—at acting as arbitrator. . . ." Egon's voice grows mockingly honeyed. "I'm far better at defending absolutely indefensible positions. I like bold decisions. In any case," he exclaims, banging his cane down against the ground, "let's try to wrap all this up as quickly as possible, shall we?"

A rumbling noise comes from the tunnel, growing louder and louder. For an instant they can see a light shining through it, like a flash.

"The six service," Dr. Nose remarks. "It no longer runs along this old circuit of tracks. Things that no longer serve a purpose are eventually abandoned." The man's stare suddenly turns hard, piercing. "And now . . . give me what belongs to us!" he exclaims, resolute. "Then you can run along and dance."

"We want our friend first," Harvey orders.

"Boy!" Dr. Nose screams, almost howling, as he bangs his cane on the ground. "You don't understand who's in charge here! Or maybe you want me to order them to nail you to that wall down there and leave you at the mercy of the rats?" he says, gesturing at the women behind him.

Harvey gulps nervously, but he doesn't even flinch. His feet are planted on the ground like an age-old oak tree. "You can order them to try . . . ," he replies, holding the man's stare.

Their staring contest lasts five, ten, twenty seconds. Then, to their surprise, it's Egon Nose who gives in first. He does so with a laugh, but a second later his voice is strangely shaken. "This kid's good!" he remarks. "There's no doubt about it! You've got guts!" He gestures to the two women holding Ermete. "Take off his gag!"

The women rip the tape off his mouth, making him scream.

"And no shouting!" Nose snaps. "Aren't you already ashamed enough, being saved by a pack of little brats?"

Sheng rubs his chin, searching for at least a little stubble to show his adversary.

"Get out of here!" Ermete shouts the moment he catches his breath. "Don't give him the map! Get out, now! He isn't going to—"

A kick makes him gulp back his last words.

Dr. Nose peers at him with disgust. "Such a sorry excuse for a man. Young Miller, I'm not so sure saving him is worth all this effort. But tell me something. Just one thing. What map is he talking about?"

"Ask your friend from Shanghai if you want to find out."

"Oh, yes. An excellent idea. I think he must know all about it. Thank you for the suggestion. And now, if you would be so kind . . ." He holds out his hand, waiting to be given something.

Harvey nods to Sheng, who hands him the backpack. Harvey raises it over his head and says, "One of them comes to get this while another one brings our friend here."

"Fine." Egon Nose nods. "I like complicated trades. Just like in the movies. You always have the impression that something un-expected could happen at any moment."

Half-walking, half-dragged by one of the women, Ermete starts to make his way over to the four kids.

"Your friend was a real chatterbox," Egon Nose continues, smiling. "He told me exactly how the tops work and about the secret you're trying to discover. It's all incomprehensible but definitely fascinating."

Ermete raises his head and whispers, "I'm sorry."

Harvey waits until the engineer is close enough and then hands Sheng's backpack over to the woman. Ermete takes the last few steps toward the kids and collapses against Harvey's shoulder, exhausted. "I didn't want to talk. . . . I didn't want to . . . ," he mumbles, his eyes blackened, his fingers injured.

Nose peers inside the backpack and pulls out a top. "So this is it, is it?" he asks, studying it carefully.

"We're leaving," Harvey states, taking a step back, still holding up Ermete. He's desperately trying to figure out which direction they should leave in when Egon Nose tosses the top into the backpack and pulls out another one.

"Ah!" he exclaims. "Are you sure about that?" He throws the second top to the ground and smashes it with his cane. The wooden toy breaks in two. "No, no . . . this isn't right!" Dr. Nose howls, hurling Sheng's backpack onto the tracks. "I don't see any gold sphere! You kids aren't going anywhere!"

A second rumble makes the station's vaulted ceiling tremble.

"Enough!" Egon Nose shakes his fists in the air, as if this is the last straw. "I've always hated the idea of hurting children . . . but you leave me no choice! Get them!"

Just then, a flapping of wings can be heard behind Dr. Nose. A crow blind in one eye alights on the ground inside the abandoned station, halfway between the man and Harvey. It peers at one and then the other curiously. Then it takes wing. Behind it, another one arrives. The wings become four, eight, ten. Other crows emerge from the darkness of the tunnel, flying low, like gliders. Nose turns around, stunned, trying to understand where they're coming from. And why.

Ten crows, twenty crows, then fifty. It seems like they'll never stop. An entire swarm of black feathers is belched out of the tunnel with a deafening screech. Beaks, wings and claws fill the cramped space inside the abandoned station.

In the confusion, a giant Indian man appears, running in from the tracks. His long hair is streaming down and his wrinkled face is that of someone who's always lived outdoors. As fast as lightning, he throws Ermete over his shoulder and orders the others, "Come with me, quickly."

Without waiting for a reply, he turns, jumps down off the platform and starts running along the tracks, in the direction the crows came from. Too shaken to even think, Harvey, Elettra, Sheng and Mistral do as he says. They're swallowed up by the darkness.

Behind them, the crows are filling the air with piercing shrieks. Egon Nose thrashes his cane around, trying to keep the birds at bay. He strikes ten, twenty of them but is finally forced to retreat. His girls are screaming like crazy, doing everything they can to keep them away, but everything they do against the wall of sharp beaks and claws leaves them with cuts and scratches.

Then, the moment the Indian man has disappeared with the kids, and just as quickly as it arrived, the frenzied black cloud also disappears into the darkness.

27

THE WOODS

T<small>HEIR ESCAPE THROUGH THE SUBWAY TUNNEL LEAVES THEM</small> breathless and panting. The Indian guiding the kids has the fast pace of someone who could run for miles and miles without growing tired. He's carrying Ermete over his shoulder, and judging from how he's moving, it looks like he can see in the dark. He slows down only when the old tracks cross over other ones coming from a tunnel running perpendicular to their own. Then he turns and says, "We only have two minutes. Don't touch the tracks." He starts running again.

There's a faint, distant glow in the new tunnel. Running in front of his three friends, Harvey spots a few lights beyond the bend. He sees a square, lit-up sign and a small green signal. Only then does he understand where they are: in the subway. The real one. He shouts this to the others, trying to get them to move faster.

"Oh man, oh man, oh man!" Sheng starts to repeat, passing Elettra, Mistral and Harvey at full speed.

Their run down the tunnel becomes frenetic. Mistral stumbles, falls to the ground and gets back up again.

"Hurry! The train's coming!" Harvey shouts to her.

The walls are black, as are the tracks. Harvey lets Elettra and Mistral pass him, too, and then starts running behind them, almost pushing them, to make them move faster. He doesn't know what direction the train is coming from, whether behind them or in front of them. *"Run!"* he shouts with all the breath he has left in his lungs.

Her heart racing wildly, Mistral doesn't think she can take another step. Harvey scoops her up, cradles her in his arms and keeps running. While he's doing so, something sticking out of the wall rips the professor's tuxedo at the shoulder.

"Oh man, oh man, oh man!" Sheng keeps repeating. He's almost caught up with the Indian man.

They run around a bend. Behind it, not more than a hundred yards away, they spot the subway station. It looks completely different from below. On the platform are five people waiting for the train.

The Indian reaches the platform and tosses Ermete up onto it. Then he turns toward Sheng, waits for him, clasps his hands together and boosts him up.

The people waiting there start shouting with fright. Elettra is also given a boost up onto the platform. A recorded voice comes over the loudspeaker, announcing that the train is now arriving.

"Come on! Come on!" Sheng shouts to Harvey, who's staggering, still carrying Mistral. "You're almost there! You're almost there!"

Suddenly, the tunnel turns white. The air is sucked away like in a giant ventilator.

"No!" Harvey shouts, lunging forward.

The Indian grabs Mistral and hurls her onto the platform. Then he grabs Harvey and pushes him up as well. A second later, the boy finds himself staring up at the lights in the ceiling of the station and the curious faces of the other people.

The train's arrived.

Harvey leaps to his feet. The Indian is there beside them. The train doors open. The man shakes his head, as if nothing at all has happened. "Not this line. We need to walk to the one train."

They're sitting down now. Their train is quickly traveling north. The night is still young, but no one feels like talking. They've just dropped Ermete off at the hospital and they're confused, scared. Exhausted. Their eyes are closed and their heads are resting back against the windows. Their torn clothing is covered with soot, dust and grease.

"I've seen you before," Harvey says to the Indian man as the train makes a stop. "Outside my house. Is that possible?"

The man nods. "I'd say so."

"But when?"

"Every morning?" the Indian suggests, braiding his long hair behind his head. Watching him do this, Harvey suddenly remembers where he's seen him. "You're the postman?"

"Yes," he admits. Then he turns to the other kids and introduces himself. "My name is Quilleran, of the Seneca tribe."

"I've heard that name before . . . ," Sheng murmurs.

"Where are we going?" Elettra asks.

"To the old tree."

"What old tree?"

"The dead tree," Quilleran replies. "In Inwood Hill Park."

208

"The woods in upper Manhattan," Harvey explains. Then he asks, "Why are we going there? And what was with all those birds in the tunnel? Where'd they come from?"

"You ask a lot of questions, Star of Stone."

"What did you just call me?" Harvey asks, almost jumping out of his seat.

"I called you by your name," the Indian repeats. "Star of Stone."

"My name is Harvey Miller."

"That's your American name," the man insists.

Harvey leaps to his feet. "Would you mind telling me what you're talking about?"

"I'm happy I saved your lives."

"Who told you we were in danger?"

"I've been following you for months." The Indian smiles.

"Following me? Why?"

"To protect you. You are Star of Stone."

"I'm not Star of Stone! I'm Harvey Miller!"

Elettra tries to calm him down and it seems to work.

"Why are you calling Harvey that, Quilleran?" Mistral asks with a small voice the moment things have settled down a little. "What does 'Star of Stone' mean?"

"It means that he received the gift of stone from the stars. He can hear the voice of the Earth and understand how to heal it."

"That's not true!" Harvey exclaims. "I've never gotten any gift, I've never heard any voices, and I've never healed anybody!"

"Every era has a Star of Stone," the Indian continues calmly, "and we've been waiting for ours."

"Well, I think you've made a big mistake," Harvey retorts.

"It's a darn good thing he did!" Sheng cuts in. "Otherwise, we'd still be down there, dealing with that big-nose and his panthers. Man, what a sight! So, are you the one who sent in all those crazy birds?"

The Indian nods.

"How'd you do that?"

"They listen to me, and I can tell them what to do."

"*Hao!* That's so cool! Is it something anybody can learn?"

"Of course. I learned it here in New York."

"Oh, please!" Harvey grumbles. Then he clenches his fists and tries to calm down, but he can't help admitting that there were, in fact, crows down there. Hundreds of crows, which appeared just in the nick of time. "You still haven't explained why you were following me," he insists, changing the subject.

"To protect you."

"Who from?"

"Your enemies."

"You know my enemies?"

"Everyone should know their own enemies."

"You didn't answer my question."

"It's late," Elettra interjects. "And I'm tired."

"We're almost there."

The subway leaves them a few blocks from Indian Road, at the northern tip of Manhattan. The only illumination is coming from the line of streetlights, which are slicing through the night. Inwood Hill Park is a patch of wooded blackness under the starry sky.

Quilleran shows the kids a path.

"The man in the subway. Is he dead?" Elettra asks as they start walking.

The city lights are swallowed up by the tangle of trees. The sounds of civilization are drowned out by the unpredictable ones of nature.

"I don't think so."

"Why did he want our tops?"

"I don't know what he wanted," replies Quilleran, who's walking ahead of them. "I'm not even sure he knows."

"You said you'd been waiting for me . . . ," Harvey says insistently, twigs snapping beneath his feet in the darkness.

"That's right."

"So how'd you know I'd arrived?"

"I saw the signs."

"What signs?"

"The garden at your house," Quilleran replies, stopping for a moment.

"What does my garden have to do with it?"

"It's the only one in the city that's blossoming." Quilleran smiles. "You have the gift of speaking with the Earth and healing it."

The little group makes its way up a hill in silence, snapping twigs and rustling grass the only sounds to be heard. No one asks any more questions. They're all lost in thought.

Around a bend, they spot a number of torches glowing in the darkness. Quilleran heads toward the lights and soon reaches them. Sitting in a circle in a clearing are eleven Native Americans, their torches planted into the ground behind them. The flames rise up, tall and crackling in the night.

"Who are they?" Harvey asks.

"The last of the Seneca," Quilleran answers.

"Why are they here?"

"To drive away the enemy."

When Quilleran and the kids arrive, the Seneca stand up and greet them one by one.

"Washington?" Elettra asks one of them, recognizing the guide from Ellis Island.

"Welcome," he replies with a smile.

"Would you mind telling us what's going on?" Harvey snaps, growing more and more nervous.

Quilleran calmly shows them a large stone with a metal plaque on it. "I wish I could have brought you here later on, by day, perhaps . . . but that wasn't possible. Things are happening quickly, and we need to act quickly, too. This is the place where a Dutch man purchased the territory of New York from the Lenape, who were our ancestors' enemies at the time, but who shared our desire to protect the Earth," he explains. "The stone you see here marks the exact spot where the tree that was to protect the city was planted."

"So where's the tree?" asks Sheng.

"It died. It was two hundred and eighty years old, and it was very tired. Its death was one of the first signs. Each city should have a tree that watches over it, just as a man must have strong roots. When this tree died, we sought the old Star of Stone, but he told us he could no longer do anything to save it and that we needed to await his successor . . . who has come at last."

The Seneca slowly pick up their torches from the ground.

"What are you planning on doing?" asks Harvey.

"We'd like to hope that things can continue. That another tree will grow and take the old one's place. That life will go on. For that to happen, we need to dance."

"I don't understand. . . ."

"Understanding isn't important. There are dances connecting to the earth and dances connecting to the sky. We'd like to dance for you, Star of Stone, and for your friends."

Harvey shakes his head, but his eyes are growing bright. "I don't understand . . . ," he insists.

"Stop wanting to understand and accept your gift. Speak with it."

"I . . . I can't."

"You can hear it. You can speak to it whenever you like. And the Earth will speak to you."

"I don't want to," Harvey protests again. But actually, deep down in his heart, he can feel something beating. He doesn't know what to call it. It's his gift. It's like a drum that can awaken unexpected strength. It's ancient, powerful, relentless.

"It's too soon. But for us, it's already late. Spring is only two days away," Quilleran continues, picking up a torch. "Allow the Seneca to do their last dance for you. Let us dance for reborn life, for the tree that needs to sprout again. Let us dance for our friends who are gone and for those who are still holding our hands. Let us dance to drive away the enemy."

"We'll dance, then," Harvey says, listening to the drum.

He slips his hand into Elettra's. Sheng takes Mistral's and then, all together, they step into the center of the ring of burning torches. Then they stop, standing before the rock, at the very place where New York's first tree used to rise.

The flames from the torches flicker in their eyes. Harvey's heart is filled with pride, drinking in the light.

Wind sweeps across the woods as if it were summoning its ancient spirits to guide the dance. Surrounded by the twelve Seneca, the circle of four friends closes in. They stand back to back, supporting each other. Around them, twelve torches begin to revolve. A single voice, guttural and ancient, utters unknown words. It's the voice of the first month of spring.

One by one, the twelve Indians sing of the twelve months of the year. As they do, they dance around the kids. It's a circle of lights and shadows, a loop of flames, a vortex of glowing blazes. It's a top spinning, a tiny light made of stars in the heart of Inwood. It's an infinitesimal cogwheel that makes a thousand other, larger ones turn. Perhaps it's the greatest machine of all, one without a name, without a center, without movement, taking a tiny step forward. It's a song of life. It's a dance for the spirits rising up among the stars.

When the dance is over, it's as though time no longer has any meaning. Ten minutes could have passed or ten hours. The woods are filled with a precious silence. The twelve Seneca men lower their torches and extinguish them against the ground. Harvey, Elettra, Mistral and Sheng unclasp their fingers, suddenly noticing they're stiff and aching.

Quilleran leads them back down the path.

In a little clearing near Indian Road, he says, "The enemies might return. But there's no need to be afraid of them. Follow the path you need to follow."

"I don't know what path it is I need to follow," Harvey says softly.

" 'It's time to understand the world. What difference does it make which road you follow as you seek the truth? Such a great secret is not to be reached by a single path,' " Quilleran recites, quoting Professor Van Der Berger.

"How do you know those words?"

"I learned them when I was waiting for you."

"Who from?"

"From the Star of Stone who came before you."

"You mean Professor Van Der Berger?" the kids exclaim together. "He was the old Star of Stone?"

"Yes."

"And you knew him?"

"For a short time. Before he left the city."

"Did he . . . did he have Harvey's gift, too?" asks Sheng.

"Yes."

Harvey cradles his head in his hands. "I . . . I don't understand anything anymore! How is that possible?"

Quilleran slides his hand into his pocket and pulls out a rectangular object. "Before he left, the old Star of Stone left me something to give to you once I'd found you."

It's an old postcard depicting the moment when Cleopatra's Needle, the great obelisk, was erected in Central Park. The back of the postcard is filled with numbers.

25, 6, 85, 42, 24, 79, 96, 73, 41, 18, 83, 119, 41, 170, 67,
102, 79, 56, 113, 90, 113, 53, 24, 79, 96, 165, 146, 124, 1,
119, 35, 113, 53, 41, 164, 16, 5, 119, 34, 67, 1, 98, 153, 119,
96, 161, 83, 143, 119, 105, 1, 98, 153, 96, 119, 1, 98, 153,
119, 96, 161, 83, 143, 119, 105, 53, 40, 149, 119.
Star of Stone, 1 of 4.

It's addressed to Harvey Miller.

28
THE METEORITE

AT THE BACK OF THE HOSPITAL ROOM ARE THREE PEOPLE: AN ASIAN boy with a pageboy haircut; a girl with long, black, curly hair; and another girl, standing at their side, with a ballerina's graceful face.

The moment he recognizes them, the man in the hospital bed flashes a little smile. It isn't a pretty smile. His lips are marked with stitches. His leg is suspended in a white sling and he's hooked up to strange machines by a series of tubes.

"Hey," he manages to whisper when the three walk up to him. "How's it going?"

"How are you?" Mistral asks, leaning over to kiss him on the cheek. Elettra and Sheng kiss him, too. His chin is stubbly.

"I've been in better shape," Ermete says softly.

"What do the doctors think?"

"It's not so clear," he says, letting out a cough. "They wanted my insurance number, and once I gave it to them . . . well, I haven't seen them since. I know my leg's broken. And a rib or two, I think. They stitched up my lip and fixed a couple of teeth. But everything considered, I could've seen worse."

"We all could've seen worse," Sheng points out.

"You got that right."

The kids look for chairs so they can sit down and tell him about meeting the Indians and about the dance in Harvey's honor at Inwood.

"Where is he now?"

"At home. He didn't take it so well."

"What didn't he take so well?"

"This whole thing about his gift. It scares him. He doesn't want to admit it, but I know it does," Elettra confides in them. "He told me about it. He told me he could hear his brother's voice. . . ."

Mistral shivers. "That can't be pleasant. . . ."

"Man!" Sheng interjects. "I'd totally love to have a gift!"

Then the kids tell him about the postcard addressed to Harvey.

"It was given to Quilleran five years ago . . . when Harvey was eight."

"When all of us were eight."

"Let's just say it took the mailman a while to deliver it to him," Elettra jokes.

Mistral stares at the liquids in the IVs. "The Indian told us he'd been waiting for Harvey. He said that Star of Stone is a name. *His* name. And before him, it was Professor Van Der Berger's name."

"The professor's?"

"He had the same gift Harvey does."

Ermete doesn't reply. He just stares at his three friends with his black eyes. "You've got to admit, the professor sure got you wrapped up in a big mess with that briefcase of his."

"Yes," sighs Mistral.

"But he didn't leave us all alone," Elettra adds. "It's as if . . . as if he warned his friends. The gypsy woman in Rome, the Seneca Indians in New York . . ."

The four begin to talk nonstop about Jacob Mahler, Egon Nose and his dancers. They discuss the fact that both of the bad guys actually seemed to be working for someone else.

"Someone from my hometown," Sheng adds.

Then they try to imagine what might've happened in the subway after the crows attacked. And what dangers might still be in store for them.

Ermete shifts in the bed, making his leg, in a cast, sway dangerously. "If only I could get out of here . . ."

"But you can't."

"Don't worry about us. We'll manage."

The kids leave a cell phone for Ermete on his bedside table. "Call if you need anything," they say. Then they stand up, determined. "We think we might know how to decipher the cryptograms on the postcards."

"That is . . . ?"

"We're going to start looking into Robert Peary, the explorer," Mistral declares, pleased, "and the meteorite he gave to the American Museum of Natural History."

Once he's alone, Ermete waits there in his bed. Then he waits some more. He turns his head to look out the window. A black crow is tapping rhythmically on the windowsill.

From time to time, a massive Indian man wearing an RN's uniform stops by to make sure everything's okay. Each time, Ermete gives him a thumbs-up to let him know he's fine, and the Indian walks off.

Toward the end of the morning, Ermete leans over to pick up the cell phone from the table. He dials a long international number.

He waits.

Someone answers on the sixth ring.

"Mom?" Ermete greets her. "Hi! How am I? Fine. Just great! Oh, yeah. It's a wonderful city. I'm . . . I'm at a museum. Yeah, at the . . . the American Indian museum. Fantastic. You can learn all about . . . their traditions. Mmm-hmm. Their traditions. What? Oh, my voice is strange because I caught a cold. Yeah, it's no big deal. So how are you?"

Elettra is sitting in the backseat of the taxi, her chin resting in the hollow of her hand. The skyscrapers are whizzing by around her. *Two days*, she thinks. Then she'll have to leave. And she won't see him again.

"Wait here, please," she orders the taxi driver once they've arrived at Ermete's place in Queens. She goes up to the second floor, opens the door and walks into the apartment.

She steps over the clumps of foam rubber and the broken furniture, looks around for the bathroom, walks in and takes the mirror off the wall, covering it with a pillowcase first to avoid seeing her reflection.

Resting on the seat of the cab, the mirror looks more solid, heavier.

"Now I need to go to the Village, Grove Court," the girl tells the cabbie through the partition.

Keeping one hand on the ancient object they found in the

mitreo below the church of San Clemente, Elettra tries to imagine what Harvey's feeling right now. She thinks she knows perfectly well what it is: a mix of anger, amazement and fear. The same things she felt when she started to realize she was releasing energy through her hands, that she could short-circuit electrical devices and make mirrors go dull. The feeling of being different, a feeling that tormented her. And the overwhelming desire to be all alone, to discover herself. Accept herself.

Elettra knows it'll take time. Harvey won't answer his phone. He needs to be alone. But she's only got two days left. . . .

Around twenty minutes later, she gets out in front of the Grove Court gates. *Quilleran's right*, she thinks, looking at the garden. Lush grass, flowerbeds in bloom, trees covered with leaves, the first white flower buds ready to spring to life . . . "The person who lives here has the gift of earth," she whispers to herself. She looks for the name Miller on the buzzers, but she suddenly realizes it isn't necessary. Harvey's standing there in the middle of the lawn. He's barefoot. His sleeves are rolled up, his hands black with dirt, his jeans streaked with grass stains. He's staring at her.

"I can feel it," he says through the bars of the gate. "I can really feel it."

New York's American Museum of Natural History is a majestic building with a broad, white marble facade that looks out over the western side of Central Park. Rising up in front of it, at the foot of the stairway, is a bronze statue of President Theodore Roosevelt on horseback.

Once inside, Mistral and Sheng cast only a quick glance at the enormous dinosaur that towers overhead in the lobby, and ignoring all the wonders that the museum contains, they head straight for the Hall of Meteorites. They've brought with them the four postcards, Mistral's notebook, a calculator and a handful of pens and pencils.

"*Hao!*" Sheng exclaims as he walks around the meteorite Ahnighito. It's an enormous, boxy mass twice as tall as they are. "Imagine the hole it must've made when it fell!"

"It's called a crater," Mistral corrects him.

"Can we touch it?"

"I think so."

"But what's it made of? I mean, if it came from outer space . . . man, can you imagine?"

Mistral stops to read an explanatory panel. "It's made of iron," she tells him, "and many other metals."

Sheng looks rather disappointed. "No unknown or alien substances?"

"Hmm . . . it doesn't look like it."

The boy rests the palm of his hand against the stone that came from space. It's warm and porous.

Mistral continues her walk around the room, discovering other curious facts. "The biggest meteorite crater is found in a desert in the United States," she says. "Then there's Wolfe Creek, in the Australian desert. . . ."

"Do they always fall in deserts?"

"Maybe the deserts were formed after they'd fallen," Mistral guesses. "A meteorite impact can raise up enough dust to block out the sun for hundreds of years."

"I read somewhere that the dinosaurs went extinct because of a meteorite," Sheng remembers.

"If a meteorite is big enough, it can change the Earth's climate, start an ice age, or . . ."

Sheng walks over to his French friend. "Do you think the text to solve the cryptogram might be one of these?"

Mistral reads the numbers on the first postcard and compares it to the words on the panel. "W-R-M-G-E," she reads aloud. "Does that mean anything to you?"

Sheng shakes his head.

The hours fly by in the useless search for a text that could help them decipher the numbers on the postcards.

"We're getting nowhere, if you ask me," Mistral is forced to admit in the early afternoon. "Maybe the meteorite Robert Peary discovered doesn't have anything to do with it."

They're sitting on the steps outside the museum. On the other side of the street is the green expanse of Central Park.

"What do we do, then? Should we try Paul Manship's projects?"

Sheng and Mistral look over the postcards again: work on the subway, the inauguration of the Bethesda Fountain, Rockefeller Center and the obelisk in Central Park.

"If I were the professor," Sheng says, reading the incomprehensible numbers for the hundredth time, "I'd have looked for a text that nobody could ever change again."

Mistral nods. "Something written that can't be altered."

"Something really old," adds Sheng.

"Here in New York there are millions of historical texts. . . ." Mistral sighs. "The public library has lots of really precious documents. There's a copy of the Declaration of Independence, and—"

Sheng cuts her off immediately. "The truth is, we're missing something. . . ."

"Wait! There's still somewhere one of the tops showed us that we haven't checked out yet," Mistral recalls, opening up her notebook. "The smallpox hospital on Roosevelt Island."

"The tower, the safe place . . . ," murmurs Sheng.

"Maybe there's a text there. An old, long text. Maybe the hospital's an important place."

"Let's try it out," Sheng agrees, pulling himself up to his feet. Then he exclaims, "Man! This is like looking for a needle in a haystack! We're overlooking something," he repeats, discouraged.

The door to Mr. Miller's study opens slightly.

"Wow! This place is spotless!" Elettra exclaims, peeking inside.

"Maniacal, isn't it?" replies Harvey, still covered with dirt.

"Look at the walls! All his books . . . his awards . . ." Elettra admires the book collection and the numerous photographs. Beneath her feet is soft, soft carpeting.

"That's Dwaine," Harvey says in a hushed voice, pointing at a photo.

"He looked a lot like you."

"I'm the one who's like him. But only in my appearance, unfortunately."

"Cut it out," Elettra says reproachfully. "What are all these maps?"

"Charts of ocean currents, air currents . . . ," Harvey replies distractedly. "My dad deals with the climate. Acid rain, tornadoes, pollution, temperature increases, melting ice caps, tsunamis . . . He has something new to complain about every night. Listening to him, you'd think these are mankind's last days. He's been that way ever since Dwaine. . . . Well, he thinks being optimistic means being stupid. He's so cold, precise, rational!"

"Which makes you feel stupid."

"Exactly," Harvey replies. "And it hurts. It's like there's no way I can get through to him."

"I understand you."

"My dad adored Dwaine. So did my mom. He could do anything. He was . . . a genius."

Elettra kisses him on the forehead. "You're a genius, too, Harvey."

"Maybe I should study geology."

"And become Lord of the Earthquakes?" Elettra jokes. Just then, the Miller family's home phone rings.

29
THE NEEDLES

Sheng and Mistral walk down the museum steps and into Central Park. Sheng starts chasing squirrels. Mistral smiles as she watches him before making her way around the bushes. The park looks like it was designed especially so people could forget about the city. There are paths, seemingly wild areas, ponds, giant fields . . . and an ancient Egyptian obelisk.

It's on a little knoll behind the Metropolitan Museum and it looks like a stone sunbeam standing on a pedestal with four large bronze crabs.

"Sheng, look!" Mistral calls.

Sheng hurries over.

"It was donated to the city to celebrate the opening of the Suez Canal, and it was nicknamed 'Cleopatra's Needle.' . . ." Mistral reads from a guidebook she purchased from a tourist stand. "Actually, it has nothing to do with Cleopatra. It was a part of the Temple of the Sun in Heliopolis, in ancient Egypt . . . along with two other obelisks."

Sheng walks around it. Each of its four sides is decorated with hieroglyphics, mysterious figures, faded with time, that look like paw prints left by ancient creatures. On its base are four metal plaques with the translation. " 'The Horus, strong Bull, beloved of Ra, the King of Upper and Lower Egypt,' " Sheng reads aloud.

"Today, the other two obelisks," Mistral continues, "are found in London and Paris."

" 'In the house of his father, the Lord of the Two Lands . . . The son of Ra, Ramesses, beloved of Amun . . .' "

Mistral's head suddenly snaps up. "Oh, man!" she exclaims. "Needles! Of course! That's why he left us the needles!"

Sheng instantly stops reading.

Mistral takes a step back and points at the obelisk. "Cleopatra's Needle was part of a group of three obelisks. . . . Three obelisks. Three *needles*. One in New York, one in London and one in Paris. New York needle, London needle, Paris needle!"

Sheng gives a start. "*Hao*, you're right!"

The girl steps over to the plaque that Sheng was reading. "The obelisk has four sides and four translations. Four texts that will never change."

"And we've got four postcards. . . ."

"Read the first number!"

"Twenty-five."

"The first letter of the twenty-fifth word is . . . G."

"Six."

"O."

"Eighty-five."

"Wait a minute . . . T."

"Forty-two."

"Another O."

" 'G-O-T-O,' " Mistral concludes. Then she says, "Go to . . . I can't believe it! It's telling us to go somewhere!"

"What comes next?" Sheng asks, almost shouting, ready to read the next numbers.

The needle is threaded with a suture. Panther handles it confidently, stitching up Dr. Nose's wounds as he lies facedown on the couch. "Oooh . . . Ow!" he moans each time the needle pierces his back. "Be careful! Be careful! Oooh! My poor, old skin!"

The woman passes the thread between her teeth, snaps it in two and walks away. "Are you done?" Egon Nose groans. "Good. Or, actually, terrible." He slowly rises to his feet, buttons up his silk shirt and turns to look in the mirror. What he sees in his reflection is a monster covered with cuts. Countless white adhesive bandages are plastered onto his face, cheeks, neck, hands.

"I'm hideous," he snarls, looking at himself. "I'm absolutely hideous. Even for a man who's accustomed to seeing himself uglier morning after morning, this is a revolting sight. Absolutely revolting."

He runs his fingers over his stinging face. For each cut, he remembers the claw or beak of the crow that inflicted it on him. His face is a mask of gashes. "But now I'm furious. I'm very, *very* angry. How can I cover up this disaster? How can I go out without being noticed? What do you think, Panther? Maybe I should pretend nothing happened, not give a damn. . . ." Dr. Nose starts looking for his cane. He grabs it and thumps it on the ground three times. "Enough! Call the others. Let's make a few phone calls and then we'll go visit our friend the antiques dealer."

* * *

228

"What do you mean you solved it?" Harvey asks on the phone, waving Elettra over. "But how'd you do it? The obelisk? Of course! Cleopatra's Needle! Why didn't I think of that? You're right!"

Elettra runs over to him and rests her ear on the other side of the receiver. She, too, can hear the excitement in Mistral's voice. "The message on the first postcard, the one addressed to you, reads *Go to the ancient school of the master of numbers. Three times three. Three times five.* So . . . do you know what that might mean?"

"School of the master of numbers? No, never heard of anything like that."

"Isn't there anything like that in New York? A math school? Three times three . . . Three times five . . ."

"Multiplication tables!" exclaims Elettra.

"Multiplication tables!" Harvey repeats.

"We thought of that, too," Mistral says on the other end of the line. "But what does it mean, then?"

"Multiplication . . . multiplication . . . ," Harvey murmurs. He hands the phone to Elettra and starts looking through the books in his father's study. "Multiplication tables . . ."

"We translated the second one, too, although we've got our doubts about one of the letters!" Mistral continues in the meantime.

"What does it say?" asks Elettra.

"The way is guarded. It takes patience and fortitude to enter."

"Patience?" Elettra grumbles. "How can we be patient? We've only got two days left!"

"The history of mathematics!" Harvey cheers, climbing up the bookshelf ladder to grab a big black volume.

"We might've found something," Elettra says. Mistral's voice is partially covered by the sound of the wind. It's as if time has started to run at a furious pace all around the kids.

Harvey nervously thumbs through the book on the history of mathematics. He checks the index. "Multiplication tables . . . nothing. Pythagorean theorem . . . Pythagoras . . . Pythagoras, the master of numbers!" he cries.

"It's Pythagoras!"

"Look up a Pythagorean school!" Mistral says excitedly after a moment.

"I'll try!" Elettra replies. "Harvey, do you have a phone book for businesses? The yellow pages, or whatever you call it here in the States?"

"Let's use the Internet instead," Harvey replies, a little surprised.

"Okay!" The girl turns to the computer and opens a browser window. "Schools . . . 'Pythagorean school,' 'ancient school' or something like that."

Meanwhile, Harvey is quickly reading over the chapter about Pythagoras. He runs his finger over the lines like a computer scanner. "The hidden meaning of numbers . . . numerology . . . school of numbers in the Orient . . . studies in Egypt . . . travels to the Orient . . . wisdom of the ancient Magi!" Harvey's voice goes up in pitch. "I think this is it!"

"Schools . . . schools . . . ," Elettra is reading just as frenetically. "This list is a total mess."

"Patience and fortitude," Mistral says over the phone. "We must find patience and fortitude. . . ."

"How's Sheng doing with the third postcard?"

"He looks like a raving lunatic. If anyone tries to get near the obelisk, he might tear them limb from limb!"

Elettra giggles. "There are three gazillion schools, but no Pythagorean school."

"Magic numbers . . . the number seven . . . the seven planets . . . ," Harvey says, still reading. "Pythagoras introduced the seven musical notes . . . and the correspondence between numbers and the universe. Number rules the universe . . . He founded his school in Magna Graecia."

"Magna Graecia school!" Mistral cries when she hears him.

"Magna Graecia is in Italy!" Elettra explains. "It was the southern part of Italy."

"In Crotone," Harvey specifies.

"Crotone school!" Elettra looks it up, but it's yet another dead end.

"His disciples," Harvey continues, "had to spend one year in silence before they could begin learning from him."

"Patience and fortitude," Mistral repeats again. "That's what's the second message says."

"It's not like we've got years," Elettra snaps. "We haven't even got weeks. Read the message again, Mistral."

"*Go to the ancient school of the master of numbers. Three times three. Three times five.*"

"That means we need to go to . . . where, to Crotone?"

"But that's on the other side of the ocean!" Harvey protests. "So why would the message be here in New York?"

"Crotone . . ."

"Crotone? Crotone? That name rings a bell. . . ."

The three kids fall silent for a long time.

"Oh, no!" Mistral wails.

"What is it?"

"It just started pouring down rain."

"Pouring down!" Elettra shouts. "That's where I've heard it before . . . from Vladimir! Wasn't Croton the name of the old aqueduct in New York? The Angel of the Waters?"

"The Croton Aqueduct!" Harvey remembers. "The fountain one!"

"Where's it based? Where's the reservoir?" Elettra asks him.

"I . . . I don't know. I mean, it's gone now."

"Well, where did it used to be?"

"How should I know?"

"Call Vladimir!"

"How can I? You're on the phone!"

Elettra tosses him her cell phone. "We might be on to something," she tells Mistral.

Harvey dials the number of the antiques shop. "Hello, Vladimir? It's Harvey. Sorry . . . I'm kind of in a hurry. Do you know where the Croton Aqueduct reservoir is, or where it used to be? I can barely hear you . . . Vladimir? You there? Croton. The aqueduct, the first freshwater system in New York. Yeah, exactly . . ."

A moment of perfect silence follows.

"There? Yeah, I understand. But how far north? Near the public library? Of course! Patience and Fortitude!" Harvey exclaims. "Aren't those the names of the two lions guarding the entrance to the library?"

Elettra says into the phone, "It's the New York Public Library! We'll see you there, at the entrance!" Both phone calls are ended, and the two race out of Harvey's house.

"Maybe we shouldn't go there alone," Elettra says as they're running to the subway. She dials a number. Quilleran's cell phone.

On the other side of the city, the moment Vladimir Askenazy hangs up the phone, Egon Nose hisses, "What was that about the public library, Mr. Askenazy?"

Vladimir groans, pinned down in his chair by two young women. "Someone wanted to know where they could find a book."

Dr. Nose leans in toward him, his face covered with a maze of bandages. "This isn't the best time to be kidding around," he hisses.

"I love stories with happy endings," the elderly antiques dealer replies.

"Make him understand the situation," Egon orders, stepping back abruptly. One of the two women grabs Vladimir's right hand.

He instantly shouts, "No! Stop!"

Dr. Nose stares distractedly at an antique statuette. He whirls his cane around and knocks it down, shattering it into a thousand pieces. "Let's try to be reasonable, Mr. Askenazy. Was it Miller?"

Nose's girl is clutching one of Vladimir's fingers in a viselike grip. He wishes he could summon the courage to make up a phony story, but he can't. "It was him," he admits.

"What did he want?"

"A copy of *The Many Adventures of Winnie the Pooh*," he hisses.

The woman instantly tightens her grip. The antiques dealer howls and slumps down over the desk.

"Very amusing, Vladimir, really," Egon Nose remarks, crushing the already shattered statuette beneath his foot. "But useless. If Miller leaves his house, my girls know about it. If he makes a phone call, my girls know about it. If your Italian friend calls his mama, my girls know about it."

Vladimir's mouth is wide open, but he can't speak. The stabbing pain in his hand is so intense that all he wants to do is pass out. Still, deep down in his heart he finds another little glimmer of courage. Or madness. Which are both crumbs from the same loaf of bread.

"There's . . . just one thing, then . . . that your girls don't know. . . ."

"And what would that be, Mr. Askenazy?"

"Why on earth they keep working . . . for a monstrous-looking man like you."

His words seem to deeply injure Dr. Nose's vain, unstable soul. The lord of New York nightlife explodes. "Is that what you think? Is it? That I'm monstrous?" His scratched face twisting with rage, Egon begins to kick and thrash his cane all around him, shattering everything he sets his sights on. "Well, it just so happens, antiques man, that this face—this monstrous face—has made it all the way to the top of this city."

Aching and tired, Vladimir half-closes his eyes. A slight smile, a crazy smirk of superiority, ripples across his lips. "Not to the top, Nose. To the bottom. To the very dregs . . ."

Dr. Nose stops tearing apart the shop. Slowly, he slips on an eighteenth-century glove trimmed with lace and strikes the antiques dealer, sending him tumbling down to the ground. He massages his hand, pulls off the glove and lets it fall to the floor.

"Set fire to the place," he orders his girls, "and leave him inside."

30

THE LIONS

PATIENCE AND FORTITUDE ARE WHITE. THEY'RE SITTING THERE, guarding the stairs of the public library, motionlessly watching the city that never sleeps. Guardian sphinxes marking the boundary between man's constant movement and the still, unchanging words written in books. An annoying drizzle has left the street gray and glistening. Sleek cars zoom along beneath the hazy facades of the skyscrapers.

Elettra and Harvey reach the majestic library first. A few minutes later, the Indian mail carrier, Quilleran, appears on the other side of the street and joins them. It's almost evening. The streetlights are about to switch on.

Harvey casts a sidelong glance at Quilleran and explains, "We're not exactly sure why we came here." Then he tells him about the hieroglyphics in Central Park and about Croton.

The man just stands there, smiling. "It's a good thing you called me." A crow with a cloudy eye perches on the head of the lion Patience, peering at them with its good eye.

Sheng and Mistral show up not long afterward. They make

their way through the umbrellas that are swarming the sidewalk on Fifth Avenue like stampeding mushrooms.

"We deciphered the others, too!" Sheng cheers, climbing the steps two at a time. "The second postcard says, *Knowledge is a labyrinth. Only the indivisible will lead the way.*"

"Breathe," Elettra says.

"And on the last one," the Chinese boy goes on, ignoring her, "it says, *The door isn't a magic rectangle. It is a grid of nine.* Oh, hi!" he adds when he notices Quilleran. "What are you doing here?"

"I'm not sure yet," the Indian answers.

They walk into the library, where silence reigns. Millions of printed pages lying on wooden tables. A multitude of file folders. Rooms, stairways, landings and hallways.

"What now?" asks Elettra.

" 'Knowledge is a labyrinth,' " Harvey recites. " 'Only the indivisible will lead the way.' "

"What did we come here to do, anyway?" whispers Mistral.

"We're not sure," Harvey replies. "We need to look for . . . for something."

"Something or someone that will lead the way . . ."

"We need a guide."

A man with bleached hair and an effeminate gait accompanies them to the first underground level of the library. "They usually don't let anyone come down here," he explains for the millionth time, straightening his glasses with lilac-colored frames on the tip of his nose. "But from what your uncle told me," he says, waving his hand toward Quilleran, whose emotionless face looks like a statue eroded by the wind, "this is a really special occasion."

Sheng smiles. "It sure is." Then he whispers to Harvey, "Why does he keep looking at me like that?"

"Guess who Uncle Quilleran's nephew is."

Sheng nods, understanding. Then he turns to Mistral. "What special occasion is he talking about, anyway?"

"It's that he'll get fifty dollars if he helps us find what we're looking for."

"So what is it we're looking for?"

Mistral shrugs. "The water pipes?"

As if to impress them, the guide rattles off a slew of information. "Our library is home to sixty million books. Thanks to our cataloging system and our high-speed carts, we're capable of tracking down any publication in under ten minutes."

The little group makes its way down a long, long corridor with a low ceiling. They're surrounded by bookshelves.

"The building that was here before the library—is there anything left of it?" Harvey asks as the corridor branches out into two aisles.

The guide shakes his head. "Well . . . Hmm . . . the building that was here before . . ."

"The Croton Aqueduct reservoir," Sheng interjects.

"Hmm . . . let me think . . . Croton . . ." The man looks around to gain his bearings and then seems to randomly choose one of the other aisles. "Follow me."

After a few detours, a few consultations and thousands of paces, the guide leads them up to an old, ordinary-looking white wall. "This should be it," he says with a little smile as he checks, for the millionth time, a photocopy he had made for them three floors above. "Yes, precisely. This is what's left of the building that

237

was here before the library: the last surviving wall of the Croton Aqueduct reservoir."

It's a perfectly normal white wall, of which not more than one square meter has been left uncovered by bookcases. To the left and right are books. The bookcases go all the way up to Harvey's head and end only a foot and a half below the ceiling. The aisle from which they've arrived is illuminated by a line of neon lights that switched on automatically as they passed by.

"Happy?" the guide asks.

"Actually . . . no," Harvey answers.

"There's nothing out of the ordinary here, on this wall," Mistral points out.

The guide rubs his hands together nervously. "In any case, this is it."

"This isn't the place we need to get to," Harvey says thoughtfully. "It's just a starting point. *Go to the ancient school of the master of numbers.*" He leans back against the wall and looks around.

"Well, we've found that." Sheng stands next to him. "And around us we've got a labyrinth. *Only the indivisible will lead the way,*" he repeats aloud.

The guide looks at Quilleran inquisitively. "Can we go now?"

"Just a moment," the Indian man replies.

"Only the indivisible . . . Only the indivisible . . ."

"Indivisible, like we need to stick together?"

"Indivisible, as in solid?"

"Indivisible, with liberty and justice for all?"

Harvey looks at the numbers marking the aisles around Croton's old wall and reads aloud, "Eighty-nine, eighty-eight, eighty-one . . ."

"Nine times nine," Sheng blurts out.

"What'd you say?"

"Eighty-one. Nine times nine. The times table for the number nine."

"And eighty-eight?"

"That isn't in any times table," Sheng says, thinking. "Wait, of course it is. It's a multiple of eight. Eleven times eight."

"Eighty-nine?"

"A multiple of seven? Seventy-seven, eighty-four . . . no," Sheng says, trying to concentrate.

"It's a prime number," says Mistral. Harvey and Sheng turn toward the French girl. "A prime number. You know, the ones that can't be divided except by themselves or the number one," she explains.

A smile crosses Harvey's face. "Can't be divided . . . indivisible . . . only the *indivisible* will lead the way!" With this, he slips into aisle number eighty-nine.

"Hey!" the guide exclaims. "You can't go down there!"

Quilleran bars his way and rests a hand on his shoulder. A very heavy hand. "Just a moment," he says. The other three kids follow Harvey.

The aisles intersect each other like strands in a spiderweb. At each intersection, the kids find a prime number showing them the way. At times it leads them to stairs going down, so they go downstairs.

The guide with bleached hair follows them, panting, protesting and looking around nervously, but he isn't actually brave enough to stop them. "If they catch you down here," he repeats at every turn, "they'll fire me."

"They won't catch us," Quilleran replies calmly.

Then they stop.

They heard a noise coming from a few floors above them. It sounded like a gunshot. They stand there, motionless. The guard is very alarmed. "Did you hear that, too?"

"Maybe a stack of books fell to the floor, or a lightbulb exploded."

Quilleran answers for all of them. "I didn't hear anything." He pushes the man forward, nodding at Harvey to keep going.

Whatever caused that noise, their descent into the maze of books continues at an even brisker pace. Soon, the gunshot is forgotten, along with all the other noises. All that's left is the rhythmic sound of their breathing and their shoes squeaking on the floor. The lights in the aisles switch on automatically when they pass by and switch off a moment after that.

There's another gunshot. This time there's no doubt about it. It's followed by a scream.

The guide stops a second time. "Did you hear it now? Somebody's shooting!"

"Yes," Quilleran says, not stopping.

The underground level around them is a dark, complex labyrinth of aisles. The Native American man gestures to them to wait. Behind them, the aisle's lights switch off bulb by bulb, until only the one directly over their heads is still on.

They wait. Everything's dark, except their tiny light. Quilleran slips off one of his shoes and, with a well-aimed swing, shatters it.

"Hey!" the guide protests. "You can't do that! That's public property!"

"Shhh," the Indian shushes him. They're in the dark. The six of them lean back against the bookcases and stand there, listening. The darkness is suffocating.

The library worker tries to insist. "Would you mind telling me—"

"I said, be quiet," Quilleran repeats with a tone that no one would dare talk back to. He looks behind him, toward the aisle they just came from. "They're coming downstairs," he whispers.

Now the kids can also hear the sound of heels coming from far, far away.

"Who's coming downstairs?" the guide whispers nervously.

"Egon's women," Harvey answers, stepping around him.

"Who?" the man asks. "What on earth are you talking about?"

"They're the ones who were shooting," Mistral adds.

The man's face grows pale. "Oh, no!" he exclaims. "Tell me you're kidding!"

"Unfortunately not."

In the distance, a door opens and shuts. Over the bookcases, they can see the ceiling lights go on in a distant aisle.

"Is there any way to seal off the floor?" Sheng asks the guide.

"To seal off the floor? What do you mean?"

Elettra waves her hands. "To put out the lights." She shows the man the distant string of neon lights switching on. "Those women are looking for us. See? Over there, where the lights are going on. As long as we're in the dark, they won't know where we are. But the moment we move . . ."

"We're trapped," says Sheng.

"We've got to go back," says Mistral.

"I'm not going back now," Sheng objects.

241

"Or . . ."

"We split up," Quilleran suggests.

"How?"

The Indian man studies the kids' faces in the darkness and asks Harvey, "Will it take you much longer to get where you need to go?"

"How should I know?"

"Some will keep going, others will turn back," Quilleran insists.

"I'm going back!" the guard cries hysterically.

Harvey studies the aisle lights in the distance. One by one, they're turning on slowly, as if the girls are unsure which way to go.

"If we split up, they'll have to split up, too," the boy whispers. "Then we might be able to lose them."

"What on earth are you babbling about?" the guide groans.

"Would you shut up?" Sheng snaps. His tone is so harsh that he instantly gets the result he wanted.

"I'm going back," Mistral repeats.

"I'm going with you," Elettra decides.

The guide raises his hands in the air, relieved. "At last!"

The little group exchanges a quick hug and the two girls begin to retrace their steps.

"Run!" Quilleran orders them.

The Indian man, Harvey and Sheng dart off in the opposite direction, leaving the guide there in the middle, stunned. "Hey!" the man protests feebly. "You can't just—"

The lights in the aisle switch on again.

242

"Quick!" Elettra shouts at him. "Get us out of here!"

The man with bleached hair doesn't wait to be asked twice.

Harvey, Sheng and Quilleran move quickly in the opposite direction. They go down one more level.

"Nineteen," Harvey reads as he turns down an aisle. He can't see any other lights on behind him. And then, "Seventeen."

They continue along, running. Quilleran turns around only when he hears footsteps behind them. Each time he stops, he breaks the neon ceiling light with his shoe. Sheng takes advantage of the brief pauses to catch his breath. The sound of his panting. Footsteps coming down the stairs. Heels. Egon Nose's women.

"We'd better move it!" Harvey says, urging them on as he checks the aisle in front of him. "We're almost there."

The footsteps are descending a stairway they just came down themselves a moment ago. Then they stop. A woman's ravenous eyes peer into the darkness, unable to see anything. Slowly, they make their way back up the steps. One, two, three, five steps. Then they fade away.

"Let's go," Quilleran whispers. They start running again.

Aisle thirteen.

Aisle seven.

Another noise behind them. The chase is on again.

Aisle five.

They hear a third gunshot far, far away. It's little more than a faint pop. But a moment later, all the neon tubes are lit up in a blinding flash of white light. The lights all go on at the same time and then burst into a cascade of tiny glass shards. A shower of them rains down all over the aisle.

"Elettra," Harvey guesses, shielding his eyes. "Something happened to Elettra!" He turns to go back, but Quilleran and Sheng stop him.

"You can't give up now, Harvey. We're almost there."

The boy tries to pull himself free, but Quilleran's grip is firm.

Sheng begs him. "Come on! We split up so we'd have a chance to get down here," he says. "And we've almost made it."

Harvey shakes his head. "We don't even know what we've almost made it to. . . ."

Quilleran doesn't loosen his grip.

Four floors above, Elettra is standing still, her eyes closed, her hands raised up toward the ceiling. All the lights around her have exploded. When she finally opens her eyes, she sees Mistral lying on the ground, face up. Thousands of fragments of glass are in her hair, on her clothes, on the floor around her.

"Mistral?"

The girl coughs. Her hand moves. She's alive. Elettra looks at the aisle in front of her. It's pitch-dark, but her eyes are still glowing. She can make out the two women's shadows not more than fifty yards away from them. They're on the ground, groaning. They aren't holding guns anymore. They've stopped shooting.

Someone lets out a sob. It's their guide. His hands are bloody. Tiny shards of glass are stuck in his fingers. Elettra leans over him. "Get us out of here, please," she says. "Before they start chasing us again."

The guide's eyes are like those of a child. In comparison, Elettra's gaze is that of a woman who's lived for centuries. "What happened?" he asks her.

"They shot at us," she says.

"No, after that."

"I defended myself," Elettra whispers, her face drained from the effort. She's surrounded by flames. The books are burning. Then, suddenly, it starts to snow.

"It must've set off a dry sprinkler system," says Sheng, four floors farther down, staring at the thin flakes of fire-resistant material that are falling all around them. "It's a good idea, in a library. No water."

Everything's dark. It's getting more and more cramped. They're venturing farther and farther down.

Aisle number three.

They walk along, the flakes still falling like snow. Shards of glass crunch beneath their shoes. Far, far off in the distance, shrieking sirens are slicing through the silence. Still, they keep going down. They turn another corner. They make their way down to aisle number one.

The last aisle.

They stop before a closed door, at the end of it all. Or perhaps at the beginning. Harvey touches the door, leans against it, looks for a handle, a lock. There isn't one. He can't see anything. Everything's as dark as night.

"It's over," he says. "The labyrinth ends here."

Sheng slides up next to him. "It's a wall."

"But it can't be," Harvey groans. "There's got to be a door. . . ."

"*The door isn't a magic rectangle,*" the Chinese boy recites.

"There are nine squares here."

"What do you mean?"

Use your hands, says a voice in Harvey's head.

"What'd you say?"

"I didn't say anything," Sheng replies.

"Why'd you tell me to use my hands?" Harvey insists.

"I'm telling you, I didn't say anything!"

Harvey shakes his head and rests the palms of his hands against the wall. He moves them up and down, searching for something. Anything. The wall isn't smooth. "There are some designs," he murmurs, groping around the dark stone wall. "I can feel . . . grooves."

Move them, says the voice in his head.

"How am I supposed to move them?"

"Move what?" asks Sheng.

Talk to me, thinks Harvey. Voices of the Earth. Spirits of places. Tutelary gods. Those who protect what must be protected. A voice he knows well.

"Dwaine, is this what I'm supposed to move?" he whispers, slipping his fingers into the gaps. "These here?"

Yes, the voice in his head answers.

Whatever they are, Harvey moves them.

Quilleran is standing behind the two boys. He turns back and peers into the darkness, worried. He hears something. Distant sirens. The rustling of the dry sprinkler flakes. Other noises coming from the underground levels. Something incomprehensible, unknown. Footsteps. Heels.

The Indian crouches down, sniffs the air, shakes his head. Then he pulls something out of his pocket and hands it to Sheng. It's a lighter.

"Wh-what's this for?" the boy stammers.

Quilleran stares at him with his sharply featured, owl-like face. "It's so you can see the door. But don't light it yet! Wait thirty seconds. With the light from the flame, they'll know where you are."

"What are you going to do?"

"I'm going to try to stop them." That's the last thing he says. He slips into the darkness and disappears. He's gone back to take on Egon Nose's women.

Sheng counts to thirty, waits a few more seconds and gives the lighter a flick. The flame wavers in the darkness, lighting up Harvey's back and the wall at the end of the aisle. Actually, it isn't just an ordinary wall. Set into the middle of it is a strange-looking grid made of tiles.

Each tile has a number painted on it.

3	8	1
5	9	7
2	6	4

Each of the tiles moves, sliding along the grid. That's what Harvey's doing. He's sliding them around with his hands.

The flame goes out and then flickers back on.

"What are those?" Sheng asks his friend.

"I don't know," Harvey replies, "but I know I need to move them."

The flame goes out and then flickers back on.

"A grid of nine," the Chinese boy remembers. He checks the tiles. There are nine of them, and they're numbered from one to nine. "Nine. Three times three . . . ," he repeats, reciting more of the clues on the four postcards.

"They need to be moved," Harvey insists.

"In what order?"

"I don't know," the boy admits.

There's a gunshot. A gunshot from very close by. Sheng puts out the lighter. They turn, breathless, their hearts in their throats. They listen. There are sounds of a scuffle. Bookshelves being broken. Quilleran has come face to face with their pursuers.

"We've got to solve this freaking riddle!" Sheng groans, flicking on the lighter again.

"But how?" Harvey wonders.

Nine tiles.

Three times three.

Three times five.

"It's a magic square!" Sheng suddenly cries, remembering an old puzzle. He points at the tiles. "The order is . . . it's got to be . . ."

The flame goes out and then flickers back on.

"I remember now!" the boy cheers. "You need to arrange them so that when you add up the numbers . . . in every row . . . and in every column . . . you always get the same total."

"But what total?"

Three times three.

248

Three times five.

"Nine," says Sheng, "or fifteen."

The noises coming from behind them grow louder, but Harvey can't hear anything. "Fifteen," he says decisively. He starts sliding the tiles around again.

The flame goes out and then flickers back on.

He slides them along the grooves one at a time, trying to position them in the right places. Sheng helps him, pointing, calculating. Harvey moves them, moves them again, slides them over and changes them back. Quilleran is battling behind them. They hear a woman's scream. Sirens in the distance.

"The four! The four! The four goes in the top right-hand corner."

The magic square is finally finished. Horizontally and vertically, the numbers all add up to fifteen.

8	3	4
1	5	9
6	7	2

Letting out a groan and a puff of dust, the wall pops open slightly.

Harvey and Sheng push on it, opening it wide enough to pass through. Before slipping in, they turn and call Quilleran's name.

No one answers.

They rest their hands on the other side of the wall and close it behind them.

Sheng fidgets with the lighter, flicks it on again and keeps the flame, their only source of light, held up over their heads. They're in a very narrow passageway. There are steps leading down. The ceiling is in mosaic tiling. There's a large platform. A metal plaque at the end of the platform reads FIRST STATION.

The little flame rises up, wavering. A vaulted tunnel disappears into the darkness. A train car is parked on the tracks.

When they move closer with the light, the boys recognize it. It's the same pneumatic train car as the model they found in the tower in the East Village. The one Vladimir told them was a model of the Beach Railroad, the secret pneumatic tunnel dug out beneath the city. Only this time, the train car is life-sized and real. And the tunnel they're in isn't the Beach Railroad but a secret, unknown tunnel. An ancient tunnel that seems to be expecting them.

The train car is made of black iron with two big, round headlights. Its wheels are protected by mudguards, like the ones on old carriages. The seats are antique velvet armchairs. On its side is the symbol of a comet. Its door is open.

Without saying a word, Harvey and Sheng step over to the train car and get inside. On the control panel is a metal ring with a red lever that has only two positions: FIRST STATION and LAST STATION.

Harvey pushes on it, but it's stuck. He shoves it impatiently. The gears grind with a noise that sounds like old bones breaking.

Nothing happens. The train doesn't move.

Then they feel a rush of wind.

A massive gust of air shoots out from behind the train car. The two friends are hurled back into the seats. Before the door can even close, the underground air-compression train is catapulted into the darkness. Toward the unknown.

THIRD STASIMON

"Irene . . . It's me."

"Vladimir? What's going on? Why are you calling me at this hour?"

"They burned it down. My shop. It's all cinders. Years of collection, research, beauty . . . all destroyed."

"And you? Were you hurt?"

"They got me out in time. My Seneca friends."

"What about the children?"

"Quilleran's there to protect them. But they're strong, Irene. Stronger than we thought. Our enemies know about Century. I'm sure of it now. They know everything. They even know where to look."

"Where are you?"

"Below the stars in the station. I wanted to see them one last time. Everyone thinks these constellations were drawn backward, but instead . . . they're the only ones that are right. The comet is coming. It's on its way back!"

"But the children are okay?"

"I think so, but I have no way of knowing."

"They're halfway there by now!"

"Century is coming back. But it won't be like it was a hundred years ago, Irene. This time, the Fox Star is going to bring a catastrophe. This time . . . it's going to destroy us."

"I'm not giving up hope."

"Mankind has grown too wicked. No one keeps their word, respects pacts. If the Earth wants to wipe us out, it'll only be to protect itself."

"No! We still keep our word. So do the children."

"But there are only two of us, Irene, and only four kids. Do you really think we'll be enough . . . to save the world?"

"You're forgetting about our friends, Vladimir. You're forgetting about our friends. . . ."

31

THE FRIEND

Lounging on the gigantic bed in the hotel room, Linda Melodia is admiring her shopping bags from various boutiques. She's arranged them around the bed like members of a royal court around the king's throne. She's holding a notebook, checking the list of the people she's bought a souvenir for. Irene, Fernando, Elettra, Linda . . .

Her own name appears seven times.

As she's peeking inside the Banana Republic bag, the phone rings. It's the reception desk.

"Someone needs to deliver what to me? Flowers? Oh, all right then. Tell them to bring them up."

She looks around for her slippers, glances at her reflection in the mirror and opens the door, wondering who it is. Her mustachioed admirer again? Could it be that after their last dinner together he's grown so bold as to bring her a bouquet of flowers? Or what if it's just a deliveryman? Should she tip him?

She makes a quick retreat to find some money, straightens her hair in front of the mirror and . . . through the open door, Linda can hear the elevator bell signaling that it's stopped at her floor. She goes back to the doorway and peers out.

She's left gaping.

It's a short man dressed in velvet, his face hidden behind the flowers, his body bundled up in an oversized coat and a pair of horrible snakeskin shoes. He isn't alone. He's accompanied by two tall, thin young women wearing platinum-blond wigs and white artificial furs.

"Hello, ma'am," a hoarse voice says from behind the bouquet. "I have a surprise for you!"

Suddenly, Linda is even more stunned, if that's possible. Could that be a nose, a ghastly, gigantic nose, peeking out between the gerberas? And what he's holding in his hand, isn't that a . . . ?

"A gun?" she shrieks, bewildered, when she recognizes the ominous black shape.

"May I come in?" Egon Nose hisses, revealing his ghastly face that was injured by the crows. "No scenes, please! Would you be so kind as to remain alive?"

Elettra, Mistral and the guide reach the ground floor of the library. They rush out a door and into a swarm of security forces, firemen and policemen trained for terrorist attacks wearing uniforms and shiny helmets.

They're pulled off to the side, briefly interrogated and given a blanket. The guide is asked what's going on in the underground levels. Everyone's talking at once. Everyone's moving around. There are faces everywhere. The two girls don't understand where they're going. The metal detectors at the entrance have short-circuited. Three policemen have been injured.

The voices come one after the other. "Who are they? What do they want? A group of burglars. Art collectors? Terrorists? They say there are three of them. Three women, all of them armed."

Elettra's exhausted. She used up all her energy jamming the electrical system.

Mistral's thinking more clearly. "Let's go," she whispers. She hugs her friend and slowly leads her outside into the open air. No one pays any attention to them. They're just two young girls.

Outside, it's a solid wall of rain sliced through by the emergency vehicles' flashing lights. Thousands of faces are pressed up against the windows of the nearby buildings. Metal boom poles are holding up the reporters' microphones. Talking heads are yapping away into television cameras with the breaking news. Special report: attack on the New York Public Library.

"Where are we going?" Elettra asks, her eyes red and weary.

"The hotel. Harvey and Sheng can meet up with us there."

Elettra nods. "We need to let my aunt know."

The cold rain is falling, running down her neck and into her hair.

The two friends have shards of glass on their clothes. Curious onlookers are crowding around in the street. Mistral leads Elettra over to a taxi. They get in. "The Mandarin Oriental," Mistral orders.

Elettra takes out her cell phone. She tries to call Ermete.

Then Harvey.

Then Sheng.

Then her aunt.

No luck. News of the raid on the library must've tied up all the phone lines. Elettra makes one last call. This time, it starts ringing.

In the hotel lobby, all the televisions are showing images of the public library. Elettra and Mistral stare at the screens as though hypnotized. The policemen have gone down to the lowest levels. They found the body of an unconscious woman. The girls pick up the keys to their rooms.

"Elettra?" a female voice asks from behind them. "Everything okay?"

Many floors above, a man with a horrible face is hissing to Linda Melodia, "If you don't mind, you'll need to give us those bags as well."

"Of course I mind!" Linda snaps, nevertheless carrying out the order. She's already been forced to unwrap all the gift packages, the contents of which are now strewn all over the bed. Then came the suitcases. She pulled everything out of them, but the madman with the anteater's nose still doesn't seem satisfied. "I don't know what you want from me, but I can assure you that you're becoming absolutely intolerable!"

The man grumbles something and waves his gun. "Yes, that's it. Those two bags. Open them and put what's in them on the bed, like the others . . . but very slowly. Even slower."

"You'll pay for this, you scoundrel. . . ."

"I said *slowly*."

"I have a date. My boyfriend will be here any moment now. And he's a very strong man."

"Open that box, please."

"This one?" asks Linda.

"Open it."

Linda takes the wrapping paper off of what looks like an old wooden box. Dr. Nose sinks his nose into the bouquet of flowers with which he appeared in the room. The wrapping paper flies off across the room and the old wooden box, covered with writings and furrows, is placed on the bed.

"Magnificent," the man says.

"What's magnificent?" Linda says sourly.

Egon steps over to the bed and strokes the box's wooden surface. "This must be it. Magnificent, don't you think?"

Linda rests her hands on her hips, peeved. "You're insane. What's so special about that dusty old thing?"

"Magnificent . . . ," Egon repeats.

Linda stares at him silently. She observes the man, who only comes up to her shoulders, with a mix of hatred and pity. "Never in my whole life have I found myself in a situation like this. . . ."

Dr. Nose gestures that she should continue emptying out the bag.

"Nothing like this has ever happened to me," Linda repeats.

"That small package, please."

Inside of it is a wooden top.

"At last! That's it!" the man exclaims. He reaches into his pocket, pulls out a similar top and rests it beside the one that Linda has just placed on the bed. "Look! They're identical!"

At this point, the woman explodes. "What are you, some kind of clown? This is all a practical joke, isn't it? Now I understand!" She whirls around toward the mirrored closet and shouts, "Elettra! Did you have me take part in one of those ridiculous American

258

programs with a hidden camera? So where's it hiding? Here? Behind this?"

Egon Nose raises his voice. "Ma'am, stop it!"

"No, *you* stop it! Enough with these shenanigans!" Linda continues, undaunted. She throws open the closet door and starts rummaging through the things on the shelves. "I fell for it for long enough! You aren't even a good actor. With that toy gun and . . . heavens! You made me put everything in such disorder! I'm sure it'll look quite hilarious on television! And do take off that fake nose!"

Egon raises his gun and aims it at Linda Melodia's back. He rests his finger on the trigger and orders her, in a deep voice, "Stop." Linda turns toward him and gestures for him to remove the fake nose. Dr. Nose begins to tremble with rage. "Not another word about my nose . . ."

Linda ignores him. "Well, are you going to take it off or not?"

"Not another word," the man repeats, holding the gun in front of him.

"I've had enough of you," Linda Melodia hisses, suddenly picking up the bronze Statue of Liberty from the closet beside her. "Take this!" she shouts, hurling it at him.

On the top floor of the Mandarin Oriental, four women come out of the elevator. They stride quickly, confidently, knowing there isn't a moment to lose. The first one has short, dark hair, big blue eyes and a long, slender neck. The second one has a cascade of dark curls. The third is black and is wearing a sweat suit. The fourth has a shaved head and on her face is the determined expression of someone who has nothing to lose.

The moment they see them, two women with flashy blond wigs spring to attention without saying a word.

"Get out of here," Mistral orders them without slowing down.

"That's my room," Elettra adds.

Egon's women don't utter a word. Their well-trained bodies are ready to pounce. Two groups form, facing each other. The hotel's acoustic system is filling the air with Muzak. Music without meaning.

"Get out of here . . . ," Mistral repeats, staring the women in the eyes.

For the first time, one of the women speaks. Her voice is cold. "We don't beat up other chicks. Normally."

The black woman standing behind Elettra bursts out laughing. "Really?" she exclaims. "Well, we do!" As fast as lightning and with equally unpredictable power, her fist smashes into Egon's lady-thug's nose.

It's all over in a second, if not less. Elettra and Mistral jump to the side as the woman staggers backward, dazed.

"Never lower your guard," says Olympia, Harvey's boxing trainer. "Right, Evelyn?"

32

THE STAR OF STONE

○

THE PNEUMATIC TRAIN HURTLES THROUGH THE OLD, FORGOTTEN
tunnels, crossing over the subway lines, between the aqueduct pipes
and the network of millions of cables that connect in the underground realms beneath New York City. It reaches a dank, leaky
area, passes through it with the last puff of air it has left and, after
a brief descent, stops with a groan at its destination. Last Station.

Sheng moves the flame from the lighter all around him. It's
an underground room with a pale blue vaulted ceiling. "Stars," he
says, recognizing the glowing specks. "We're heading in the right
direction."

"But to get to what?" Harvey asks, passing in front of him. The
underground station's platform has only one exit. It's a carved,
egg-shaped opening surrounded by the twelve signs of the zodiac.

"The path of stars?" Sheng guesses, the lighter raised.

On the other side of the opening is a short corridor that finishes in a steep, narrow staircase leading up. They take it. It isn't
very long, and at the top of it is an open door. On the wall beside
it is a relief sculpture of a man, his face twisted with grief, who's
slaying a bull.

"Mithra as he's killing the bull," Harvey says, remembering. They step through the doorway. The room on the other side is very large. To the left and right of the entrance, on the walls, are large carved bronze panels. Sheng's lighter lingers beside the muscular shapes of ancient heroes who look like they're leaping out from the stone. There are women of incomparable beauty, their faces partially hidden behind veils. There are animals, snakes, ravens and bulls lurking in the shadows.

Even with the help of their only light, the two boys can't make out how large the underground room is. They walk down one side of it, pausing to look at the scenes carved into the walls and read their captions.

" 'Deucalion and Pyrrha after the flood' . . . ," Sheng reads, studying a man and woman walking on a rocky outcrop surrounded by water. Over her shoulder she's throwing stones, which are turning into tiny men.

The next panel depicts a brawny, bearded man who's carving a rock with wind whirling around it. " 'Hephaestus creating Pandora, the first woman.' "

On the next side is Prometheus, surrounded by flames as he crafts a man out of clay and water. After him is a man sleeping in a large garden with animals peering into it. " 'Adam, made of clay, about to awaken,' " Sheng reads.

Next comes Niobe, who's desperate because she's been turned to stone.

They're all legends that connect man and stone.

The room is shaped like a circle. Harvey suddenly stops. "Did you hear that?" he asks Sheng.

"No. What was it?"

The voice in Harvey's head just said something. *Look for the center,* it told him.

"We need to look for the center," says Harvey, pointing to the heart of the room, which is still pitch-dark, "and see what's there."

"Whatever you say."

The two friends stand next to each other, shoulder to shoulder, and move forward. After a few steps, their little flame starts to illuminate cords and vines hanging down from the ceiling. They look like big stone spiderwebs. Little by little, as they move closer to the center of the room, the tangle grows denser. Sheng touches one of the cords. It looks like fossilized wood, but it turns out to be fragile and snaps easily. All together, it looks like a jungle with a thick mane of stone. "Harvey," he whispers, frightened, "what are all these . . . things?"

"I don't know," he answers, making his way through the spiderwebs trailing down from above.

"It's like being surrounded by tree roots!"

"Maybe they really are roots," Harvey says in a hushed voice, moving closer to his friend. The voice he heard a moment ago is silent now. "Give me some light, Sheng." The tangle of branches is incredibly dense. The space has grown cramped, stifling. Harvey's forced to walk with his head bowed down.

They've almost reached the center of the room. The lighter illuminates a strange object on the floor. "What's that?" Sheng asks, moving the little flame as far in front of him as he can.

"I'm not sure," Harvey whispers, pushing the branches aside to take a better look. "It looks like . . ."

"An egg?" Sheng says, finishing his sentence.

It's a red rock shaped like a vase the size of a soccer ball. The top of it looks cracked, like a broken eggshell. It's resting on a structure held up by three stones. A dolmen. Depicted around the vaselike rock are dozens of little men. Above it is a stylized shower of falling stars.

Sheng lights up the altar and red marble stone. The lighter goes out and is flicked on again. It goes out and is flicked on again. The mystery of the room and the object remain unsolved. "Do we take it?" he asks, looking over at his friend.

Harvey stares at the stone before him. He doesn't seem to have even heard Sheng, whose voice is being covered up by a sort of murmur, an intense whispering that's growing louder and louder inside his head. They're voices. Thousands of overlapping voices talking to him with the same tone, mixing together. Harvey hears them but doesn't understand them. All he can make out is an emotion, which is crystal-clear. Crystal-clear and nameless. It isn't like the other times. It isn't Dwaine. Among the roots coming down from the ceiling, he can sense absolute antiquity, a time that came before the founding of New York, before the Indian villages. It goes much, much farther back in time.

Pure antiquity, a state that belongs to no calendar, is echoing through his head like the song of the Earth itself. It's what existed in the very beginning. It's something that belonged to the first men.

Where were the first men born? In Africa? Asia? America? He doesn't know. He never studied that at school. Or if he did, he doesn't remember it anymore.

His head is crowded with names that mean nothing to him,

that he can't sort through no matter how hard he tries. Neanderthal man, *Homo erectus*, *Cercopithecus*. Which of them is the oldest? Which ones are the ancestors of mankind?

"Man descended from the apes . . . ," he says aloud.

"You got that right," Sheng replies in the darkness.

The noise inside Harvey's head has grown more insistent, almost painful. He raises his hands to push the branches aside. The stone is coarse, rough. It's a pure object, untouched by men's tools.

The little men surrounding it. The stars falling from the sky.

"Man descended from the apes," he repeats. "Or from the stars."

The stone is hollow. Harvey feels around inside of it, his fingers discovering a series of small lumps that form four backbones, like arches in a vaulted ceiling, which join together at the bottom of the vase.

There's something at the bottom. Four tiny objects. Harvey grabs them and rolls them out into the palm of his hand. Sheng moves his lighter closer. "Smaller stones?"

"No . . . ," Harvey whispers, turning them over in his fingers. "They're seeds. Tree seeds."

The voices become even more insistent. *Take the Star of Stone!*

Harvey claps his hands over his ears, trying not to hear, but then he gives in, grabs the stone and picks it up.

"What are you doing?" Sheng asks him.

"I think we're supposed to take it with us," he answers.

"Take it where?"

Harvey turns around. The wooden vines caress his face. "We'd better get out of here," he says as the light flickers out.

"Yeah, but go where?"

Sheng tries to get the lighter working again, but all it does is let out a few meager sparks. "Oh, no!" he groans.

"There's got to be a way out of here," Harvey says beside him. He pushes the vines aside and grabs Sheng's arm. "Come on. Follow me."

"Which way?"

"In this direction. I think it's the right one."

"How can you tell?"

"The voice of the Earth just told me so."

Sheng tugs on his friend's arm, stopping him. He switches on his camera, which starts up with a high-pitched whine. "The flash," he explains. "We can use it to see something. . . ." A second later, a burst of white light fills the room.

With Harvey leading the way, they reach a second door in the circular wall. They slip down a tunnel and find a passageway heading upward.

Harvey is clutching the Star of Stone to his chest. In his pocket are the four seeds. Sheng sets off his flash every ten seconds, intermittently lighting up their path. He doesn't ask questions. He doesn't say a word.

From time to time they stop. Each time, Harvey seems to listen to something and then says which way they should go.

33

THE DOOR

THE DOOR TO LINDA MELODIA'S HOTEL ROOM SUDDENLY BURSTS open. The woman peers out, sees what's happening in the hallway and cries, "Elettra!"

"Auntie!" Elettra shouts.

Linda dodges one of the women from Lucifer, along with Olympia's punches. Then she leans back against the door, too stunned to do anything else.

Mistral holds out her hand. "Quick! Let's get out of here!"

Four girls are duking it out right outside her hotel room. Soaking wet, Elettra and Mistral shout at Linda to follow them.

"Get out of here!" Olympia shouts to her, too.

The woman stares at the black girl. *Who's that?* she wonders. But she doesn't have time to find out. *Enough is enough,* she thinks. *And quite frankly, this is* definitely *enough.* She dashes down the hallway. The moment she catches up with her niece, she asks, almost shouting, "What's going on?"

"Are you okay?"

"Yes, but . . ." Linda points to the room she just left. "What is it these people want?"

Elettra grabs her aunt's hands and pulls her away, almost dragging her. "It's a really long story! We've really got to get out of here!" She tries to accompany her to the elevator at the end of the hall. Mistral, on the other hand, moves toward the hotel room door.

"Mistral!" Elettra calls to her. "Come on, quick!"

The French girl doesn't listen to her. Her back flattened up against the wall, she moves even closer. The door is still open. The map and the tops are inside.

She can't leave them there.

She goes in.

A stairway. A stairway leading up. Flashes of light coming from above.

Harvey and Sheng scramble up the steps. They push against a wall of wooden planks nailed together and make an opening that leads into a big, empty room. Sheng steps out from the darkness, coughing. He kneels down on the floor. Behind him, Harvey staggers around the room, exhausted. He leans against his friend's shoulder, staring at him. Sheng looks back at him. They're covered head to foot with cobwebs. Giant threads of spider's silk.

"You okay?"

"I think so."

Sheng pulls himself up to his feet. The room around them has peeling walls and a ceiling with patches of mildew. The floor is covered with debris. The windows are open, empty gaps. A doorless doorway leads out into a silent corridor. There are lights coming from outside.

The two boys lean out into the corridor to take a look. They're in a giant abandoned building. Dozens of empty rooms. Rust, crumbling walls. Echoes of laughter. Shadows. Stairways leading nowhere. Silence. Light streaming in through the damp air.

"I've got to get out of here," Sheng says, looking around. The rhythmic noise they hear is the rain. It's muffled, melodious. "I've got to get this stuff off me."

They walk down two giant hallways, which were once painted. Vines are peeking out from the gaps in the walls. The light streaming through the boarded-up windows reveals the glistening paths of snails on the walls. It's a crazy building without any real dimensions.

It's the smallpox hospital on Roosevelt Island.

Mountains of wrapping paper. From the hallway between the door and the bedroom, all Mistral can see is wrapping paper. She steps closer. She sees the open suitcases, the clothes scattered all over the bed and the floor, the bouquet of flowers . . . and a man's body lying on the floor. She can hear him gasping for air. Half-hidden behind his fingers, the man's eyes open wide. His nose is bleeding and his hand is splattered with blood.

"Ohhh . . . ohhh . . . ," Egon Nose howls, trying to get to his feet. "Ohhh . . ."

He gropes around for something.

The gun.

Without a moment's hesitation, Mistral darts forward. As if in a dream, she dives onto the bed and flings the mountain of paper onto the man lying on the floor. She recognizes Elettra's bag, the wooden map, the tops. She scoops it all up in her arms and flies off, leaving a rustling pile of crumpled paper behind her.

"Hey! Little girl!" Dr. Nose shrieks, rising to his feet. His enormous nose is dripping blood all over the carpet. The door to the room is open. His women are retreating from the blows of two strange girls. Egon Nose raises his gun.

In the atrium of the hospital is an old, boarded-up door. The wood is rotten and it soon gives way beneath the boys' kicks. They dive out through the hole they've opened. Rolling to the ground, they feel refreshing raindrops splashing onto their faces.

"We did it!" Sheng cheers, looking up at the sky. He throws his arms wide open, enjoying the sensation. "Yes!"

Harvey gets to his feet and starts walking through the mud, just as happy. The rain washes away the cobwebs and drowns out the buzz of whispering voices he's been hearing in his head. He clutches the red stone to his chest. He doesn't know what it is, why it was there or why he took it with him.

Sheng's laughing.

"What's so funny?"

The Chinese boy points at the building they just came out of. "The tower, remember?" he asks. "The safe place!"

Harvey looks up, shields his eyes with the palm of his hand and reads the peeling sign over the door. "Smallpox hospital . . ." He holds the stone tighter. He can't hear any voices. The rain drums down on his head.

The two friends stagger into the garden, which is overrun by brushwood, in search of lights, some glimmer of civilization.

"We came out on the opposite side of New York," Harvey says when he sees the Manhattan skyline rise up from behind the corner of the hospital. It's a series of dark shadows with tiny points of light. A vast city of glass and light reflected in the river.

Harvey looks at Sheng, who stumbles on the lumpy ground, and laughs.

Stumbling, falling and getting back up again, the two finally reach the edge of the garden. Then, exhausted, they sit down on the ground and stare across the river at the city that never sleeps. Harvey slips a hand into his pocket, takes one of the four seeds he brought with him and lets it fall to the ground.

The two friends hug in the rain, laughing.

34

THE SEED

THE RAIN FADES AWAY IN THE MORNING. As NEW YORK IS DRYING off, Quilleran walks down the street at a slow pace. He has a gunshot wound in his side. It hurts, but he's happy.

He has a paper tucked under his arm. News of the attack on the library is on the front page. Three women spread panic through the underground levels of the building and have been arrested, but the reason behind what they did isn't known. They were looking for someone. For some kids . . .

It seems the girls were following the orders of a man by the name of Egon Nose, a shady nightclub owner. He's also been arrested, caught on the top floor of the Mandarin Oriental Hotel after threatening an Italian woman.

For those who don't know the background behind these two events, there's no clear connection between them. It's simply a day of unusually crazy news.

Quilleran goes down the steps to the subway. A quarter of an hour later, he comes out again on Roosevelt Island. He walks south, heading toward the abandoned smallpox hospital. A black crow, blind in one eye, perches on his shoulder.

"Hello, Edgar," the Indian greets him, feeding him a pistachio. Then he takes out a mint-flavored candy for himself.

Edgar flies off. The smallpox hospital is a black skeleton surrounded by an untended garden. Quilleran climbs over a low wall and makes his way through the weeds, trampling debris and other abandoned items that the grass has swallowed up. He reaches the bank of the river, which is flowing by peacefully. At the very edge of the garden is a recently upturned clump of earth. Rising up from the middle of it is a tiny tree shoot.

"The first tree has sprouted again," the Indian man whispers the moment he sees it. He peers around at the footprints that Harvey and Sheng left behind and then goes to caress the tiny sapling. It has only a single tiny white leaf, but it holds within it inestimable power. "This is truly magical," Quilleran says softly. "Nature's magic is both incredible and simple."

Out there, somewhere on the other side of the river, behind one of the thousands of windows, are Harvey and his friends. "Keep searching, kids," the Indian says. "Keep searching, Star of Stone."

At 11 Grove Court, Harvey Miller finds an old brass key in his brother's desk drawer. He goes out into the hallway, heads to the kitchen, grabs a chair, drags it over to the grandfather clock, climbs onto it and opens the glass clock face.

He slides the key in and, without hesitating, turns it. The old mechanism seems to think it over a moment, after which the whole clock begins to tremble as the cogwheels make their tiny revolutions. Harvey sets the clock's hands to the right time, gets down from the chair and nudges the pendulum in the chamber below, definitively starting up the mechanism. He looks up at the clock his brother rebuilt, full of admiration. "Welcome back, Dwaine . . . ," he says softly.

Antiques dealer Vladimir Askenazy walks along, hunched over more than usual and smiling feebly. He's just come out of the Mandarin Oriental, where he went to say goodbye to the kids and make sure everything was all right. As for himself, he hid his concern and tried to reassure them.

Maybe . . . , he thinks, *maybe we can do it.*

Mistral managed to get back the map and tops from the hotel room, and the scoundrel Egon Nose was arrested. He'll probably be released with a slap on the wrist, but if everything goes as planned, the tops will already have left New York by then.

Harvey and Sheng returned from their journey belowground, bringing a red marble stone and three seeds with them. They still have time to discover their true meaning and their relationship with the Ring of Fire.

Maybe I'll discover that, too, thinks Vladimir. He's tired. Very tired. He wearily makes his way to the bank, gets in line at a window and clenches his teeth. There are still so many things to do. Many open wounds that someone needs to try to heal.

When it's his turn, the antiques dealer pulls a roll of banknotes out of the pocket of his overcoat. He hands it to the teller, who counts them. Two thousand dollars.

"Deposit it into this account," Vladimir orders, handing over a slip of paper with a long number written on it. "It's under the name Agatha Meyrink." He waits for the receipt, puts it in his pocket and wearily walks out of the bank.

The Chanin Building isn't very far away. Vladimir goes there on foot, steps into the elevator and presses the button for an apartment number he knows very well. Agatha Meyrink opens the door a moment later. She stares at him, a bewildered look on her face, and asks, "Who are you?"

Vladimir makes a little smile. "A friend of Alfred's," he replies.

Agatha looks him up and down for a few seconds and then adds, "I've already seen you somewhere before. . . ."

"That could be," the antiques dealer answers, holding an old camera out to her. "I've come to give you this back."

Agatha retreats a step. "Alfred's camera?"

"I believe it is." Vladimir nods.

For a moment, Agatha is still suspicious. "Why is it you're all looking for Alfred these days, after so many years of silence?"

The man lets the camera fall to his side. "I wanted to tell you what happened to him." His frank, firm tone of voice tells Agatha a great deal more than his words do.

"He's dead, isn't he?" Agatha asks, slumping against the doorframe, as if the burden of all those years is suddenly unbearable.

Vladimir doesn't reply, but his silence makes the answer clear.

"Where did it happen?"

"In Rome," the antiques dealer says.

Agatha steps aside, gesturing for him to come in. "How do you know that?"

"I was one of his last friends," Vladimir answers, limping over to the living room.

"Help me remember," Agatha says softly. "Where have I seen you before?"

"I know you have a picture of Alfred, here in the house."

Agatha remains silent.

"I'm in that picture," Vladimir admits, leaning on the arm of the chair. "I'm the shadow, the photographer."

Harvey, Elettra, Sheng and Mistral are in Ermete's hospital room, sitting on the edge of his bed. They tell him everything that's happened in a confused, excited way, in an outpour riddled with doubts and second thoughts. On the engineer's lap are three objects: the mirror set in a copper frame, which they call the Ring of Fire; a shiny red egg-shaped rock, which they call the Star of Stone; and three dried seeds. Harvey explains that he planted one of them in the garden where they ended up last night.

Mistral is convinced the egg-shaped stone is a meteorite. She says she's seen one like it, with the same red color. On the other hand, Ermete thinks it's a sculpture, a symbol: the primordial egg from which all forms of life were born.

"What if the primordial chicken came first?" Sheng asks jokingly.

The mood of the five friends is relaxed. They're starting to get used to the fear and rash decisions forced upon them, like when Mistral went back to get the tops.

The others ask her at least three times to tell them how she managed to escape from Egon Nose. "I just hid in the bathroom," the girl says, "while he ran out of the hotel room as fast as lightning!"

"And got a pummeling from Olympia!" Elettra continues.

Naturally, the kids have one more problem now: Linda Melodia's questions. "Actually, what my aunt just can't get over," the girl from Rome explains, "is that some stranger ruined all of her perfectly wrapped presents."

"It's pretty obvious that there's something I need to do. . . ." Harvey sighs when he's finished describing in detail how they made their way down into the maze in the library, crossed through the door with the magic square and took a ride on the pneumatic train.

"Something *we* need to do, Harvey. Not just you. All of us," Sheng interjects.

Harvey continues. "Professor Van Der Berger's known about me ever since I was little and he named me as his successor, whatever that's supposed to mean. To the Seneca Indians, I'm Star of Stone, just like he used to be. I don't know what to make of that, but I know the professor believed in it. He wants me to go down a path paved with strange clues, to track down a place we don't know anything about yet. To discover a secret."

"I say we should do it," Mistral says, stroking the stone resting on the bed. "Even if it might turn out to be pretty frightening."

"We could get really hurt," adds Sheng.

"Then there are these seeds," Elettra murmurs. "Are we supposed to plant them all?"

Harvey shakes his head. "I don't know, but we'll find out soon enough, I guess."

"Oh, no!" Ermete groans, lying in the hospital bed. He tenses up and points at someone who's just appeared in the doorway.

The four friends whirl around, scared.

It's a tall black woman with a lean physique and a determined look on her face. She's staring at them.

277

Harvey's the first to recognize her. "Don't worry, Ermete! That's Olympia, my boxing coach."

Olympia smiles and walks into the room. She has a bruise on her right cheek where one of the two women managed to punch her. "Sorry to barge in. I called the Millers and they told me I'd find you guys here."

They introduce her to Ermete and thank her for coming to their rescue. She doesn't ask many questions. She slugs Harvey lightly on the shoulder. "See you tomorrow, then, okay?"

Harvey smiles at her. "Okay."

When they're alone again, Sheng goes to shut the door to the room and Elettra pulls the map out of a bag. "Before we split up again," she says, "there's something we'd better do. . . ." She takes out the top with the rainbow, which Mistral got back from the hotel room.

When he sees it, Ermete smiles. "There it is, at last. . . ." Then he frowns. "Don't you think we should give it back to Vladimir? After all, it was stolen from him."

"We tried to," Sheng explains, looking at Harvey. "But he doesn't want it."

"And so," Mistral continues, "we thought *you* should keep it." Elettra hands Ermete the ancient top with a rainbow engraved on it. A little embarrassed, Ermete cradles it in his fingertips. .

"What do you think this top points to?" Harvey asks him.

"I don't know," the engineer admits. "To answer that, I'd have to spend a little time looking through my books, and maybe what's left of the professor's books, too."

"If you had to take a wild guess?"

"A rainbow is a bridge, and a bridge connects two things that used to be distant. It's a passageway, a link, a connection. It's a way to get over something that would otherwise divide two things," he answers hesitantly.

"Go ahead . . . cast it!" Sheng urges him, gesturing at the wooden map. "Let's see what it points to."

"What kind of paper map should we put on top of the wooden one?" asks Mistral.

"I thought we should think big! Let's use one of the whole globe," Elettra replies. She spreads a world map showing all the continents on top of it.

Ermete nods, makes himself more comfortable in the bed and positions the top at one edge of the map. "I'm ready," he says. With this, he spins it.

The top whirls around over the seas and continents until it reaches a remote area in the middle of Siberia, almost on the border with China. There, it pauses, spinning around slower and slower.

"Siberia?" the kids exclaim, looking at each other, bewildered.

A moment before it stops, the top bounces, swiftly crossing over the Russian steppes, the Ural Mountains, Eastern Europe and a part of Western Europe, finishing its trek in . . .

"Paris," Mistral murmurs, fascinated.

Sheng twists his lips with disappointment. "Why couldn't something happen in Shanghai, huh?"

"So the top jumped from Siberia to Paris," Harvey observes. "Why?"

No one has an answer.

"Fire connected Rome and New York," Harvey continues, brushing his fingers over Prometheus's mirror. Then he picks up the red stone. "Maybe the next connection is going to be stone?"

Before anyone can reply, the hospital room door bursts open. Linda Melodia appears in the doorway. She has a platinum-blond hairdo.

"Auntie!" Elettra exclaims the minute she sees her. "What have you done to your hair?"

The woman smooths down one of her locks sensually. "Nice, isn't it? I thought a New York style would do me some good! But please, let's not talk about me. Hello there!" she says to Ermete. "You must be the friend from Rome Elettra's told me so much about."

"That's me. . . ." Ermete smiles from his bed.

"Heavens! What happened to you?" Aunt Linda asks, reaching the bed with only a few long strides.

Sheng makes the tops disappear, but he doesn't have time to hide the mirror or the stone.

"Oh, what pretty souvenirs!" she exclaims. "Where did you find them?" Before they can even react, she snatches them up, looking for a label or logo. "They're filthy dirty, though," she proclaims, placing them on the nightstand. "You'd better not keep them on the bed."

Elettra tries to get rid of the woman, but it's no use. "Listen, Auntie, we were just saying goodbye to Ermete. Pretty soon . . ."

Linda Melodia shakes her head vigorously. She looks around for a chair, finds one and plunks it down at the foot of the bed. From there, one by one, she looks all five of them in the eye. "That's enough, my dears! Now, make yourselves comfortable and explain everything, and I mean *everything*, about the tops and the wooden box."

"Auntie . . ."

Linda raises a finger threateningly. "Otherwise, the first time I get my hands on them, I'll throw them all away in the trash!" The kids exchange long, worried glances. "Who wants to start?" Elettra's aunt asks.

35

THE HERMIT

MOTIONLESS BEHIND THE PICTURE WINDOWS OF HIS SKYSCRAPER, late at night, the man shows no signs of wanting to sleep. He hates sleeping. He hates sleep. Most of all, he hates dreams.

He's standing there, looking outside. A light drizzle is streaking the windows. Gray clouds on the horizon are concealing the most distant neighborhoods of Shanghai. The minutes go by quickly.

And still, no phone call.

The man waits patiently, even though patience has never been one of his qualities.

Jacob Mahler is dead.

Egon Nose isn't calling.

Clack! goes the automatic calendar on his desk at the stroke of midnight.

March twenty-first, the first day of spring.

The man takes off his black Bakelite glasses and clutches them in his fist. He'd love to shatter them, but he doesn't.

He's been expecting a completely different outcome. He expected that, come spring, he'd already have a great deal of the

282

Pact under his control. Instead, he's lost his best agent in Rome as well as contact with his trusted man in New York.

March twenty-first. And he still doesn't have the map.

"Don't think you've gotten anywhere," the man hisses. "You don't know anything yet. You haven't understood anything yet. We're two sides of the same coin, young Mr. Miller, Miss Melodia and Miss Blanchard. As for you, little Chinese boy, sooner or later you'll come back to see your family. Sooner or later . . ."

The kids are following a path that others have prepared for them. A path that's not very clear and has been a carefully guarded secret over the course of the years. A path that's mysterious in some respects, even for the man standing at the window of his skyscraper. But it's still a path. One of the many that leads to the secret behind Century.

"What difference does it make which road you follow as you seek the truth? Such a great secret is not to be reached by a single path. If you find it, you must guard it with care and keep others from discovering it as well. This is the secret behind Century . . . ," the man whispers before stepping away from the window.

He takes a few steps into the room, reaches its only door and walks through it. The moment the door closes, the air-conditioning system begins to sterilize the room to eliminate every last germ.

The man walks down a hallway. "Century tells us where we came from and where we're going. And for how much longer . . ."

The hallway is almost two hundred yards long. It has neither doors nor lights. Tall and narrow, the walls are covered with drawings and writings in childish red scrawled handwriting. The man walks all the way down to the end, where there's a tiny door. He needs to hunch over to step through it.

On the other side of it is his bedroom. The man undresses with methodical, routine precision. The cuff of his shirt is splattered with blood. He shattered his glasses after all, and he's still clutching them in his fist. He lets the pieces fall to the floor.

"He who knows the secret behind Century," he says, resting back on the bed, which is too short for him to lie down on entirely, "rules the world."

He doesn't shut his eyes. He almost never sleeps. He hates sleep. Most of all, he hates dreams.

"I want to rule the world," Heremit Devil says, the expression on his face unchanging. Painted on the ceiling of his room are the stars. But they're all depicted wrong.

36

THE CHILDREN OF THE BEAR

Winter has swallowed up the cardinal points in Siberia. The woods are icy. The rivers slice through the rocky heart of the valleys. Nothing is moving. Tunguska is an expanse of broken rocks, moss and lichens, motionless forests where the pine needles are as sharp as razor blades. The paths are scanned by the blue eyes of wolves and marked by the passing of white foxes.

A single train reaches this land, braving the cold with its pinnacle of black smoke. The noise of its wheels on the tracks can be heard from dozens of miles away. The train is a black iron drum, its thumping beat echoing through the whiteness. It does this every year at the beginning of spring.

In Tunguska, there's one thing that isn't to be spoken of. It isn't easy to discover, let alone reach. It's a forest that no longer exists. It used to be very large. Its outer perimeter was once formed by slender pine trunks that tilted backward. Little by little, the smaller trees disappeared and the age-old pines became those that were tilted. They grew at impossible angles, as if they'd been swept back by an overpowering wind.

Then the trees disappeared. Their trunks were driven down,

one beside the other, their roots pointing toward the center of the forest. In the center there was only snow, which covered expanses of molten, superheated rock. They say a comet fell in Tunguska in 1908. But that's only a rumor. It's best not to speak of what really happened.

Two figures are walking through the forest that no longer exists. They're wearing heavy, hand-sewn furs. Crystals of snow are clinging to their eyebrows. Their boots are sinking down into the glistening mud. Their eyes are mere slits. It's a woman and a man.

"I saw the star," she says. She stares at the figure accompanying her with eerie-looking eyes. They call her the Seer, because she can see things with those eyes that others can't see.

"What was it like?" her companion asks her.

"It was white. Like a foxtail. I saw it coming. But I couldn't see if it was bringing life or destruction."

"More destruction?"

"Not here. Somewhere else. But it won't be like it was a hundred years ago. This comet will be much, much larger."

The wind sweeps across the land, finding no obstacles.

"Who could ever know if it's going to bring life or destruction?"

"The ones who summoned it. The Children of the Bear." The Seer huddles up in her furs and points at the white expanse of the forest, which was destroyed by the impact of a falling star. "Every hundred years, the bear gives birth to four children. They're her chosen ones and they're born in the north. They're the ones who summoned the comet. And now they have to guide it."

"But how . . . how do you know these things?"

The Seer's eyes narrow. "They told me. I've seen them. In the mornings and evenings. In the river and in the plain. I've seen it in the snow. I've heard it in the songs no one sings anymore. In the lost music. The world itself told me."

"Here?"

"Here," the Seer replies. "Because this is where it happened a hundred years ago, when the old children of the bear came. They summoned the comet and they didn't know how to guide it."

"How could anyone guide a comet?"

"By respecting the Pact." The Seer kneels down to touch the ground. "The pact that allows us to live with her. The pact between man and the Earth."

The two fall silent for a long while, and then the man helps the woman to her feet. "Why did you bring me here?" he asks her.

"Because you need to go find the Children of the Bear."

"Where should I look for them?"

"In the city of wind and words."

"I don't understand," the man replies. "There's no such city."

"Yes, there is," she insists. "They call it Paris."

"You want me to go to Paris for you?"

The Seer shakes her head. Very few teeth remain in her smile. "Not for me. For all of us. You need to find the Children of the Bear and give them something."

She pulls out a leather pouch sealed with a rawhide string stiffened by the cold.

Inside of it is a wooden top.

Engraved on the wooden top is a heart.

CREDITS

© Iocopo Bruno (p. 4, photo 1; p. 4, photo 2; p. 5, photo 4; p. 5, photo 6; p. 5, photo 7; p. 9, photo 20; p. 10, photo 25; p. 11, photo 27; p. 11, photo 29; p. 12, photo 30; p. 12, photo 32).

© Chang/istockphoto.com (p. 4, photo 3).

© Corbis (p. 5, photo 5).

© daniellesmith/istockphoto.com (p. 4 top; p. 7, photo 12; p. 8, photo 15; p. 9 top; p. 11 top left; p. 12 middle right; p. 13, photo 34).

© Denis Finnin, American Museum of Natural History (p. 9, photo 21).

© flexidan/istockphoto.com (p. 8, photo 17).

© FreeTransform/istockphoto.com (p. 12, photo 31).

© Jello5700/istockphoto.com (p. 9, photo 22).

© lfreytag/istockphoto.com (p. 13, photo 38).

© Lingbeek/istockphoto.com (p. 11, photo 28).

© Marbury/istockphoto.com (p. 6, photo 8 bottom).

© Mikadx/istockphoto.com (p. 13, photo 37).

© Nazreen/istockphoto.com (p. 11, photo 26).

ABOUT THE AUTHOR

PIERDOMENICO BACCALARIO was born in Acqui Terme, a beautiful little town in the Piedmont region of northern Italy. He grew up in the middle of the woods with his three dogs and his black bicycle.

He started writing in high school. When lessons got particularly boring, he'd pretend he was taking notes, but he was actually coming up with stories. He also met a group of friends who were crazy about role-playing games, and with them he invented and explored dozens of fantastic worlds.

He studied law at university but kept writing and began publishing novels. After he graduated, he also worked with museums and cultural projects, trying to make dusty old objects tell interesting stories. He began to travel and change horizons: Celle Ligure, Pisa, Rome, Verona . . .

He loves seeing new places and discovering new lifestyles, although, in the end, he always returns to the comfort of familiar ones.